Shadows

Philip T McNeill

Published at CreateSpace

Beth!

To Alfie – despite you scratching my arms, biting and chasing my fingers as you walk across the keyboard, I still got this finished

SHADOWS

Prologue - 1642

The church bell rang at just after three in the morning, the sound echoing around the village square and searching out attention from the cold stone walls.

At the boundaries of Ashton village, a large procession of twinkling lights could be seen flickering through the bordering trees as they wove their way along the twisting track that would eventually lead to the main throughway. As the bell pealed once more, their pace quickened.

Mary Fielding sat up in her bed, large eyes adjusting to the darkness of the long burnt out candle. The bell was still ringing frantically, trying to wake the inhabitants of the settlement, and Mary pulled the sheets around her, trying to trap heat and courage together.

She was eight years old but was still afraid of what could lurk in the shadows. The noises of the pigs rooting around outside her window was frightening enough, but she had heard Elizabeth at the mill house talk of wolves occasionally picking off animals at night. Perhaps that was what the bell was for?

Now she could hear footsteps marching up the main throughway, expensive boots crunching across the gravel and dust. It sounded to Mary as if an army were storming through Ashton, but then came the harsh rapping of fists on wood, followed by muffled and incomprehensible raised voices. The mysterious visitors had stopped and again, the small girl's mind spiralled. They were probably looking for shelter for the night. Or maybe they were even hunting an escaped convict?

The young girl was tempted to run to the window and peer into the throughway, but dared not dip her toes into the inky blackness that surrounded her bed. Her conversations with various playmates at the farmers' market had left her well aware of the creatures under the bed that waited to snatch little girls who were awake when they should have been sleeping. Instead, Mary sat where she was, tightly huddled in the linens, waiting for her parents to check on her.

The curious sounds outside were now joined by the discord of splintering wood and breaking crockery, giving Mary the fanciful image that these people were for some reason knocking on doors then releasing a bear into the house to tear it apart.

The bedroom door flew open and Mary shielded her eyes, waiting for the bear's gleaming teeth to close in on her. When the pain did not come, she opened one eye carefully, breathing a sigh of relief as she saw her brother Jacob holding a fresh candle.

At fifteen, he was apprenticed at the blacksmiths, and usually regaled the family with workshop stories, but now he carried a look of concern, the candlelight wavering in the draft from the hallway. He had roughly pulled his britches on so that his nightshirt was only half tucked in. His feet were bare.

"Mary," he whispered. "Don't make a sound. Come across to me."

"I can't," the girl replied with a whimper. "The thing under the bed is waiting." Jacob gave a silent smile as he padded into the room and swept his sister up with his free arm. Once in the hallway, he handed the candle to her for reassurance.

"My feet are cold," the girl began absent mindedly. "I need my boots."

"But we are quieter without them." At this point, Mary paused. Why should it matter if they were heard?

"Jacob, what's going on?"

"Papa says we are to ride to The Circle and wait for them there." Mary's eyes were wide. *A two-mile ride in the blackness of the forest?*

"Now?" she exclaimed. "But why?"

"Just take my hand." Mary did as she was told, her fragile fingers fitting perfectly into Jacob's rough palm, letting him lead her through the house despite her having the candle.

The two of them froze as yet another door was knocked upon. Too close. It could be next door, or two doors down perhaps, reasoned Mary. They treaded barefoot down the staircase and made straight for the yard which held the stable, the woodshed and the outhouse.

Jacob could feel his sister dragging behind, pulling against him, and he understood her desire to see their parents, but he was old enough to follow orders without question. His father had charged him to protect Mary, and that was what he would do.

As the two children hit the sharp air, faces flushed, Mary saw that the family horse was already saddled, bags hanging from either side. She stepped forward and peered into the closest satchel. She could see bread, cheese and other supplies, but there was also a book of her father's, bound in black leather with a silver buckle. The book had no title, but was branded with a star in a circle. Although she had never been allowed to look inside, Mary knew that with the book came a set of pendants with odd designs. The young girl turned back to her brother, who was shuffling his bare feet nervously on the cobbles.

"Is it...?" Mary breathed as heavy fists pounded at the door. Before Jacob could grab her, she sprinted back into the house, the meagre flame swishing into nothing as she ran with the candle.

"Mary, no!" shouted Jacob, lunging desperately forward.

Mary hurried through the cottage, hurtling into the front room just as the door was forced open. Mr and Mrs Fielding were backed against the wall next to the fireplace as a number of men armed with pikes strode into the room and knelt, brandishing their weapons as if the Fieldings were criminals about to bolt.

Two of the pike men stepped aside as another man flowed into the house. It was obvious that here was their authority, as the man was dressed in fine amber britches and scarlet waistcoat. A cloak was draped across his shoulders, and his head adorned with a tall and wide-brimmed hat. He was bearded, and despite the early hour, his eyes gleamed with satisfaction, confidence and, Mary fancied, a little excitement.

"William and Elizabeth Fielding," he began with an air of command. "In the name of the Church, I hereby exercise the right to search this property on suspicion of witchcraft. This village is uncertain in its reputation." Mary felt her heart sink into the soles of her feet. She knew this had something to do with the book hidden in the knapsack. She shrunk back against the doorframe, watching her parents expectantly. Her father stepped forward.

"Do what you like Hopkins," he spat. "You'll find nothing here."

"You know me sir?" asked Hopkins curiously, raising an eyebrow with a hint of amusement.

"Aye, by word only," continued Mr Fielding. "Matthew Hopkins, self appointed Witchfinder General. You've cut a bloody trail from Essex, so I'm told." Hopkins nodded with satisfaction.

"Then you know not to cross me, good sir." At this, he nodded to his men, who sprang forwards and began rooting through the shelves and dressers, pulling plates mercilessly to the floor to peer behind them. Jacob arrived behind Mary just as their mother stepped forward angrily.

"Now really, Mr Hopkins, is there any need to-"

"Silence, woman!" Hopkins roared, dealing her a swift and lashing backhand across the cheek. The pikes remained angled towards Mr Fielding, daring him to challenge them. He remained still, although his eyes burned with hatred.

"Here sir," called one of the marauders. He was crouched next to one of the drawers, a cluster of dried lavender gripped firmly in his hand. Hopkins' eyes lit up hungrily.

"Nothing but sweet fragrance," muttered Mrs Fielding, massaging her face, which was already beginning to discolour. Her husband looked towards his children.

"Jacob, take your sister away. We'll sort this." The look in the man's eyes told Jacob all he needed to know, and he dragged his sister from the room, clamping his hand over her mouth. He could feel her tears running over his fingers, and he hated himself for tearing her away from everything she knew and loved, but he too had heard the stories of Matthew Hopkins, told long after Mary had been put to bed. He knew what was coming.

The young man led his sister out into the yard and lifted her gently into the saddle. He untied the horse and then looked her in the eye solemnly.

"I have to unbolt the gate," he said calmly, hoping she would emulate him. "Stay absolutely quiet until I come back for you." The girl nodded with shining eyes.

Jacob made sure that the horse was settled before running around the corner of the house where the tall oak gates stood. As slowly as he could, he slid the rusting bolt across, wincing every time the metal screamed in protest.

Breathing heavily with nerves, he eased the gate a fraction, pressing his face against the gap, a single aquamarine eye taking stock of the throughway outside. He could still hear a commotion coming from the house and from further up in the village, but none of Hopkins' associates could be seen in the vicinity.

He turned on his heels, now black with the grime of the stones and ran back to his sister. As he rounded the corner of the building, he jolted to a stop, eyes widening as he saw one of the pike men advancing on Mary. From her position on the horse, she hadn't seen him come out of the house.

Jacob Fielding was torn. There was no use in shouting, as Mary wouldn't know what to do with the animal, and if he moved then the soldier might turn to him instead. Of course he had no choice. He promised he would protect his sister no matter what. He took a deep breath, ready to rush into the cold steel. Perhaps he could fend off the older and stronger man for long enough for Mary to get clear.

As he moved from the shadows, Mary noticed the movement and turned her head. She must have seen the advancing soldier in the corner of her eye because suddenly she screamed a high pitched piercing sound. Petrified, the horse sprung onto its front legs, lashing out with powerful flanks and forcing its back legs into the air. The soldier was struck in the chest and was flung across the yard, landing in a crumpled heap against the far wall. More men spilled from the house as the horse panicked and fled straight towards Jacob.

"Jacob!" Mary wailed as the horse surged forwards. The young man crouched, trying to anticipate which way the horse would run. The frantic animal wheeled around before heading for the open gates. Now was his chance!

Jacob launched himself upwards as the horse passed, flinging out his arms as he seemed to fly through the air. His fingertips caught in one of the bag straps and he fell roughly to the ground, bouncing off the cobbles. The pain was unimaginable as his legs were scraped and battered; thundering over the rough stones, but eventually the boy was able to pull himself onto the back of the horse, clinging desperately to his sister, his britches streaked with dirt and blood.

The two of them rode for half an hour without looking back, until they were well embedded in the looming and twisting shadows of the forest. Jacob took the horse to the top of the nearest rise, a route he had walked many times on his way to the next village. He kicked his heels in, sending the animal bolting along the leaf-strewn path. After a mile and a half, the track began to climb up once more, until eventually the two children and their steed cantered out into open moonlight once more. They were at The Circle. Twelve pillars of rock jutted from the soft grass like broken teeth, all leaning slightly inwards so that if one stood within the stones and looked up at the right time, the moon would seem to be pierced and held in place by the twelve pinions. At the moment, the glowing orb was hovering on the circumference.

The Circle had been around for as long as Jacob could remember, and no doubt had been here for as long as his father could too. He was always impressed by the fact that all sounds, sights, worries and cares seemed to peel away as soon as he crossed the threshold between the rocks, but now he didn't step into the ring. Both children had their attention fixed solely on the hollow where Ashton nestled.

"How long did Papa say to wait?" whispered Mary with a whimper.

"I don't know," her brother replied anxiously. "But keep your head held high dear one." As they watched in silence, Jacob felt the fleeting hooks of doubt snagging in his mind. His Papa had been so hurried that he hadn't explained how long to wait or what to do if nobody came. He would have to look after Mary all alone…

The village suddenly came alive with dancing flames as the thatched roofs were torched and left to burn. The wind picked up, bringing with it the echoes of mournful wails and anguished yells as innocent people were forced to watch their livelihoods blaze. Mary said nothing, and Jacob wasn't sure if she truly understood what had happened. He wasn't looking forward to explaining when they got to – wherever they ended up.

With a final look at the flames encroaching on the now indigo sky, Jacob and Mary Fielding swung the horse around, and rode into the morning.

"There's no such thing as magic. Magic implies something that cannot be explained. However, it is written that everything on this earth has an essence, an aura that cannot be seen. With training, this essence can be felt and manipulated, creating the impression of magic. Much of what society believes to be magic is either this connection with the elements, a basic knowledge of herbs and stones, or a state of mind."

The Book Of Shadows

<u>Dex's Run</u>
<u>November 17 – Present Day</u>

Chapter 1 - Pax

The moonlight gently filtered through the forest canopy,
casting silvery spears into the comforting ground. As
midnight drew closer, a tiny flare of light seemingly ignited
itself, throwing a soft glow onto the undergrowth. One by
one, five candles arranged in a circle began to glow, each
one embossing the surrounding trees with gold until the
entire area seemed to shine metallic. Finally, at the fifth
candle, a cloaked figure was thrown into relief, crouching in
the centre of the circle of light.

Dex shifted his cloak to cast a glance at his watch.
Five minutes to midnight. For a second, he was struck by
the surrealism of the contrast between pagan and modern.
Although he was setting up a primitive tripod with a glass
dish on top, the luminous blinking display of his digital
watch kept him grounded in this century. *And for the rest of
the world, that would be normal,* he mused. After all, it was only
him and a handful of others that had access to the
knowledge and power that he was about to exploit.

Three minutes to midnight. Dex stood up and
surveyed his work, his crystal blue eyes scanning the
cluttered clearing. As he glanced around, a gust of wind
blew his cloak out behind him, revealing a side-pack and a
belt laden with pouches and vials. He ran his fingers over
the bottles until he settled on one, half filled with a pale
green liquid, and it was this Earth Oil that he poured into
the glass dish above the tripod. He placed a candle under
the dish; the heat causing a rich earthy fragrance to
permeate the clearing as Dex tilted his head back, listening
to what the forest was feeling.

One minute until midnight. The wind was rustling through the branches, bared by the chill of the oncoming winter - a soft rattling broken only by the sound of a fox somewhere in the darkness. Dex was reassured by the light, almost childlike chattering of the creature. After a few moments, the fox itself curiously padded into the tiny clearing and sniffed the hem of his cloak. Dex reached out a hand and gently stroked the animal's head as it closed its eyes in pleasure. Relaxed, with nothing to fear except the prospect of returning to the den without a kill, the fox set his mind at ease. The forest was in harmony and there was no need to worry. A bird hooted softly and the fox trotted out of the clearing in search of this new creature. Dex lowered his head, his eyes remaining closed as the wind dropped to a faint whisper.

Midnight. Dex knelt down and lifted a cord from around his neck. On the simple leather band hung a circular disc with a crooked line engraved across it, the elemental symbol for the power of Earth. Kneeling on the velvety moss-covered ground, he set the disc before him and began to whisper.

"Ina kioymarinatoh firel paroywonelrai oyfia Ehraifir tohoy firel kiunasarel oyfia firel fioynarai."

It was done. He sighed, releasing the tension he was feeling, and then froze. The forest was now completely silent - nothing stirred in the wind and the fox was nowhere to be seen, leaving only the inescapable void of sound. Dex raised his head, his wide blue eyes shining as they passed through beams of moonlight. What was the forest trying to tell him? He reached out for meaning, for an indicator of his danger. The shrill bark of the fox rang through the dense blackness and all hints of calm vanished - this was a cry of terror. Dex was in trouble. It was *him*...

Dex snatched his necklace from the ground, overturning the oil burner as he did so. As the steaming liquid hit the forest floor, a shower of sparks shot up from the carpet of curling leaves. If his position was at first a secret, it certainly was no longer. Dex ran out of the clearing, his cloak billowing out behind him.

Driven by fear, Dex sprinted as fast as he could, instinctively picking his way through the trees. The darkness had set in almost as soon as he had scrambled away from the circle of light, and he had to rely on his mind. Straining to seek out the essence of the forest around him, he used his own aura to shift leaves and branches out of his way as he ran. The trees did not obey Dex - man and nature worked together in a partnership of respect, for which he would have to pay later. For now, Dex was content that he had not hit anything, and was spurred on by the cry of pain rising from behind him as his pursuer crashed into the brambles that had sidled round to cover the escape route. Dex and the forest fought together to put as much distance between him and his enemy as was physically possible until Dex burst out of the trees, rolling down a small embankment onto a dusty track. In one smooth motion, he rolled into a crouch, facing the edge of the forest, panting, his eyes wide with fear.

The trees were wavering slightly in the breeze, each shadow twisting and blending into man-shaped forms, but still nothing emerged from the tree line. Was he imagining it? Maybe because he was expecting to be interrupted? No. He had heard a cry as he was fleeing – he was definitely not alone.

As he scanned the inky blackness of the forest, the wind picked up, carrying faint whispers onto the track.

"Scott…" Dex spun around, the voice seemingly off to his left. Nothing but empty space, cold and uninviting.

Next came a hollow laugh, this time in front of him, hidden beneath the overlying shadows. The branches were constantly moving in the breeze, creating a shifting mottled pattern. It was impossible to discern anything, human or otherwise camouflaged in the undergrowth. Dex began to wonder if this was as far as it went. If all he was up against was some creepy noises, then he could muster the strength to man up and find the others – his companions were also in the forest, and he hadn't heard anything from them. Perhaps his enemy wouldn't show himself after all…

As if to answer his fleeting doubts, a flock of crows erupted from the forest canopy, shrieking and cawing in blind panic. There was a flash of intense violet light, and the birds dropped to the ground, stone dead. Dex raised his hands to shield his eyes as he careened away down the dirt track, abandoning all hope of secrecy. The darkness of the forest was on his right, and to his left was an expansive field of some tall grassy crop. Either side would not afford much cover, unless… there was another option. Spurred on, Dex sprinted forwards into the night.

It wasn't long before he came to what he was hoping for. As he reached the corner of the field, there was a crossroads with another track cutting across to follow the new boundary. Dex hurried into the centre of the junction and held out his palm. As if magnetically repelled, a small amount of grit displaced, leaving a small hole. Next, he flicked his fingers across his belt again, this time bringing out a small rectangular tin that had once contained his Top Trumps cards. Before he had left his home earlier, he had prepared the tin especially for this kind of situation. He flipped the lid and checked the contents – a handful of greyish soil, some old bones and a passport photo of himself, smiling and blissfully unaware of the picture's ulterior purpose. Satisfied, Dex closed the lid, dropped the tin into the hole and swept his hands over the indentation, covering the container as he did so.

"I invoke the Pax," he whispered nervously. All of a sudden, the atmosphere changed, and Dex could feel the presence of somebody else at the crossroads. He turned around to see a tall hooded figure waiting silently by the edge of the track. The figure pulled back his hood to reveal a man who looked to be in his late twenties. His hair was a medley of browns – shades of darkness with lighter patches that glimmered in the moonlight, and his eyes burned with the same marine blue as Dex's. "Why are you a man?" Dex asked, rushing his words. "Shouldn't you be appealing to me, like a fit girl or something?"

The Pax smiled. "I am linked to your mind, it is true." It seemed to Dex that the being was speaking incredibly slowly on purpose, and he kept casting a nervous glance over his shoulder. Luckily, the dirt track remained empty. Nothing was following him. Yet. "Deep down," The Pax continued. "You seek reassurance that you can still grow up to be successful and powerful despite your… parental setbacks. So here I am in this form." Dex blew out a breath, the shock of being told what was in his subconscious leaving him speechless for a second. "What can I do for you?" The Pax asked. "And be quick, I don't belong here in this world. There should not be those with the power to summon me."

"Well there are," said Dex defiantly. "And I'm one of them. Another one is after me, except he's not the same. He's different. More powerful. I need you to protect me."

The Pax tilted his head slightly as if in thought. "Ah, I know the one you speak of. He has The Spirit. I was bound by one such as him. I cannot help you."

Dex opened his mouth vehemently. "No!" he shouted. "That's not how it works. You're a Pax; you have to make a deal with me. I'm here at the crossroads, you have to!"

"You don't know what I am, my young friend. I was once like you, alive and indignant. Until I was chosen and given this task to last me beyond my death. I can't go against the forces that keep me here, anymore than you can."

Dex's face fell. "So you'll do nothing?"

"I will give you these words of advice. I know your group was divided. I know this because it is in your head. It is not me you should be calling on – it is your brothers, but don't waste time. His coming must mean the end for this world." Dex blinked and the apparition was gone, along with his hope of striking a bargain. *Although maybe The Pax was right,* he thought. He should call on his friends, and he cursed himself for not trusting them enough in the first place.

Chapter 2 - Confronted By The Chase

"Anything occurring naturally on Earth, whether plant, animal, element, metal or stone is alive. Something that can be recreated an indefinite number of times identically lacks life. Each living thing has its own unique essence and when a species becomes extinct, that particular variation of power is lost forever."

The Book Of Shadows

Dex left the crossroads and stalked into the field. The grass rose a couple of inches above his head, which at just over six feet meant it must be nearly time for the crop to be cut. As he moved deeper inside, the looming stalks arched over to cover him from view. The young man wove his way in and out of the patches of nettles littering the field, sensing them before he came across the stinging plants. Eventually, he emerged into yet another clearing, in what he guessed must be the centre of the field. This was the perfect spot to call for help, not exposed like the crossroads had been. The dense grass would block out any sound he would make, but unfortunately it would block out any sounds anyone else might make also. *No matter*, he thought. *The grass had other ways to communicate.*

     Dex crouched down and began to rummage through his side-pack. The full moon hung directly over him, the great guardian of the night. There were no stars. He reached into his bag, grimacing as he felt his way around belongings that had broken in his hasty roll out of the trees. Eventually he pulled a candle out of the bag. One tall, red candle. His blue and yellow duplicates were snapped, but it didn't matter, one was enough. For a second, Dex sighed at the irony that the one candle left was the red one, but he wasn't going to complain too much. Any one of his brothers would help him unquestioning, no matter what had previously happened between them.

The once soft, dappled moonlight now seemed to burn down from the sky, warping the candle into a twisted menacing limb. Dex roughly forced another hole into the mud and stood the candle in it. He fumbled in his pocket for a box of matches and lit the candle, watching expectantly as the golden flower blossomed and wavered in front of him.

"Harerel maryoh kiailoh," he urged quietly. Help would come. It had to. Something flickered in the corner of Dex's eye. The grass was wavering gently, as if rocked by some invisible hand. The wind? No.

"Don't move." A cold voice from behind. "Or you'll end up like those birds." The words seemed to pierce Dex's heart, every syllable stinging like a vengeful scorpion. He straightened up, daring himself to look around at his enemy. Despite trying to remain composed, his breathing quickened – he had been dreading this moment, as it would surely mean the end for one of them.

"You follow instructions well, don't you," he stated, hoping to distract his stalker long enough until rescue arrived. That was the only way the confrontation would swing in his favour.

"Nobody instructs me! If you really expected me to come, you would be fighting back about now. It's obvious you're unprepared."

Dex tried to ignore the taunting lilt. "How did you find me so quickly?" he asked, trying to buy yet more time.

"It wasn't too hard. I asked the forest. That's what you do isn't it?" The mockery in his enemy's voice was unmistakable, and Dex realised that it was too late to think about distractions.

"Yona kiainartoh harunaraito marel," he said

defiantly as the attacker laughed acidly.

"Come now, speak English. You know I don't speak your language… but I *can* hurt you." Dex's heart sank as he realized that he had been understood. Yet another secret that was no longer just for him and his friends. Slowly, he turned around to look into the deep, grey eyes he knew would be there. It was a shock how *well* the other man looked, his hair neatly spiked and his black clothes freshly pressed. The only give away was his unnatural paleness like brilliant porcelain.

"It will soon be over, Chase," whispered Dex softly. The other man laughed, his grin contorting his face into a mask of torment as Dex took a step backwards and closed his eyes.

"Interesting, but I've left that name behind."

"I forgot, you call yourself Deus now, don't you."

"It's Theban Locte; I thought that would be a nice touch." Chase's eyes narrowed suspiciously. "What are you doing? Look at me!" Dex wasn't listening. An idea had sprouted in his mind; he just needed to wait for his enemy to make a move. Dex forced himself to concentrate on the soil beneath the other man's feet, and slowly, his enemy began to sink into the earth. Chase panicked, hauling his foot out of the soil, spraying chunks of mud around the clearing, but Dex was ahead of him. He felt, rather than saw Chase strike out with his fist, and crouched down as the arm flew over his head. Rolling to the side, Dex grabbed a fist full of nettles. He trusted his mind, for the Earth told him they were growing there. In the mutual connection between the two forces, the nettles did not sting the man's hands as he rubbed them together, pulverizing the barbed leaves.

Dex opened his eyes suddenly as Chase ran towards him, the platinum glow of the moon backlighting him like a bullet exploding from a gun. Dex did not move as Chase charged forwards. In the final instant before collision, Dex grabbed him around the neck, the venom of the nettles taking effect. Chase screamed as the poison bit into his throat and neck, the two men trapped in an embrace of flailing arms and swirling cloaks. Dex forced his attacker to his knees, squeezing harder and harder as his enemy choked, gasping for breath. Chase clawed at Dex's thighs, the final attempts at freedom from a man defeated. As he resignedly closed his eyes, wishing for the end, Chase sensed a heat pulsing from the other man's hip, and reached out for the side-pack strapped to Dex's belt. Oblivious to the scratching, Dex clutched harder and harder, forcing his enemy closer to the mud.

An ice cold shock shot through Dex's body and he released his captive, screaming in pain. The agony clouded his mind. Unbearable and piercing. The pain. *The pain!* Blood splashed to the ground as Dex fell to his knees, the other man grinning maniacally. Chase raised his hand, tormenting his victim with his weapon, Dex's own athame, stolen from his side-pack in the heat of battle. The silver blade, stained crimson with Dex's life, glinted in the pale moonlight, the colours fading quickly from Dex's world. The stricken man slumped onto his back and looked despairingly through increasingly blurred eyes as Chase stepped forwards.

Suddenly, a reddish shape bounded out of the tall grass and leaped at Chase, who was caught off balance. The fox from the forest had sensed Dex's pain and had come to his aid, knocking Chase off his feet. He cried out as the small claws ripped at his chest while he flailed in the dust. With a loud bark, the fox clamped Chase's ear in its jaws and was now shaking its head, splattering the mud with droplets of crimson. To Dex, the scene looked like

someone had spilt water on a painting, the colours rapidly
bleeding into each other. A yell rang out across the field as
Chase finally forced the fox away, causing it to rip his ear as
it was pushed from him. The ravaged man jumped to his
feet with one hand pressed against his head, blood running
in rivulets across his fingers. He looked menacingly at the
fox as it scrambled up. Leaning back on its haunches, the
brave animal leapt through the air, again aiming to knock
Chase to the ground, but this time the man was prepared.
He bent his fingers like talons and swiped upwards,
slashing through the empty air in front of him. The fox
halted mid pounce and then fell to the ground as if it had
been simply swatted out of the sky. Dex stared, trying to
make sense of what he had just witnessed. His vision was
slowly fading, but even he could tell that Chase had not
actually touched the creature. His enemy's power was so
great that he had been able to eviscerate the poor animal
from five feet away. Dead before it had hit the ground, the
fox now lay much like Dex did, sprawled in the mud,
soaking in an ever increasing pool of blood.

Almost consolingly, Chase strolled over to where
Dex lay, a satisfied grin spread across his face. It was as if
his ear had not just been ripped off.

"Even your little friend couldn't save you," he
taunted. "So much for the mighty forces of Earth." With a
swift movement, Chase had slit open Dex's shirt, revealing
his chest, the heaving motion becoming slower by the
second. Dex lay paralysed, his eyes wide as Chase placed
his hand over his victim's heart. Chase leaned in, his
bloodshot eyes millimetres away from Dex's. The faint blue
of life, pushed back by charred portals of vengeance. Chase
shot out his hand, grabbing the necklace that hung round
the fallen man's throat. His nails scratched Dex's skin as he
yanked, tearing the cord triumphantly. Chase tied the cord

around his wrist and dangled the pendant in his victim's face.

    "I'm going to feel you die," whispered Chase, his voice softer than a kiss. Dex's heart stopped as the forest fell silent.

Chapter 3 - The Dream Of Infinity

There was a blinding flash as the bonfire erupted, a column of flame shooting skyward. The four men were thrown backwards, falling perfectly into their compass directions, a quartet of directional chaos. The ritual had worked, and the links forged between the young men was stronger than any of them had predicted. But something was wrong. There was blood on the autumn leaves littering the woodland floor. Next, a figure began to sink beneath a churning brown mass, a cross between an earthquake and a sea storm, swallowing up the helpless form as it lay broken and burned on the cold earth. And screaming. The screaming never stopped…

Nineteen-year-old Rich Benson awoke with a start, his face shining with sweat. The bed sheet had been twisted into a tight coil around his waist and his heart was still beating rapidly from the recurring nightmare. Rubbing his short blonde hair, Rich slowly sat up and glanced at his alarm clock. The blurry haze of red light eventually focused, showing the time to be only 6:15 in the morning, but there was no point in going back to sleep. The trauma of recent events had woken him with the force of being plunged into icy water, and even if he did manage to slip off, he would only be awoken again, the same hellish visions lurking behind his eyes, ready to appear as soon as they were closed. It was like one of those falling dreams, except he never woke up before the fatal smash. He considered consulting his dream dictionary, but there was no point in that either. He knew what the dream was about, he knew the torture of reliving that night every single time he went to sleep, the infinite depths of the vision always able to petrify his very core, no matter how many times it played through his mind.

The incident itself only happened two weeks ago, on Halloween, of all nights, so these dreams could just be because it was still so fresh. *That was it,* Rich thought. *It's only natural to keep thinking about something that terrible when it only happened a fortnight ago. After all, people who witness murders and stuff say they never forget the images.* Far from reassured, he convinced himself that although the visions might never leave him, they might get less severe. That couldn't come soon enough, because currently, he could feel every jolt as if he were still there.

Rich sighed, sliding himself off the bed, his feet tingling as they touched the cool floor. He moved over to a small shelf set about waist height into the wall and lit a yellow candle. Usually, he would be shattered at this time of the morning, but the dream had the power to snap him immediately into full consciousness like being slapped in the face. Besides, after two weeks he was used to seeing the early hours.

The room began to glow with a soft golden tint as the candle burned stronger. A thin swirl of smoke snaked its way to the ceiling where it pulsed outwards, an ethereal jellyfish floating through a sea of air. Bathed in gold, Rich leaned back, his eyes closed, contemplating the day ahead of him. Things had definitely changed since Halloween. He and some friends had been taking part in a ceremony that would empower them with the ways of the Craft. It was this ritual that had ended in the tragedy that he was constantly reliving every time he fell asleep. The ritual itself had been successful: it had cost life and friendship, but was successful none the less. As a result, he was endowed with the powers of the element of Air, taking upon himself the Craft name of Altair. Ever since that night, Rich had been able to sense the slightest of changes in air pressure and temperature. Valuable information could be obtained from reading the pressures in the air and in your head, and the clarity in Rich's mind suggested that the weather at least would be good today. Birds began to chatter outside of the window, the cheerful sound reminding the young man that another day was beginning, the eternal cycle repeating as always, nothing to disrupt the workings of time.

Rich stared at the thin line of smoke rising from the candle he had lit. He had been dying to test what he could do with his new powers, and smoke was sort of linked to air wasn't it? He screwed up his face, his blue eyes half closed as he held out his hand. Almost instantly, the smoke began to bend towards his hand and weave between his fingers. He was actually controlling the way the smoke moved through the air! Thoughtfully, he lowered his hand, releasing the smoke from his mind and letting it continue its simple journey skywards without interruption. Rich started to grin as he realized the potential that he now had. What else could he do if he concentrated hard enough? He had already seen his friend Scott do some amazing things with the forces of Earth. Could he do anything as impressive as that? Glancing at the clock again, he decided to try once more. He still had a few minutes before his father woke up, so he held out his hand again, closed his eyes and thought harder. As before, the smoke began to bend towards Rich's hand, but this time, he willed it to take a specific form in the air in the centre of his bedroom. When he opened his eyes moments later, his name hung in the air, perfectly formed out of the twisting tendrils of smoke. Rich smiled again as the smoke disbanded into a solid line for the last time before he snuffed out the candle.

A floorboard creaked outside the door, the tell-tale sign that his father was now awake. He was always up this early as he worked for Spyrus, the biggest medicine manufacturer in the country, and needed to drive into the city every day. Rich thought enviously of his friend Josh, who was living in the University Halls of Residence. He could play with his powers whenever he wanted, and not have to worry about being disturbed by parents. But here it would only bring questions which, since Halloween, Rich would have had trouble answering. The young man stopped wondering and sighed. Thinking of his friends was difficult, especially as he did not know if he would ever talk to them again. The accident that had given him his powers had caused rifts within the group, which had now split up. The four of them had gained tremendous power but had lost the friendship that had created it. They were each destined to experience their gifts alone as it soured and decayed in front of their eyes like rotting fruit.

As the glowing figures of the alarm clock transitioned into 6:30, something warm and fluid trickled down Rich's face, the metallic taste as it touched his lips unmistakable. A nosebleed. He opened his eyes and wiped his mouth as more blood rolled down, hot splashes on his chest.

"Shit!" Rich breathed as he clamped one hand over his nose and ran to the mirror in the next room to inspect the damage. The blood was still pouring from his nose as he fumbled with the tap. Only a rusted screech emerged - the water was denied. Blood swept down, spiralling into the sink, creating candy swirls against the shining whiteness. He tipped his head back, still pinching the bridge of his nose to stem the flow of the blood. Eventually the bleeding slowed to a halt, and Rich admired the image in his mirror. The blood had fallen onto his chest in three diagonal lines, as if he had been mauled by huge talons. Rich stared at his reflection, and as more scarlet poured from his nose, the three slashes gave off the impression that it was them that were bleeding freely, like freshly inflicted wounds. The image was so striking that Rich had to put his hand to his chest to check that he hadn't in fact cut himself. Relieved, he wiped the blood away, smearing the image into a deep crimson smudge. He took one last look at the blood in the mirror before peeling off his shorts and stepping into the shower to wash away the scarlet illusion.

Chapter 4 – Blood Brothers

"Belief is key to the Wiccan practice. Only can the aware be attuned to patterns of life and death. It is in these patterns that clues reside and as a result, events should not be dismissed as coincidence. Instead, coincidence should be dismissed as imaginary. Everything has meaning."

The Book Of Shadows

Nosebleeds never really used to bother Rich that much. He was prone to them when he climbed to a high enough altitude, and even when the weather was about to thunder, but those nosebleeds usually stopped after a minute or so. After the water in the shower had turned a brilliant red and the blood was still pouring as he wiped himself down with a towel, he began to worry. There are only about eight pints of blood in the human body at any one time, and if he kept on losing it like this, he would be unconscious in around twenty minutes. He knew he should go to a hospital where he could get some sort of coagulant, but something held him back. He didn't know why, but he didn't want to bother the doctors with something like this, as if he was ashamed to ask for help. He also knew he couldn't bother his father for the same reason, not to mention that he would be on his way to work by now, and would be less than pleased if his son called him back for anything but the most serious of reasons.

Instead, his mind turned to his friends. The pattern of the three slashes seemed too perfect, giving him the nagging feeling that this was a problem in his spiritual life, not his physical one and that made Scott Fielding as the intellectual of the group the best person to consult. Mind set, Rich pulled on some clean clothes, stuffed his nostrils with tissue and ran out of his house, heading for the university campus, hoping to find his wise friend, or at least Josh, who would make up in playful humour what he lacked in knowledge.

By the time Rich arrived in the main corridor of the university, the tissue had long since disintegrated, and his white T-shirt now bore the same crimson gouges that had adorned his chest earlier. The bleeding had at least slowed down to a few drops every so often but students still stopped in their tracks and stared as he blundered past, each step becoming harder and harder to take as the loss of blood finally hit him. Compared to the generic grey of the corridor, the droplets of blood that had hit the floor stood out like vibrant splashes of colour in a black and white world. It looked like a bright trail was pointing to where the stumbling teenager was heading, for anyone to follow. As it was, Rich did not care. All he could think about was finding a toilet and grabbing some more tissue and maybe some water before continuing to look for his friends.

A few moments later, Rich was in the male toilets, desperately wiping the blood off his face with a hand towel as the sink filled with water. Once the basin was full, he threw the sodden paper into the bin and plunged his whole head into the cool liquid. The bleeding seemed to have stopped for now, and he wondered how much blood he had actually lost.

There was a low creaking sound coming from one of the cubicles behind him and he heaved his head out of the sink to look around. Nothing there. Maybe he had lost more blood than he thought. He struggled to focus, blinking several times but still he saw nothing that could have made the sound. Groggy like the worst kind of hangover, and hearing things too! He shook his head and once more submerged himself in the sink, not caring that pink tinted water was sloshing onto the floor, and also not noticing the cubicle door slowly opening behind him. A figure stumbled out of the cubicle and lurched towards Rich, who sensing movement, lifted his head and spun round to face the mysterious person. He gasped a mixture of surprise and shock as he came face to face with Matt Blake.

Matt was one of the four who had performed the tragic ritual, and represented the element of Fire. He had chosen the spiritual name of Phoenix, and had also not spoken to Rich at all since Halloween. To Rich's horror, Matt was also covered in blood, the same three lines seemingly scratched across his chest, in exactly the same position as his own. Matt slowly lifted his head to stare uncaringly at his former friend, who could only stare back, unsure of what to say. Should he be sympathetic to his old companion? Or should he play the harsh angle because of their falling out? In the end it was Matt who set the tone of the conversation.

"Well well well," he slurred. "You had a nosebleed too. Half six at a guess? What a coincidence." He seemed to be having trouble getting his words out but his sarcasm was still alarmingly prominent, and Rich guessed that he must also be suffering from severe loss of blood. At least, like him, Matt was no longer actually bleeding. "Although I wouldn't say it's worth drowning yourself over…" Rich scowled. Even now, Matt was trying to put him down.

"Doesn't this strike you as strange?" Rich started, hopefully trying to score an agreement, something that could start them back on the road to reuniting the group. Matt could be a dick, but the four were better together. The other man continued to look blank. "This can't be just coincidence. It can't! What if this is to do with… you know, Chase." At last, Matt's face changed expression. He grinned slyly and shook his head.

"Yeah, and the others are also round here somewhere, squirting blood like bastard water pistols," he snapped sarcastically. "Get over it, Richard. What are you even doing here anyway?" Rich explained that he was looking for the others, and then asked the same question. After all, Matt did not go to university either, he spent most of his time playing bass guitar, practising with his band, Crystal Homicide or lounging about at home. "I'm slowly bleeding to death, idiot," he replied icily. "Go home Rich," he continued. "They won't talk to you. Josh is taking a time out, and Scott is too self-involved to talk to anyone else." Rich's heart sank. So his feelings were true. His friends did not want to get back together, and Matt had made it blatantly obvious that he didn't care anymore. Anger streamed up inside Rich as he thought back to just two weeks ago, when the four of them were the best of friends. They did everything together, and now thanks to this mess, it seemed they would never speak again. As he thought about his destroyed friendships, he struck upon an idea.

"I'm going to the police!" he announced. "I'm going to tell them what happened, just like I should have done on Halloween. I don't know what this is, psychosomatic or whatever, but we are feeling the guilt, and we have to pay for it!" Rich turned to leave but Matt feebly grabbed his arm, trying to pull him back. Rich could sense the weakness of Matt's grip, even as he tried to discourage him.

"Don't be an idiot!" Matt whispered, unable to raise his voice any higher. Rich looked on his former friend pityingly as he realized that while he may have been bullied into keeping his silence when the accident actually happened, he was stronger now. He gently lifted Matt's hand from his own wrist and laid it on the side of the blood-splattered sink. Matt seemed to have given up, and simply slumped down so that his head was resting on his arm, his whole body propped up against the side of the sink as Rich strolled out of the toilets, the door closing behind him to leave Matt in silence.

Ten minutes later, Rich stood in the campus security office, staring at the large lady who bustled about the cramped office. The woman had barely noticed him as he hovered in the doorway. Eventually, he gave an awkward cough, aware of how strange he must look, covered in blood. The officer shot him a troubled glance, immediately taking in his appearance with a frown.

"Oh God, another one," she complained. "And what have you done? Broke your nose whilst trying to vandalise a toilet?" Rich was taken aback, not expecting a greeting like this.

"Um?" he faltered. The security officer shook her head, sending an odd ripple through her large body.

"If that's all you've got to tell me, then you can move along," she said with a wave of her hand. "I'm up to my eyeballs in trouble - have you seen what one of your coursemates has done? Set fire to the oaks and broke some ribs trying to run away by the looks of it. It's always the same with you people, you think you're being funny but all we get out of it is broken windows and hospital visits." Rich considered turning to leave as the lady continued to rummage through her papers but stopped himself, forcefully locking his knees to stop himself from backing out. If he left now, Matt would have won again.

"I'm not leaving!" he said, almost shouting. "This is important. Somebody…somebody's died." Chest heaving, Rich leant back against the door-frame.

"Thousands of people die every day. I don't have time for them either." Once more, the woman made to continue with her sorting.

"You don't understand," Rich murmured softly. "I've killed somebody. A student." He took a breath, satisfied with the look of incomprehension on the woman's face as she sunk into her chair.

"I think you better start talking." This was all she said, a strange glint in her eyes. Rich explained everything from Halloween onwards, and afterwards, the officer looked blankly back at him. The office was adorned with the usual posters with snappy slogans encouraging students to stay safe and protect their belongings, and it was these that Rich looked at, anything to avoid staring into those unbelieving eyes. He was glad that the security officer had just assumed that he was a student. His story would have even less credit if the officer knew that he did not even belong to the university. Eventually, the security officer made a loud clucking noise.

"So let me get this straight," she started, the disbelief already obvious in her voice. "You're a witch. You and some other witches went to the woods on Halloween and *accidentally* killed Chase Rivers and now you're having a nosebleed about it. Right. Show me a trick, Harry."

Rich raised his voice. "No! Aren't you going to take this seriously?" How could a responsible adult act so flippantly when there was a death involved? He eyed the officer malevolently as she stared back. It was clear that she had not been expecting such an outburst, and was choosing her words carefully.

"It's you that should take things seriously," she said with a hint of annoyance at being shouted at. "I already told you the kind of shit I've been dealing with today, and you still feed me this... this rubbish." Rich opened his mouth in anger, ready to start shouting again as the woman changed her approach.

"Listen, honey," she began. *Great!* Rich thought. Not only did this woman not believe him, but she was now treating him like a child. He knew that he could not win now; he had met people like this before. As soon as they think they are better than you, there is no chance that you can ever get through to them. "All I'm saying is that I would take it seriously, but I know it's impossible. You see, Chase Rivers was in his lecture this morning. It's right here on his attendance record." The officer nodded at her computer screen. "Not bad for a corpse, right?"

The bottom of Rich's stomach dropped away, leaving him with an empty feeling. Chase could not have been in any lesson this morning - Rich had seen the body, had seen Scott bury it in the woods. He was completely lost; his thoughts had become a raging hurricane, trying to tear him from the debris of logic to which he clung. The security officer was watching him carefully.

"Anything else I can help you with?" she asked. "Because I've still got to sort out an accident report for the clown who burned those trees." Rich snapped back into focus. He could still try and convince her, show her his powers, but he no longer wanted to. The officer had made him feel stupid and he just wanted to be alone to sort through the mass of questions he now had.

"Err no," he said, before leaving the office.

Chapter 5 - Follow The Signs

Rich walked slowly home, the dream constantly replaying in his mind. The only thing that could have given him a nosebleed was the blast as the bonfire exploded, but in reality, it wasn't him who had bled. He shook his head and looked around him. He had come further than he expected, and was already outside the park. There was a cool breeze in the air, and he lifted up his head so it blew across his face. The faint scent of pine needles played across his nostrils, mixed with another aroma, one that the young man could not place. Still, he did not sense anything deeply malign about it, so carried on walking. The sun was shining brightly through the park railings, casting a striped pattern of light and shadow across the pavement in front of him. At least he had been right about the weather being fine.

A group of teenagers were walking towards him on the other side of the road, typically loud and foul mouthed. Rich lowered his head and quickened his pace. As the group came closer, a gust of wind blew straight into Rich's face, forcing him to look up, straight into the eyes of the last teenager. The spiky haired teen was grinning, his eyes shining with malice. Rich's throat seized up and he staggered back against the fence as if recoiling from a blow to the chest, and then it was over - he could breath again, and the mysterious teenager carried on walking as if nothing had happened. Shaken, he ran after the stranger, grabbing him by the shoulder and roughly spinning him around.

"Ow! What you doin'?" the teenager cried. He was younger than Rich had thought at first, but he could only let go and stare silently, as the confused child took one look at Rich's bloodstained chest then ran after his companions. The kid didn't even have the face that had jolted Rich just moments before. Long after the teenagers had disappeared around the corner hurling light-hearted abuse at him, Rich stayed leaning against the railings, blankly staring through the fabric of the world, into the endless depths of his own fears – for a second, he had been convinced that the boy was Chase Rivers.

Rich ran the rest of the way home, and after checking that his father wasn't home yet, barricaded himself in his room. He now sat with rune tablets laid out in a cross formation in front of him. The four used to consult the runes together, but Rich had never felt the need to use them on his own before. He sighed. It was not like he had any alternative, as he thought back to his conversation with Matt. He was alone whether he liked it or not. The random runes that he had picked from the leather pouch did not fill him with happiness. Inverted Fehu told him to beware of those around him, inverted Thurisaz warned to consider the past; Raido signified a reunion and Eiwaz foretold an encounter. He half hoped that they were hinting at the reforming of him and his friends, but the appearance of Thurisaz was eating away at his vision. He was certain that if he were to reconcile with the others, they would have to forget the past, not give it more attention. After staring at the runes for a while longer, he could divine no further meaning from them and reached for his transcript so he could record the results. Each member of the four had a notebook, in which they recorded any findings or results from scrying and divination, but his transcript had been neglected for a number of months. He had written in it on Halloween, but before that, he had been too busy, and after that, he had been too troubled to even consider writing in his transcript. For a moment, he wondered if the others still kept up their journals. Did they even bother with their new powers, knowing the tragedy that they had caused?

There were five odd marks, like small burns, on the front of the notebook. He scratched at one with his little finger, but shrugged when the mark would not rub off. He was always spilling wax on his stuff; he must have knocked a candle over at some point. Shaking his head, he hastily scribbled the rune pattern onto a blank page, and copied the meanings alongside it. Afterwards, he rolled his pen away and sat cross legged, with his eyes closed. The inverted Thurisaz rune told him to consider the past. What had happened in the past that could affect him so? It had to be the accident on Halloween. That was the only thing he could think of. It must be a spiritual matter that connected the four friends, for he was now certain that all of them had had nosebleeds, so therefore wouldn't anything of great importance be written in the transcript? If only he had kept his up to date more thoroughly. Rich cast these negative thoughts aside and turned his notebook to the last page - "The Initiation".

"Sowen – October 31 – The Initiation

Oh my god! This should have been a special day, the day that The Four were finally brought together, but instead, everything has fallen apart. The ritual was going fine until Chase showed up right at the very end when we were doing the naming part. The power was so great, I don't think even Scott expected it. We were thrown back and not really hurt but Chase got the full blast. I don't know what to do with myself. Scott sorted out the body and everything, but I can't help thinking that we killed someone. Is our freedom and empowerment worth someone's life? They seem to think it is..."

The Transcript Of Altair

Rich became lost in thought once more. Reading what he had written back then made him sound so cold and heartless, but that wasn't how it was. No one can predict how they will act when faced with tragedy. He shook his head and turned his mind to the runes. Look to the past, a reunion, beware of those around you? What could it mean? Chase was dead, he suffered first-degree burns and there was no way he could have survived. But why was Rich dreaming about his death every night? Why did the security officer swear that Chase was in his lessons today? And why did the runes seem to relate to this particular event? Everything was too confusing and his head began to throb, so he closed his transcript notebook and undressed. Now in his shorts, he slipped into bed and closed his eyes, knowing what would await him in the world of sleep.

There was a blinding flash as the bonfire erupted, a column of flame shooting skyward. The four men were thrown backwards, falling perfectly into their compass directions, a quartet of directional chaos. Now a grinning face with spiked hair, fury burning in his eyes, laughing. The ritual had worked, and the links forged between the young men was stronger than any of them had predicted. But something was wrong. There was blood on the autumn leaves littering the woodland floor. And laughing. The laughing never stopped...

Rich woke up, a cold sweat coating his face, like he had been drowned in freezing water before waking. The same dream as always, yet different somehow. The grinning face of the mysterious teenager had taken the focus of the dream away from the tragedy of Chase's death. It was almost as if the accident meant nothing compared to the events now afoot. He headed once more to his mirror and studied his drained reflection. He had started to regain a little colour after his nosebleed, but he still looked pale and distraught. In the corner of his eye, he could see his altar shelf reflected behind him, with one tall blue candle standing higher than anything else. Towards the centre of the candle, it became distorted where a handprint had been melted into the wax. It was Josh Thomas's handprint and they had all made these candles for each other back when they were friends. The idea was that by melting your handprint into the candle, you were linked to it and so if one of your brothers needed your help, they could simply light their candle and they would feel your call. Rich knew that if he tilted his head slightly, he would be able to see similar candles in red and green, bearing the handprints of Scott and Matt. Even now, the Wiccan's former friends were not beyond contact. He could still not shake the idea that there was something serious going on. Surely that would justify his trying to talk to the others. After all, they would want to know, wouldn't they?

It was 02:30. Rich walked over to his shelf and lit a match. He hesitated as his hand hovered over the tip of the green candle. He had made up his mind, he was going to get in touch with the others, but did he really need to waste the candle? He did have a telephone after all. He shook the match until it extinguished, picked up his mobile and sat on his bed as he dialled Scott's number. The phone rang twelve times before he reluctantly hung up. The intellectual was probably asleep, resting his overused brain, he reasoned. Not particularly wanting to talk to Matt after their encounter earlier, he decided to call Josh next. This time, he was not disappointed as his former best friend drowsily answered.

"Err, hello?"

"It's Rich." There was a moment's silence before a reply came.

"Oh," Josh said negatively. "What do you want?" Rich sighed but could not criticise. After all he would be annoyed if someone had called him at half past two in the morning.

"I tried phoning Scott, but he didn't answer."

"Good for him. Rich, it's late and I'm not in the mood to chat, so just get on with it, ok?" Rich paused. Was he just heading for a repeat of the conversation with the security officer? No. Josh was there, he would understand. Rich told himself this as he took a deep breath, swallowing any reservations he had.

"Fine," he began. "I think something is going on. I went to Campus Security and she said that Chase was in his lessons today. Then I saw him on the way home, only it wasn't him."

"There. It wasn't him," Josh interjected. "I don't see any problem here."

"No! I mean it was him, but when I looked again, it wasn't! And what about him turning up at uni today?"

Josh sighed, obviously losing his patience. "For God's sake, Rich. Everybody knows lecturers just fake their registers when they can't be bothered to do them. Chase wasn't in uni today, and you didn't see him in the street. The mind plays tricks. Just forget it. Now if you're finished, I did plan to sleep tonight." Josh was going to hang up, Rich could tell. A wave of fury began to sweep over him. Why would no one listen? So he had never been the most involved member of the group, but now he had something valid to say, he shouldn't just be blanked completely. Before he knew what he was doing, he began blurting frantically into the receiver.

"But the nosebleeds!" he shouted. "Me and Matt had nosebleeds! It made the exact same pattern. It can't be coincidence!" He stopped himself, gasping for breath after his rant. On the other end of the line, Josh was silent. "Josh?"

"It's nothing. Goodnight Rich." The phone clicked

as Josh hung up. Rich stood holding the receiver for a moment, staring vacantly. He had been sure that Josh would listen to him. They were the closest friends before the accident, and he could still not get over the fact that the past now counted for nothing. He dropped the phone down and slumped face first onto his bed. Before he knew it, he was crying into his pillow, thinking about all the things he used to have. He would sacrifice all the power he had now for just one day where he could hang out with his old friends and a bottle of cheap cider under the climbing frame they used to inhabit at the local playground.

Rich dried his eyes and sat up, surveying his room. It had been a while since he had tidied it. He smiled to himself, remembering something his father had told him.

"It's better to do something to keep yourself busy, so you don't dwell on whatever's got you down," he had said. Rich looked at the clutter on his floor - a tangled mess of clothes, papers and rubbish. Tidying it would definitely keep him occupied until daylight. He bent down and picked up a book from beneath a shirt he had thrown down a couple of nights ago. The book was old and worn, and he didn't recognise it. He turned it over in his hands, trying to find a place for it in his mind, but he drew a blank. The book definitely wasn't one of his own. He read the title: *Back To The Beginning*. Flicking through the pages, he was not surprised to find them all empty. The sign was obviously in the title alone. He was sure he had never seen this book before, but its meaning was clear. He had to go back to the beginning, to where it all started. This was the one way to see what was going on, if any of it was true. His face was set as he pulled on some trousers.

Half an hour later, Rich was standing in a clearing deep inside the woods. The trees blocked out most of the moonlight, giving the clearing an eerie glow, but he knew this clearing well enough even without full sight. He knew that to the right would be a corner of stonework remaining from the settlement that used to be here hundreds of years ago. There were some other remnants: fragments of walls and outlines of plots, but time had claimed the rest of the village.

He could see lots of odd shapes scattered around the clearing, and remembered that last time he was here, all four of them had left so quickly that a lot of the candles and oils that they had used were still littered across the ground.

As he picked his way through the debris he reached a blackened circle of soil, the place where their bonfire had been. Rich knelt down and held his hand above the ashes, closing his eyes. The air was moving in a strange manner, circling to the centre of the pit and then shooting up as if a fire still burnt there, sending waves of heat into the sky. Without thinking, he stepped into the centre of the charred ground. The air swirled around him, encircling him in a tornado as it shot towards the stars. The air currents made a whistling sound as they shot past, the sound getting louder as the air gathered speed. Soon, the whistling was so loud that Rich had to force himself not to bolt. As the sound rose to a high-pitched screech, a new range of noises emerged within. First there was a bang, then a scream, then the faintest of panicked whispers. Amongst the chaotic blend of shouts and screams, Rich thought he recognized his own voice…

Something jabbed Rich in the back. He opened his eyes and snapped around. Everything was silent and even in the dark, he could tell there was no one there, but the air currents had again changed. They now seemed to stem from a point across the clearing, fanning out and rising up, as if something on the other side of the fire pit was repelling them. He got to his feet and edged towards the disturbance. That was when he saw it. At the edge of the clearing, the ground was churned up, as if it had been ploughed by an uneven blade. He stared as he took in the roughly hewn rectangular hole and the mounds of earth surrounding it. Chase Rivers was definitely not dead and buried, and by the looks of it, he had clawed his way out in an extremely bad mood.

Chapter 6 - The Devil's Handshake

Rich took a step back in shock, his blue eyes wide and
unblinking. He silently cursed himself for not bringing
anything with him, as now was the perfect time to use the
calling candles he had been tempted by before. Even
though his craft was not the kind that used a magic wand,
he wished he had something with him that he could
brandish. He always felt a lot braver when he had a stick in
his hand. He paused for a moment, thinking about how
childish that sounded. He knew he should run home and
tell the others, but again something was preventing him
from taking the sensible course of action. He had always
been in the background of the group, going along with
whatever the others decided. If he hurried to them straight
away, he would forfeit any chance he had of dealing with
the problem himself.

The air had changed again, yet Rich could not define
it. It was as if the wind was blowing from every direction at
the same time, creating a frenzy of air currents that were
impossible for him to single out. He turned away from the
grave and once more surveyed the clearing he was standing
in. The moon had moved and was now shining directly
down into the clearing, replacing the blue glow with
shimmering silver light. Without warning - without even
slowing down first - the air in the clearing stopped dead
and the clouds in the sky seemed to bunch together
menacingly. Rich spun around, trying to find the cause of
this unusual occurrence and stopped, staring upwards as a
column of cloud dropped down to the tops of the trees and
then split into two separate strands. The main body of the
swirling grey mass now covered the moon, as if it was not
allowed to witness what was about to happen. Rich stayed
rooted to the spot, the hairs on his neck tingling as the two

lumps of cloud twisted and morphed in front of his eyes. Within seconds, the cloud had taken the form of a pair of giant hands, each one as big as Rich himself. The fingers were bared, as if to shoot out and grab something, and each one ended in a metre-long talon. The hands hovered menacingly, leaving him to ponder whether the huge claws could actually hurt him, what with them being made of mist. He decided he didn't want to find out.

Suddenly, the connection between Rich's mind and his legs seemed to become re-established, his brain pounding the same message out over and over again. Run. Run. *Run!* He turned and sprinted towards the edge of the clearing as, at the exact same moment, the left hand scythed down, gouging a huge trench into the soil. The Air Elemental didn't look back as he drew nearer to the safety of the trees, the idea of escaping still the only thought in his mind. One of the huge hands slammed into his back, throwing him forwards onto the ground, the trunk of the nearest tree just out of his reach. The young man cried out as he rubbed mud from his eyes and tried to stand, but the hands were one step ahead of him. The left hand gently pinched his leg between its huge thumb and index finger, and began to drag him back into the centre of the clearing. Rich's torso burned as it scraped along the rough ground but at least he knew that the air-hands could indeed touch him. He decided that this was of little help as the left hand settled across his legs, holding him in place as the right hand rose high above and clenched into a terrible fist the size of a garden shed.

Rich closed his eyes, preparing for the inevitable. He knew he was going to die, and strangely, he wasn't thinking about the fact that he would be dead, he was wondering how it would look to whoever found his body. The hands would almost certainly disappear after their work was done, so would it just look like Rich had been the victim of some terrible gang beating? Before he could answer himself, the fist slammed down into his face and he felt his nose shatter, the warmth of blood once more covering his jaw and chest. As the stunned Air Elemental blinked blood out of his eyes, he was surprised that he was still alive. Maybe the hands didn't have that much strength, but he secretly suspected that they simply wanted to prolong his suffering for as long as possible. He wasn't going to let that happen, as he was struck by a sudden thought. If the ethereal fists could touch him, then surely he could touch them? As the right hand rose again, preparing to slam down once more, Rich kicked out at the left hand pinning him down and felt it give way a little. The monstrous right hand plummeted, whooshing through the air as it sped on its way, but this time, he was ready. At the last moment, he kicked upwards and then rolled to the side. As he had reckoned, the left hand was unprepared for any resistance, and he was safely out of harm's way as the huge fist plunged into the ground with such a force that the trees themselves shook. If he had been underneath that, his skull would have been crushed. Face pounding with pain and blood coursing down his chest, Rich rolled onto his feet and turned to face his opponents, hoping to see that the tremendous impact had damaged them in some way. Unfortunately, the two oversized hands were still in perfect condition, and to Rich's horror, were both shooting straight towards him, fingers flexing eagerly. He screamed as the hands clamped around his body and hoisted him off the ground. The three twisting forms continued to rise until they were well above the trees, embedded in the night sky like a writhing constellation of stars. The hands began to shake him like a rag doll, his head snapping back and forth as he was buffeted in every direction. It was as if the young man was floating unsupported: everywhere he looked he could see the stars, even if he looked through the hands themselves, which were oddly translucent, like looking through smoke. Rich began to feel sick and thought how sweet it would be to just close his eyes and let death take him. *No.* He couldn't give up now! He had to fight. He racked his brains for anything he could try, and then the thought struck him almost as hard as the hands were shaking him. He was a Wiccan, and he was the Air Elemental. He was Altair. He just hoped he could pull off something this big…

Rich closed his eyes and tried to clear his mind for a second, a difficult task considering that the giant hands were now jerking him so hard he thought he could feel his bones rattling inside his skin. Not at all satisfied that he had the right level of concentration but forced into action by the hands tightening their grip - deciding to choke the life out of him - Rich muttered a small phrase in the Wiccan language the four of them had invented.

"Ainarai, barel inanar marel," he said, hoping that he had translated it right. The language was still relatively new, and he didn't exactly have time to work it out in great detail. He was reminded of this as the hands squeezed with fresh ferocity. His ribs would crack if he didn't free himself soon. He tilted his head back as far as he dared and opened his mouth. As he had hoped, wisps of air began to flow into his mouth, refreshingly cool as they slipped down his throat. This air was not going into his lungs so he did not have to stop to breathe out: this air was headed straight for his spiritual core. He kept his mouth open until he had gathered enough of the thin strands of oxygen, then closed it, curling himself into as much of a ball as he could, despite the huge slab-like palms crushing him.

This is it, thought Rich. This was going to be the true test of his powers. He paused for one last moment of preparation and then screamed, uncurling himself with such a snap that his arms hurt. With a loud clap of thunder, the air that Rich had taken into himself burst outwards like a huge shockwave. The enormous hands were ripped to pieces as the blast surged through them, until they were nothing more than a few tendrils of mist rapidly fading away in the clear night sky. Rich looked out across the forest, bathed in darkness, and then at the university campus on the outskirts, and the lights of the city twinkling just beyond. The tower of the Spyrus Corporation jutted into the night sky like a lightning rod, its many floors still bustling with activity, a true business that never slept. He marvelled at this once in a lifetime view for a split second before his own air left him completely and he began to plummet towards the cold, hard soil below.

Rich was falling faster and faster, his arms flailing as the forest canopy rose up to greet him. He had completely forgotten to plan for his survival once he had freed himself from the giant claws. He screamed as his fingers clutched at the air, pointlessly. Or maybe not. To his surprise, the air seemed to be getting more and more tangible, until he found himself holding two slipstreams between his fingers. It was as if the air had sensed his need and heightened his connection so he could land safely. He was now sliding comfortably; using the slipstreams like a skateboarder might use grindrails in an elaborate stunt. Rich grimaced through his bruised face as he imagined the atmosphere as a huge curtain and himself sliding down it like a small child. He considered how easy it would be to fall if he lost his concentration even for a second. By the time he reached the ground, he was floating at his own leisure, hopping lightly off the airstreams and landing softly on the forest floor, sitting down with a bump. He truly had become a master of the air, he thought as he swelled with pride.

Unfortunately for him, his tormenter had chosen another method of torture to finish him off...

Like a fish being snatched out of the water, Rich was grabbed and hoisted into an upright position. Still no one was behind him, but his back burned as if two flaming hooks had been embedded there. His right arm was pulled out, stretched until his shoulder clicked. The pain was unbearable, and he could not help but cry aloud. His index finger began to wave, as if being toyed with by an invisible cat, and then a loud crack rang through the clearing, as the finger was snapped backwards. Crack! Crack! Crack! One by one, Rich's fingers were snapped and left hanging loosely, twitching with every blow the tortured soul received. His own tears were the last things he felt before the darkness closed in.

In The Beginning
October 31

Chapter 7 - Antichronology

An unusually warm October sun shone down upon the main quad of The University of Central England, an inconspicuous campus nestled in the heart of the country. The quad itself was surrounded on all four sides by tall buildings, themselves an intricate maze of corridors, staircases, lecture theatres and classrooms. The wide lawn was traversed by a number of tarmac paths, which snaked their way across the grass like a net, holding nature down into the constricted order of the university. In each corner of the quad stood a towering oak, reminders that every year students may pass through the quad and things will change, but these trees would remain, a constant strength. Each tree now bore a mass of bright orange crepe streamers, catching on the breeze and reaching out eerily into the air. Large pumpkins leered out at passers-by from every available window ledge, a tacky reminder that it was Halloween.

Students were milling about the quad, admiring the decorations. Amidst the crowd walked Scott Fielding and Josh Thomas. Each had a rucksack slung over his shoulder, and both of them were wearing short-sleeved t shirts to celebrate the fact that the sun was indeed shining despite the oak trees having decided long ago that it was officially autumn. Scott's bright blue eyes narrowed as he took in the Halloween decorations, and he made a small disapproving clicking noise in his throat as he turned to look down at Josh, a full head shorter than him. Josh remained mercifully silent for the time being as he was well aware of his companion's disdain for the commercialisation of witchcraft. As the pair of them reached the centre of the quad, Josh nudged his companion, who tore his contemptuous glare from the leering pumpkins. Heading towards them from a gap between two of the buildings was the other half of their group. Matt Blake was confidently striding across the grass, his shoulder length blonde hair flowing impressively behind him as he walked. He was looking intently at a little scrap of paper, but as soon as he saw the others he pocketed it. Just behind him was Rich Benson, who was grinning in their direction. Matt was stony faced as always, usually preferring to keep his silence than betray any signs of emotion. It always amused Josh to see those two on campus. They were not actually students, and he often wondered how they managed to spend so much time at the university without ever being questioned by any of the other students, let alone the staff. Still, he supposed, it's not like anyone would be expecting nineteen year olds to spend any time at a learning facility if they didn't have to. Matt was doing a part time course at the local college, but he rarely turned up because he was always on the UCE campus instead. The two new arrivals fell into step with the others and they began to talk as they crossed into the shadow of the Heffernan Block.

"Hey guys! How was lessons?" Rich asked, a sly grin on his face. He always liked to ask about lessons, considering he never had to do any himself. Ever businesslike, but with an unmistakable smile, Scott rolled his eyes while Josh grinned mischievously.

"Fine. How was doing sod all?" Josh's smile grew even bigger as his best mate pretended to look hurt. Teasing each other about their education habits was considered a traditional greeting between them. The two jokers fell behind slightly and immediately started laughing and talking about something on television the night before as if they were carrying on a conversation they had already started.

"They don't show repeats of *Holby City* you idiot!" Josh roared as the two of them burst into fits of laughter. Matt leaned forwards, using the noise as cover.

"Is everything ready for tonight?" he whispered. Scott tensed, and looked around, to make sure that nobody was listening. To anyone else, this would seem like an unnecessary precaution, but Matt knew that he was simply being careful. Talking openly about this sort of thing could get people into trouble.

Unknown to anyone else, University was only half of these young men's lives. For most of the time, they went to lectures, went out with girls or chilled in the sun, but the rest of their time was spent in the shadows. A world of secrets and whispers took the other part of their lives. Matt, Scott, Josh and Rich were Wiccans. At least they would be after tonight. So far they had talked and theorized a great deal, but had only done research, nothing practical. Tonight, Halloween, was going to be a ritual that would finally initiate them into the craft, and hopefully empower them with actual magical skills.

Scott paused, seemingly deep in thought before he nodded in confirmation. He turned around to face the comedians, who were still laughing heartily. A slight frown flickered across his face when they did not immediately acknowledge him, but it was gone in a second.

"You two know about the plans for later, right?" The question was as good as rhetorical. Despite his slightly stuffy impression, he trusted the others completely. This didn't stop him however, from constantly asking if they knew what they were doing. Josh looked blank.

"Something's happening tonight?" he asked curiously. Scott opened his mouth, ready to dish out his condemnation, when he spotted that both of them were stifling laughter.

"Of course we know!" exclaimed Rich, in between chuckles. "What do you think we are, stupid?" It looked as if he was about to get an answer, so he continued. "We have to meet at the top f-" He was cut short by a sharp nudge in the ribs from Josh. He was nodding his head to the side frantically, and as the other three looked across, they saw Chase Rivers running towards them across the grass. Chase was a year younger than them, only eighteen, and none of them knew him that well. As he got closer, a smile spread across his face, his dark hair gelled into perfect spikes. Matt, Rich and Josh hastily plastered bemused grins on their faces, but Scott made no effort to hide his annoyance.

"Hey, hey! Smile!" Before they knew it, Chase had whipped a camera out of his pocket and blinded them all with the flash. Rich thought the young man would be in for a great picture as he looked around at the increasingly fake expressions that he knew he also wore.

"Hey…. you," Josh said, still grinning strangely. He had obviously forgotten Chase's name, but the younger guy didn't appear to notice. There was a minute of awkward silence, with Chase looking expectantly around the group until to everyone's surprise, Matt stepped forwards and gave him a friendly pat on the shoulder.

"Hey Chase, how are you doing?" Josh and Rich looked at each other, trying not to laugh. Scott looked like he wanted to do anything but laugh, yet he managed to keep his mouth shut.

"I'm ok," Chase replied. "Oh, I checked that essay you asked me to. I changed a few things but otherwise it was fine." He fished around in his bag for a second, pulled out a roll of paper and handed it to Matt with a small smile.

Josh sniggered as he exchanged a knowing look with his friend. "What are you guys up to?" Scott's eyes flicked maliciously towards him, but he didn't see.

"We were just talking about tonight." Matt answered. "We have this thing where w-"

"We're not up to anything," cut in Scott, his face contorted into what he hoped was a blank expression, but what looked more to Josh like he had gone brain dead. He was fully aware that his friend had difficulty hiding the fact that he was annoyed, in fact he was almost exactly the opposite of Matt, who could have just fought in World War Three and no one would be able to guess. Scott walked off, avoiding Chase's grey eyes. The two jokers followed, casting Matt a strange, questioning look before he himself turned to look apologetically at Chase.

"Well, I guess I'll see you later," he muttered before hurrying to catch up with the others. Chase stood where he was, looking dejectedly after the group he desperately wanted to be a part of.

"Yeah... later."

Matt jogged slowly into the building at the end of the path. He didn't know which building it was, as he had never bothered to learn much about the university. He preferred to learn what he wanted to, not what he was told, and so had left school as soon as he could. He found himself in a long corridor, with identical doors running along each plain, generic wall. It did not take long to find the room the others were in, as they had chosen the one furthest away from any of the others. He walked into the room, closed the door and then sat with the two clowns who were sitting on tabletops. Scott was standing in front of them in a strange parody of the student-teacher relationship that was seen every day in this building. Matt cast a disapproving look at their self appointed Moses, who was ready for an argument, a scowl on his face.

"What was that?" Scott demanded angrily. Matt shrugged.

"What? He helps me with work sometimes, he's a clever guy."

Scott shook his head. "You're disgraceful. You're just using him to do your homework aren't you? You don't even like him!" The accusation grated with Matt. *Coming from the guy who probably did all of his homework the night he got it anyway*, he thought venomously.

"You're the one who just froze him out," he said quietly.

Scott was quick to defend himself. "It's not that I don't like him," he said. "I just think that this should be kept between us. That's all. No outsiders." He looked away, apparently thinking that the conversation was over.

"Whatever, I didn't realise this was members only." Matt muttered. Scott snapped back round to glare, a definite scowl on his face.

"Of course it is! It has to be." Matt did not look away, but instead chose to stare concretely, both pairs of blue eyes boring into each other. Rich looked back and forth between the two of them. Neither was wavering in his resolve, so he decided to interject.

"How do we know this is going to work?" The rocky glare swung round to him, exasperated. Rich thought he saw the faintest of smiles as Matt looked down at his feet, but it didn't matter. Neither of them had won and the tension would soon be forgotten.

"If you believe it, it will work," said Scott matter of factly. Josh shook his head.

"Yeah," he said sarcastically. "We've all read the Book of Shadows, but what do you *really* think?" Scott glared for a second, and then looked down at the floor. Rich sighed. He had only asked that question to distract the two rivals, he didn't intend for Josh to ask a stupid question that would only annoy Scott further. To his exasperation, Matt looked up again, a sly grin creeping across his features.

"He doesn't know what he really thinks," began Matt. "He's scared to admit the truth. This is stupid. Witchcraft? Hocus Pocus? I guarantee the only thing we'll get tonight is a cold." Rich scowled at their companion, who was still grinning. What the hell was he doing? They were becoming increasingly ruffled, and the ritual was happening tonight! They didn't need a falling out right now.

"Then why are you here?" snapped Scott acidly.

"Call it a lack of anything better to do." At this, Scott looked as if he was going to jump across the desk and hit him. Instead, he swallowed his rage and turned to each one of them in turn, a defiant look on his face.

"This is going to be the culmination of all the research we've done." Scott said, glaring. "Everything we hoped for will happen tonight. Think of the power we will have!" he said as he turned to look at Rich, who gave him a smile. "Real life witchcraft! None of this kids' crap! We will be the real thing! Just think about it. No more being beaten at stuff or being called weird!"

At this point, Scott paused and scanned the others once more. He was sure all of them had some bitterness about something that had gone wrong in the past. *The What If factor*. Something that would have worked if only they had had that extra edge. For him, it was the embarrassment of Year 9 Sports Day. Every child had been forced to sign up for something, regardless of ability, and Scott had been put up for the 800 metres. Generally, he had no problem with running, but in front of the whole school in a compulsory situation was not his idea of fun. He had come dead last, a panting chubby mess in front of a jeering crowd.

Ever since that day, the young man had grown to resent sports of any kind, seeing them as a form of public humiliation. *But if he had the power...* He could have given himself more traction, could have maintained his heart rate or got rid of his stitch. He wouldn't have made himself win of course, but anything than dead last.

"Are you saying we should use it to cheat at stuff?" asked Josh, seemingly reading Scott's thoughts.

"There's nothing wrong with using a talent that you've worked hard for. And anyway, what do you think the unused part of your brain is for? It wouldn't be like using drugs or anything, it's just using your head."

"If it works," cut in Matt. The look on Scott's face suggested that this sniping comment was the last straw.

"It *will* work. See you tonight," he finished, staring at the disbeliever, who was once more looking at his feet. With that, Scott picked up his bag and strode out of the room. Josh shook his head as he gave a relieved whistle that the little meeting was now over.

Chapter 8 – Haven Rematch

Scott stormed straight past his English classroom, trying desperately hard to swallow back the silent rage exploding within him. He ignored the staring faces in the corridor as he pushed people aside, hurrying for the exit before he lost control. As he erupted into the sunlight, he broke into a run across the grass of the quad, heading for the far corner. He quickly slipped into the narrow alleyway between the two buildings on the opposite side of the lawn and ran into the forest that backed onto the campus. To the untrained eye it would have looked as if he was just aimlessly blundering through the trees and bushes, but he knew exactly where he was heading.

At the beginning of the four friends' interest in witchcraft, they had discovered a small clearing which they had affectionately named The Haven. It was an ideal place to meet up and talk about their findings, and to even practice a few of the things they had learned. None of it had worked of course, but that was another reason why tonight's initiation was so important. It would make everything worthwhile.

The anger rose once more as he emerged into The Haven. It was larger than it looked, but was cramped by the tree stumps that they used as seats. Breathing deeply, Scott thought back to when the four of them had spent all of their free time beating back the undergrowth and arranging the logs into a rough circle. It had been their summer holiday project, and they had even brought a tent and crashed there for a couple of nights.

Despite them visiting it regularly, the forest was already beginning to claim back its territory, with brambles and nettles creeping into the clearing from all directions. Someone had even dumped a load of rusty metal poles next to one of the trees. He walked over to the poles and picked one up, feeling the weight of it in his hands. *I'll show them,* Scott thought resolutely as he started hacking into the brambles around the edges of the clearing. The satisfying sound of the pole whipping through the air only fuelled his rage as he began to strike harder and harder, smashing the encroaching plants into tattered, bleeding wrecks. *How dare he!* Scott's mind screamed, focusing particularly on Matt as he decapitated a cluster of white-headed flowers. *He has got a point though...* whispered a smaller voice in the young man's head.

"No!" he shouted aloud as he swung the pole around his head and brought it crashing down into a patch of nettles. Scott turned around, scything the pole through the air until there was a loud clang that echoed startlingly loudly through the trees. His arms shook violently from the vibrations of metal hitting metal. His face shining with sweat and anger, Scott looked up straight into the eyes of the very person he was fuming at. His friend and now rival had also picked up one of the flaking, copper coloured poles, and was wearing a slightly confused frown as he stood there, blocking Scott's swing.

"I just wanted to apologise," Matt said. "I shouldn't have kept ragging you." Scott didn't even register the words as the rage burst into action once more. Matt had deliberately picked up another pole and blocked the swing. Why didn't he just cough or something to announce his presence? Was Matt challenging him? Scott's mind laughed cruelly. He had taken fencing lessons when he was twelve years old. If Matt wanted a fight, he would get one.

Matt stared at his bitter friend thoughtfully. He didn't expect him to realize how hard this was to do, as apologizing was not really in his nature, but he at least expected Scott to say something - anything to acknowledge that he had accepted the apology. Out of nowhere, Scott swung the metal pole he was holding upwards and around, brandishing it like a sword. He then lunged forwards as if to skewer him with it. It was only Matt's lightning fast reflexes that saved him as he jumped backwards out of the weapon's reach. Wide-eyed, he looked up questioningly, but it seemed that his friend had lost it, already bringing the weapon around for another attack. Matt tightened his grip on his own pole and raised it across his chest as his opponent leaped forwards, swinging his bar towards Matt's head. Again just in time, he lashed out and The Haven once more rang with the sound of metal on metal. Stuck in this position, straining against the force of Scott's strikes, he was suddenly overcome with the urge to smile. Scott had always been Mr. Predictable, and now here he was going utterly mental, laying into him with a metal pole.

"I think you've definitely got some anger issues that you need to work out," he taunted as he launched into his own string of swipes that sent flakes of rust flying around the clearing like odd, copper butterflies. Scott looked taken aback, both at Matt's words and by the fact that he was actually fighting back.

"Why do you always have to undermine me on everything?" Scott shouted as he knocked the other pole to the side and lunged forwards again, this time catching his adversary in the side as he tried to spin away. Matt shouted out in pain and he froze, suddenly afraid. His anger was subsiding rapidly with the thought that he could have hurt his friend. To his relief, Matt looked up at him with a grin, already raising his pole ready to continue fighting.

"I didn't mean to undermine you," Matt said as he flicked his pole into his left hand. "I was just voicing my opinion." Scott swept low, aiming to catch his opponent's legs, but his reach fell short. "I guess I just don't believe things as readily as you," Matt admitted as he sliced his pole downwards, deflecting another powerful swing. "But don't get me wrong; I know exactly what to do when the time comes." Matt's hair kept falling down in front of his face, so he had to keep swinging his head to be able to see properly. As such, it meant that he looked a lot like he was dancing rather than fighting.

"I don't know why I'm so confident about this," considered Scott as he again slashed upwards, ripping Matt's t-shirt. Stunned, Matt looked down at his chest as the red cotton darkened with the blood seeping into it. "That's two nil isn't it?" rallied Scott. The rage he was feeling when he arrived had now vanished, and he was actually having fun facing off with one of his best friends. Matt smiled slyly as he again straightened up, preparing to fight. Scott tried to lunge forwards once more, but his rival was already racing towards him. As Matt passed the outstretched pole, he spun around and brought his own weapon crashing across Scott's shoulder blades. Scott reeled forwards from the impact, but Matt had already grabbed his pole with his free hand. Somehow, he had got his foot behind Scott's legs, and as he forced his adversary backwards with his own weapon, Scott pitched over Matt's foot and landed hard on his back. Matt wrenched the pole out of his hand and raised it above his head while he swished his own weapon down and pointed it at his throat. Scott was winded, shocked and surprised that he had been beaten down so easily, especially after he had dominated most of the encounter.

"Two all then," said Matt, still smiling. He threw both poles down to the ground and stood over his friend, his eyes flashing with intensity. "See you tonight." Scott stared as Matt strolled out of The Haven. He shook his head, bemused yet impressed. He had thought that he had the power, with his anger and the fencing lessons, but Matt had been in control all along.

As Scott lay on his back, panting loudly, he realised why there was so much friction between Matt and himself. It dawned on him that he considered Matt his equal, and that was a worrying notion. It was all too easy to lord it over Rich, who would follow anyone to the end of the world as long as he was awake, and Josh would only question him if he saw the point, but Matt was different. He had knowledge, expertise and cunning but he showed none of it, after all he had somehow gotten Scott to calm down and reconcile with him before blatantly thrashing him in their brief exchange.

Climbing wearily to his feet, he brushed the flecks of rust from his chest and shrugged to himself. Perhaps Matt was his equal, maybe he was his superior even, but in a few hours that wouldn't matter. Nothing would.

Scott's mood picked up as he headed through the city towards a side street that was off the main high street. Away from the glass fronts and fancy displays, this street was a lot quieter, with only a few people hurrying across the road in order to get to the better-known shops. The young man loved the fact that right next to all the corporate brands and logos was a feast of smaller establishments that had one off finds at bargain prices. He thought it was a fitting match considering the double lives he and his friends were about to embark on – regular on one hand, with a host of hidden values on the other.

It was to one of these shops that Scott was now heading. He had discovered it quite by chance, whilst looking for a present for an old girlfriend, and had always kept it stored in the back of his mind. Now, it seemed like the perfect choice for his needs. *Buckeye's* was a tiny building with cream coloured woodwork, and a window display of fairy statues dancing around a fountain. *No wonder it was off the beaten track*, he mused.

He stepped into the shop, a tiny bell ringing somewhere above him. He was immediately assaulted by the strong scent of incense, the air thick and hazy with the smouldering sticks. Directly in front of him was an island counter piled high with more of the happily dancing fairies. The young man had often wondered why anybody in their right mind would walk into town with the specific intention of buying a fairy statue, and judging by the layer of dust that covered the ornaments, not many people did.

To the right was a wall covered with shelves, all holding books with titles like '*Charm Yourself Thin*' and '*Teen Witch's Almanac*'. On the opposite wall was another set of shelves holding a varied assortment of candles and oils. Most of it was tourist rubbish, dragons and skeletons and the like, but there was also the odd hidden gem like the essential oils. Scott found himself wondering if the proprietor and the patrons knew the true potential of the items they had, or if they just thought they looked cool. The young man walked straight to the back of the shop where there was a small counter and a door with a red curtain hung over it. Scott had never been up there, but he knew that the owner of the shop sometimes did private tarot readings in the flat above the shop – for a charge of course.

The owner was currently sat at the counter, a large steaming mug of tea clamped in her hands. She was definitely a showman, her hair dyed red with a patterned scarf tied elaborately round it. She wore huge hoops dangling from her ears, and too much make up on her face. It was like looking at a mixing palette that smiled and smelled of rose water. Her ringed fingers clinked as she set the mug down and turned to Scott with professional warmth.

"Let me guess," she grinned, showing smoker's teeth. "Handsome young thing like you… must be a love spell right? You want to keep her coming back for more? Let me see, I've got Lovers' Candles, Cupid's Arrow – that's a good one – Gentle Lovers' Remedy-"

"No, no," Scott cut in. "Nothing like that." The last thing he wanted was to spend twenty pounds on a bag of crap. The woman raised an eyebrow. "What I need is a chalice. A good one."

"Well why didn't you say?" The woman beamed, taking him by the arm and leading him to one of the shelves. A few moments later, he had selected a sturdy crystal goblet. "Anything else?" At this, Scott pulled a scrap of paper from his pocket.

"I need frankincense, myrrh, benzoin, sandalwood, cinnamon, vervain, rosemary and bay – oils if possible but powders will do." The shop owner paused for a moment, taking in the list.

"Well," she exclaimed. "Your house is certainly going to smell… interesting." Scott nodded, turning away whilst she fetched the ingredients, humming a cheerful tune as she flitted between the shelves. To her credit, she seemed to know instantly exactly where all the items were but she obviously didn't have any idea what she was actually selling. A few minutes later, Scott left the shop, his arms loaded, but his wallet considerably lighter. The woman watched him go, her smile plastered on her face until the bell rung once more to signify his departure. She immediately dropped her shopkeeper's airs and scrabbled for the phone that was nestled underneath a mess of newspapers. She hastily dialled with baited breath.

"A message for the other side. It's happened. Yes, all of the ingredients, and the chalice. It must be soon. Tell them to look for the host any day now." The woman hung up the phone and sat back, peering into her now empty teacup with satisfaction.

Chapter 9 – Definity Theory

"Knowing the name of something defines the action you must take to focus on it."

The Book Of Shadows

The antique grandfather clock in the hallway chimed eight o'clock as Scott paced back and forth. If his father were here, he would no doubt tell him off for scuffing the carpet but he had left when Scott was thirteen. A lot had changed since then, and Scott often wondered if his father ever thought about him, about how he had turned out.

He was disturbed from his musings by the doorbell, a classical tune pealing through from the doorstep. With a deep breath, Scott pulled the door open and tried to smile as he saw Rich, arms wrapped around himself against the chill.

"Come in dude," he said, moving to one side so that his visitor could enter. As Rich stepped into the house, he was forced to look around in awe, despite having been there many times before. Every wall was covered in ornate frames holding classic art, every surface an exhibition of various trinkets that Scott's mother had brought back from her travels. All Rich knew was that she was a rep with some company and was frequently out of the country showcasing their latest products to an international market.

It was like someone had crammed a museum and a library into a normal house, and every time he entered he somehow felt like he was spitting on diamonds just by being there. As he followed his friend up to the loft, he felt the pressure lift. This was the only room in the house that truly had any of Scott's influence, and although Rich would be damned if he threw anything on the floor like he did in his own room, it certainly had a less hallowed feel to it. The room was roughly divided into two parts, the part in which Scott slept and played on his Nintendo, and the half that held all of his books and his altar, which was looking oddly depleted. As Rich scanned the room, he saw a big rucksack propped against the sofa.

"Wow," he breathed in mock amazement as he held up his own bag, dwarfed in comparison. "I have bag envy."

"I've been all packed for hours," Scott shrugged. Rich nodded as he took a seat, careful not to hit his head on the sloping ceiling. "Can I ask you something?" Scott said, his lip trembling with uncertainty.

"Sure man," Rich said, wondering what the matter was. It was rare that Scott deviated from his passion for order and had a heart to heart.

"Are you with me?"

Rich didn't even have to think about it. "A hundred percent." Scott looked relieved. "I know you're feeling rattled about the others and I'm telling you not to worry. We're all in this together, whether it works or not."

"It will work!" Scott said, his voice rising slightly. "Why doesn't anyone believe me?"

"I believe you," reassured Rich. "But you're missing the point. For me it's not about the power, it's about our friendship. That's where we get our strength from right? And I know I don't spend half as much time with you as I do with Josh, but he's my playmate, you're my mate-mate." Rich chuckled to himself as his friend smiled. "So don't worry…. mate." The two of them started laughing.

"How do you always do that?" Scott said, shaking off the last of his amusement.

"Do what?" asked Rich.

"You always seem to know what I'm thinking."

Rich grinned once more. "Well that's my power of Air and Intuition isn't it! You'd better watch out, after tonight I'll probably be able to read your mind."

"Get lost," Scott laughed as he playfully pushed him backwards into the wall. Rich opened his mouth in mock outrage.

"Oh you shouldn't have done that, Fielding. Prepare to die!" he shouted as he lunged forwards, locking his arms around the other's slender waist and pulling him to the floor. The two of them were still scrapping when the other half of the group walked into the loft.

"Is this a private party, or can anyone join in?" Matt said sarcastically, before stepping over the tangle of youth and slumping into the sofa. Scott propped himself up on his elbow and turned questioningly to the newcomers.

"How did you guys get inside?" he asked as Josh flashed him a mischievous grin.

"Jeeves let us in, don't you know!" Scott rolled his eyes. "Nah man, you left the door off the latch like an idiot. Someone might come in and steal all your mum's crap." Josh grinned as he hoisted Scott off the ground and then sat down next to Matt. "Oh, I brought wine like you asked. Nothing amazing, just some plonk. Vintage yesterday probably." As Josh chuckled, Scott brushed himself off and took a moment to reconstruct his serious composure.

"I've been thinking about names…" he began. "And I'm going with Dexamenas. It's a centaur name apparently - what do you think?" He looked at the others, awaiting some kind of response. Eventually Rich nodded and he breathed once more. "It sounds strong and regal, Dex of Earth."

Once more, Matt chipped in with his undermining comments. "Regal and strong? And what are you calling your ego?"

Scott scowled. "What are you choosing?" he
snapped.

"Phoenix. I chose it a while ago - imagine burning
fury and ambition. Plus Phoenixes are supposed to live
forever." Matt puffed out his chest, as if to emphasise that
he could be victorious over Scott even in name choosing.

"You might as well have chosen God…" Scott
muttered under his breath. From his position on the striped
rug, Rich could once more sense the tension between his
friends reaching its peak.

"It took me ages to find one that suited me," he
interjected. As he had hoped, the others turned their
attention from each other to him. "I thought about what it
meant to be an Air Elemental, and I came up with freedom.
Riding on the wind and all that. But then it struck me that
it goes higher than that, it's everything around us. I went
for Altair. I found it on a website about astrology. It's
supposed to represent everything connected."

"So you chose it because…?" Josh said, obviously
unclear as to what Rich was getting at.

"Because that's what we'll be. Connected through
the ether. I chose the name to emphasise our friendship."
Rich blushed slightly. "That's all," he muttered.

"Well I think it's a good choice," encouraged Scott.
"What's yours then Josh?"

"Remind me again why we have to choose names?"

Scott sighed loudly. "It's the second law of names,"
he began impatiently, as if he had explained this a thousand
times and Josh was somehow slow to catch on. "If you
know your *true* name, then you have greater control over
your own actions. Also, if you know somebody else's…"

"Greater control over them," chipped in Rich
eagerly as Scott nodded.

"That doesn't sound like a plus to me," complained Josh. "Why are we telling each other?"

"It's meant to be a show of trust," continued Scott, the irritation beginning to show on his face. "We each have a piece of the others now."

"Well in that case, I'm having Dylan. It sounds the least stupid and the most like a real name."

Scott pursed his lips sternly as the others laughed. "Good to know you chose a name for all the right reasons," he said dryly. Josh looked at him, his grin fading rapidly.

"Hey," he defended. "I'm here tonight aren't I? I'm totally putting in when the time comes, but until then I'm keeping light-hearted. It's just a name, its not going to change who I am."

Scott sighed, knowing he would not be able to argue his point. "Fine," he conceded. "But we have to use these names when we are doing Wiccan stuff alright?" He looked around at the three blank faces, none of them comprehending what he was driving at. Sometimes it annoyed him that he seemed to be the only one with any imagination. "Two different names, to represent the two different lives we'll lead. If we go around mixing them together, then who knows what could happen. There's that adage about power corrupting, you know." Josh sighed, backing down from the onslaught of dedication. Sometimes his friend was a bit ferocious when it came to getting his way, but he figured Scott always knew that he would only disagree with him when there was a valid reason, unlike Rich who would burn his own house down if enough people told him it was a good idea.

"Alright, alright," Josh said, palms raised in surrender. "Josh now, Dylan tonight. Dylan of Water I shall be. Now let's get magical."

"It's not magic, there's no such thing as magic," Scott chided as Matt checked his watch.

"We should get going," he stated bluntly.

Josh turned to him with a smile. "Aww, are you excited Matty?" Matt narrowed his eyes in reply.

"There's just one more thing," said Scott as he reached for what seemed like a bundle of faded and scuffed velvet. The colour had once been a deep purple, but the fabric was worn and grey, holes beginning to show where the cloth had been handled repeatedly. All eyes were on him as he dropped the rags into his lap, unfolding the layers until they could see a set of necklaces gleaming in the lamplight.

Rich leaned forwards curiously, taking in the four metal discs threaded onto simple leather cords. Each sliver of silver had a line etched on it, and the young man recognised them as the elemental symbols. He picked out his own disc, complete with curving cloud shape and held it up closer, marvelling at the precision.

"Did you get these done specially?"

Scott shook his head. "They came with the book – the original. My granddad must have kept them. They were tucked into his copy of the book when I got it. I figured we should wear them, seeing as they're meant to go with all this."

Not even Matt said anything as the others picked out their corresponding pendants and slid them over their heads. As the cool metal nestled against his throat, Scott took a final look around the group before getting to his feet and heading for the door.

Chapter 10 - Unity Leaps Fourth

The sun had set long ago, and everything was ready. The excitement was palpable as the four friends made their way through the darkness, treading familiar routes along woodland paths. The only sounds were the rustling of branches in the breeze and the soft crunching of twigs underfoot. Soon, the ordinary would become extraordinary, and lives were about to change. The four initiates edged forwards slowly, picking their way around the dense undergrowth that surrounded the clearing they had chosen, until at last they were met by the startling emptiness that signified their arrival. They had considered using The Haven, but in the end decided that it was too small for this particular ritual. Ashton Clearing, as this space was known, also held some old ruins of a village that had been destroyed by fire at some point. The stonework that remained was blackened and twisted with ivy and creepers, but Scott always thought they added an extra touch of mysticism to their purpose.

As he stood on the brink of change, the young man found himself remembering the stupid conversation they had had about choosing a location, which as usual had caused an argument between him and Matt. His companion had suggested using the Stone Circle that lay outside of town, but Scott had thought that was too obvious. To which Matt had pointed out that Halloween was obvious enough so they might as well go the whole hog. Scott had played his trump card, the one that won every time. *It was his idea, his book that started it all, and his rules.* End of discussion.

"Ready?" Breathed Rich, looking expectantly at Scott, who snapped out of his memories.

"Hmm…" he began, taking a breath and assessing his inner feelings. "I could do with a slash." He grinned sheepishly as Rich wagged his finger.

"I told you to go before we left."

"Nerves, I guess," Scott shrugged and hurried into the undergrowth until he could no longer hear the rustling of his companions. When he had relieved himself, he looked to the sky, the moon peeking through the canopy sending criss-crossing beams of glimmering light playing across his body. *Please,* he thought. *Let this work. Just show me something... anything.* Scott had no idea who he was appealing to, but he felt reassured all the same, glad that he could take a moment away from the others so they wouldn't witness his petitioning. The last thing he needed was more fuel for the pyre that Matt was all too ready to throw him on. *Anything will do…*

In answer, a panicked fluttering sound erupted from the bushes to his left. More curious than afraid, he brushed the leaves aside and saw what looked like a writhing mass of feathers, black, indigo, bottle green and white. It took Scott a few seconds to realise that it was a flock of magpies, scratching and pecking at something that they had pinned to the dirt.

Instinctively, the young man began to count the birds. *What was the rhyme? One for sorrow, two for joy. Three for a girl, four for a boy. Five for silver, six for gold and seven for a secret never to be told.* That was as far as he could remember. *What if there's more than seven?* He wondered, imagining some scientist explaining how it was physically impossible for more than seven magpies to be in the same place at the same time.

The frenzied animals kept flapping their wings and hopping over each other, so Scott clicked his fingers loudly. Startled, seven magpies launched into the air and faded to inky black, leaving their prey tattered and bloody in the soil. The young man took a step forward, taking in the jutting broken wings, the dishevelled feathers and the exposed throat. It was the eighth magpie. Scott opened his mouth in disgust, forgetting his plea and turned to bolt back to the clearing.

Josh was waiting impatiently as Scott hurried into the ritual space. He looked alarmed and flushed.

"What took you so long eh?" he said with a smirk and a wink. Scott put the magpies to the back of his mind and instantly composed himself with a shake of his head, set his rucksack down and pulled out four black cloaks. The velvety material flowed easily across the skin as he handed the cloaks to the others, which they donned without question. Josh had briefly considered mentioning how embarrassed he would be if anybody saw him wearing a cloak, but after his faux pas back in the loft, he decided to keep quiet. Scott was determined that everything should be right, and this included looking the part, not just playing the part. Next, he started unpacking the candles and oils needed for the ritual. As he did so, the other three arranged the candles in a circle, and began to light them.

"Why can't we just use torches?" he heard Matt grumble. "We never use electricity, it's always bloody candles." Scott considered marching over and lecturing him that a.) It was traditional to use candles, and b.) Candles represented the element of Fire for ritual purposes, but he held back for the same reason he hadn't mentioned the magpies – they were so close now, and Scott didn't want even the slightest hiccup to upset the balance. When everything was unpacked, he turned his attention to the centre of the circle, and began to start a fire.

Rich watched as his friends hurried around the clearing, the final display of nerves before they had to be steeled. Scott was casting his eyes over the proceedings, and the Air initiate was suddenly struck with the desire to help. Perhaps he should give his friend a final show of his loyalty in case Scott's resolve was wavering? He reached into his own, smaller backpack and fished out his copy of the Book of Shadows.

"I brought my book, just in case you need to look at it," he said casually. Of course Scott would probably have the whole ritual committed to memory, but it wouldn't hurt to have something to refer to. With a wary smile, his companion took his own identical book from his bag, and held it up.

"I'm covered, cheers." Rich nodded and set his book on the ground as Scott gave one last look around the ritual space. Finally everything was ready.

Josh knew the time was near. He slowly moved to his place by the fire, the direction of West. As the others took their places, he cast a nervous look at them. Matt looked like he usually did, stony and unreadable, although Josh was sure he noticed the slightest hint of a scowl cross the other's face as he was handed his cloak. Rich had a small smile on his face, a reminiscence of the supposed childlike state they were going to leave behind. Even Scott looked apprehensive, and he was usually always so focused and determined. Josh's legs felt rubbery as he stood there, the heat of the fire washing over his face. Should they really be doing this? After all, witchcraft had never exactly been smiled upon. He thought back to history lessons at school, about how hundreds of people had been killed for supposedly practicing dark magic, when really they had just had an advanced knowledge of botany. The Salem Witch trials were history's biggest case of Chinese Whispers. Surely times had changed a little since then? As nerves sunk into his consciousness like stinging tendrils, he glanced across at Rich, whose face was set. Unwavering, thought Josh. It seemed as if Rich had no doubt simply because Scott had told him it would work, his loyalty to his friends never failing. In the face of such blind faith, he could not back out and let the others down. *Fate was about to twist*, he mused as Scott began to speak.

> "North, South, East, West
> Lend to me your powers best
> At each point shall shine a star
> The sacred runes play their part
> Tetragrammaton, Adonai, Elehun
> With three hundred and sixty
> This circle is done."

As the incantation was finished, the wind died down and the clearing was silent. Rich looked over at the master of ceremonies, who was checking the Book of Shadows whilst pensively fingering the hilt of a silver blade tucked into his waistband. As if reaching a decision suddenly, he drew the blade and pointed it at Rich's throat. Although the blade did not glance against his flesh, he could feel the power that it held, radiating against his neck.

"It is better that you should fall upon this blade," began Scott. "Than enter the circle with wrongful intent. How do you enter?"

Rich looked up at his friend, whose eyes were blazing, the orange of the fire casting a contrasting reflection in the shining blue. He looked at the others. They were all watching him intently. He was the first to be confirmed, he had to set a good example otherwise everything would be for nothing. But it wasn't just that. Standing there, with the cruel steel glancing across his throat, he found that what he had said earlier was true. He was in this one hundred percent. He took a deep breath and replied.

"I enter the circle with intent to follow the craft and cause no harm unless it is right that I should do so."

Relieved, Rich watched as Scott nodded and passed the blade to him. He grabbed the hilt, shaped like a woman standing amid the spread of an eagle's wings and held it up to Matt's throat to repeat the question. Each of the four had to ask and receive the question; otherwise the bond between them would not be forged equally. When Matt was confirmed, he took the knife and held it up to Josh's neck, before he in turn did the same for Scott.

When all four men had confirmed their intention for joining the circle, Scott began the next step of the ritual. Setting his newly purchased crystal glass firmly on the soil, he pulled a pin from somewhere in his cloak and held it over his index finger, fully aware that all eyes were on him. He had never been good with pain, and the thought of having to injure himself on purpose was weighing heavily on his mind. The moment seemed to extend for an age, the pin wavering over tender skin.

Why did it have to be blood? he found himself complaining. There was always some mention of blood, or bones, or something else disgusting – why couldn't it ever be something normal and easy? Of course he knew the answer – witchcraft was all about testing your limits. How far would a person go to get what they wanted? If it were too simple then nobody would be worthy of it. As Scott thought, he became aware that he was trying to distract himself from the pin pricking issue.

"Shit!" he cursed, embarrassed by his weakness. He shrugged apologetically at Rich, who was staring back thoughtfully.

"Hey," he said gently. "Look at me; I'm not bothered about it." Scott looked into his friend's eyes as Matt snuck up behind him with a pin of his own. Smirking as Rich held Scott's attention, he jabbed the pin hard into the waiting finger, catching a few drops of blood in the glass.

"Jesus Christ!" Scott yelled, instinctively jamming his finger into his mouth. He glared at Matt, who had plastered the biggest smile possible across his face.

"You're welcome!" he simpered. Scott frowned as he removed his finger, waving it in the cool breeze.

"If that's what your smile looks like, I'm glad you never do." Matt ignored the insult and held the glass in front of the other's face expectantly. The Earth Initiate stared at the crimson splatters for a second before remembering that he was supposed to have said something when his blood went into the glass. "I commit myself to the craft, Wicca in body and in spirit," he rushed, hoping that it wasn't too late.

Once again, the action was repeated around the circle, everyone adding their essence to the chalice albeit with a lot less fuss. When Josh had added his blood, he took up his bottle of wine from the ground and filled the glass to the brim. He grinned sheepishly as he passed the cup along. This was the part that none of them had been looking forward to. They all knew it must be done, yet they all dreaded it. Scott held the glass and peered into the crimson depths for a second. *It still wasn't too late to change his mind*, he thought as the blood created brighter swirling streams within the wine. No. He had come this far, and would not be swayed this late in the game. He also wanted to show that he had recovered from the inability to prick his own finger. The last thing he wanted was some sort of nickname to arise from it. Although he couldn't think of any off the top of his head, he was sure that the others would be able to create one, given time.

"I drink of my brothers and embrace the fact that we

are one. Blessed be." Without hesitating, he lifted the chalice to his lips and took a deep gulp. The metallic taste of the blood was almost hidden by the sharp acidity of the wine, yet it still held a noticeable linger at the back of his throat. He gulped and shook his head, his eyes scrunched up as he passed the glass along.

Josh watched as one by one his companions drunk from the chalice and noted their reactions. Scott seemed to be disgusted by the taste, flinching and shaking his head as he drank. *Although that could just be the fact that the wine only cost three pounds*, he thought with a smirk. Rich looked as if he liked it, and, typically, Matt did not look bothered at all, his expression hardly changing as he drank the life essence of his new brothers. Josh took the glass from him and immediately drained it. He lowered it, smacking his lips as if trying to place a familiar taste, yet none had ever drunk this concoction before. He placed the glass on the ground and took out a piece of paper with the word "Dylan" written on it. The other three did the same, each with their own individual magical names written on them.

Once more, like a ripple moving across still water, an action went round the circle. First the leader said his piece, and then it passed on until it came to Josh.

"I take unto me the name Dylan and all that it encompasses. Let the spirits of Water be my witness and my guide, so mote it be."

When he had finished, Scott looked around the circle and nodded. As one, the four threw their papers into the fire….

Chapter 11 – The Burning Question

"Everything in life has a double meaning. Never accept that one meaning is correct. To universally accept the fact that a colour means one thing is wrong, for Red can mean both danger and love. But also do not forget to consider both targets of the meaning. After all, danger could be for someone else, or it could be for you. Just like anything else in life, all options must be considered before a decision is made."

The Book Of Shadows

It was half past ten when Chase Rivers was dejectedly lying on his bed, flicking through the television channels. Nothing was on. This room, his bedroom, meant nothing more to him than a place to sleep. He had never had any fun in there, had never had friends round, and he didn't even own a computer. The walls had once been painted purple, but the paint was now flaking quite badly. The worst places had been covered by a couple of posters, the jagged logo of Crystal Homicide an island in a sea of shabbiness. Chase turned the television off and sighed deeply. This was how he spent most of his evenings. Alone. He didn't even have any work to do for Matt. Deep down, he knew that the college guy was just using him to get the grades, but even the few moments they shared when they exchanged essays were better than nothing.

He reached into his pocket and fished out a small scrap of paper. It was a note from his mother that he had found hastily scribbled and left on the kitchen table.

Gone for a week. Maybe more. Feed yourself.
Mum
P.S Where's my bastard hairdryer?

Typical! thought Chase, glumly. There was no message telling him to be careful, or to have fun, or to do anything except find his mother's hairdryer, which he hadn't even seen for about a month. In a sudden flush of anger, he vowed that if he did find the elusive implement, he would smash it. Mrs. Rivers never spent much time with her son, as she had taken to drinking and going away with various different men ever since Chase's father left home. *That's no excuse though,* he thought, as lots of people had single parents that had kept themselves respectable after divorce. Chase had been looking after himself since he was nine, so he wasn't surprised by his mother's absence, but even if the two of them hardly spoke, he always felt better when she was at home. She was like a security blanket, except one that swore and slept around.

Chase sighed again and crumpled up the note, throwing it onto the floor. It looked like he was in for another night of crying into his pillow and hugging it like a long lost friend. Of course there was the dog, but he didn't count.

In a rare act of charity, Mrs Rivers had come home years ago with a puppy for her son, and Chase had named the black Labrador Pepper. *Black Pepper.* Of course as soon as he was old enough to realise how stupid the name was, it had stuck and the dog would answer to nothing else. Now though, Pepper was at the comfortable age where he would lie around the house all day, less of a companion and more of an ornament that made the occasional noise. Even that one gift seemed to have faded and lost its shine.

Sometimes he liked to think that he was stuck inside a nightmare and that when he woke up, his mother would have breakfast ready with a smile, and his numerous friends would all be waiting for him to come and hang out with them. He was always disappointed. Usually when he was feeling like this, he put on his favourite program, *Buffy The Vampire Slayer,* the only DVD he owned, but even to him, the idea of watching vampires and magic on Halloween seemed clichéd. Instead, he resigned himself to sitting in the quiet of his loneliness.

The silence was suddenly broken by the shrill ringing of Chase's mobile. He was unused to hearing the sound and it took him a few moments to actually realise that it was happening. He fumbled awkwardly in his pocket, hoping that he wouldn't miss the call. All that the tiny screen said was "Unknown Number" but he didn't care, he would talk to anyone to relieve the boredom, even if it was a phone salesman.

"Hello?" he said, aware that he must sound like an eager child. There was no sound on the other end of the line save for a muffled breathing. Chase began to get impatient. "Anyone?" he challenged, exasperated yet hopeful at the same time. There was the ghost of a syllable before the line went dead, the potential conversation replaced by cruel monotone. He was certain however, that someone had begun to speak before they hung up. Could it be his mother, drunk somewhere? The only thing to do was to wait and see if the mysterious number called again. With a sigh, Chase rolled onto his side and curled his legs up to his chest.

Chase was being hoisted onto the shoulders of a big crowd of people, all shouting his name. He had just scored the final point of a crucial volleyball game, which had won the National Volleyball Cup for the University of Central England. An extremely handsome and popular young man came up to him and asked if he wanted to join the England Volleyball Team. Was there such a thing? When Chase answered, the man beeped at him. That wasn't quite normal. Soon everyone was beeping at him instead of talking, the beeping rising to one deafening high pitched tone. Beep! Beep! Beep....

Chase awoke with a start. The pillow he had been hugging now lay on the floor by his bed and it was now twenty to twelve. He had been asleep for an hour and a half, but what had woken him up so suddenly? His pale grey eyes scanned the room for anything unusual. His alarm clock wasn't set, and there wasn't a microwave in the house. For a moment, he paused and wondered what made him think of a microwave in the first place, but his musings were soon interrupted by the green glow emanating softly from underneath his bed. He felt around for a moment and emerged holding his mobile phone. And then he remembered why he had dropped off in the first place, hoping for another phone call. This time someone had sent him a text message. Who would want to contact him in the middle of the night? Curious, Chase pressed a button to read his message.

B prt of the grp.go 2 the forest

Puzzled, Chase stared at the message for a few minutes, as if some hidden part would reveal itself. However, it was clear that whoever had sent the message was not going to give any clues. *That's a point,'* he thought. Who *had* sent it? He checked the number, but again all his phone would say was that it was unknown. There was definitely something strange going on. Chase hugged his knees as he flicked through all the possible meanings of the message in his head. It could be someone playing a joke on him. It could even be that the message got sent to the wrong number, after all, just one wrong digit when dialling could reach a completely different person. *'Yeah,'* he thought. *'That's what it is. Just a wrong number. A mistake.'* Chase lay back down, his heart still beating faster than usual at the prospect of the message. He rolled over onto his side and caught a glimpse of the crumpled note that he had thrown down earlier. Suddenly, he was overcome with a sense of defiance. His mother could leave home and go gallivanting around the country having fun, so why couldn't he? He rolled off his bed and onto his feet. *Sod it,* he thought, as he grabbed a hoodie from the back of his door and walked out of the room.

A short time later, Chase was walking along the thin path that ran alongside the forest. Typically, the street lamps that had been placed for safety weren't working, so the young man was going slowly, trying not to walk into anything. The trees seemed to bend outwards as if beckoning him to come closer. It was cold, and Chase had reluctantly pulled the hood over his immaculate spikes in an attempt to at least trap some heat. His initial enthusiasm had died off, and he was wondering what he was actually doing there. The message hadn't said which part of the forest to go to. Surely if someone wanted to see him that badly, they would have told him exactly where to go. The message also hadn't specified a time, so in theory he might have missed... whatever it was he was heading into. Then he saw it.

The faintest flicker of orange stood out against the pitch black of the forest. Like a firefly flitting between the trees, it would vanish and reappear suddenly as branches blew across it in the wind. As Chase stared more intently at the glimmer of fire in the darkness, he could tell that the shadows moving in front of the flames were not trees. They were people. Curiosity reached out to him, fixed like a noose round his neck and started to pull. He stared harder and harder until it felt like he could make out aspects of the figures. Two of them were blonde, and one of them had some kind of knife. *Wait.* He shouldn't be interfering. He could get hurt. What if it was some sort of devil-worshipping cult thing? On Halloween, it couldn't be good.

Chase closed his grey eyes briefly, snapping out of the focus he had on the mysterious fire. He then looked around, blinking wildly. He had no idea where he was. After turning, he saw the line of wooden posts that marked the pathway about ten metres behind him. Looking forward again, the flicker of the flames was definitely closer. Had he somehow walked into the forest without knowing it? Or had he been drawn there? Did something want him to discover this group of shadowy figures? Chase glanced down at the floor where a bunch of berries had been trodden into the ground, their red juice shining in a patch of moonlight. It was crimson blood mixed with the brown earth. He tilted his head as he stared at the berries in the soil. The more he scrutinised, the more the shape of the splatter seemed to change. At first it was just a random mess of red, but now it looked like a skull, screaming up at him from the forest floor. Was it a sign? Perhaps someone was in danger? He lifted his eyes for a second, and then blinked. The smeared berries had returned to their original haphazard arrangement, although Chase was certain that he had seen the face in the scarlet.

A yell split through the wavering shadows, cementing Chase's apprehension. Somebody *was* in danger. He fumbled in his pocket for his phone, holding it up to the scant moonlight but the blinking image of a telegraph pole was unmistakable. The signal must be obscured by the trees looming over him. Whatever he was thinking of, he would have to do it himself without the reassurance of the police being a phone call away as there was no way he was going to turn away now and leave the iron curtain of the forest just to get reception. What if he missed something vitally important? Cursing his phone network, he edged closer, worried that the mysterious strangers would see him. Chase was tall, but he figured the shadows of the trees would hide him as he crept closer. Maybe whoever sent the message was the one who needed help, or at least someone who knew what was going on and thought that he would be able to do something about it. *God knows why*, he thought. *I'm a nobody.* As he crept closer, he could hear voices. They were talking about committing to something. Some sort of craft with wicker baskets or something. *What is this?* The young man found himself standing in the shadow of a fragment of wall, aged stones stacked together and held with primitive cement. He remembered that there had been an old village here hundreds of years ago. Was that anything to do with what was happening now? Chase took one more step and then emerged into the clearing....

As one, the four threw their papers into the fire. As the little scraps of white floated down into the flames like moths attracted to the fatal candle, a figure burst into the circle from behind one of the ruined walls. The four cloaked men turned to face the newcomer, his jaw jutting with determination. It was Chase. A similar expression of confusion, anger, fear and surprise appeared on five faces as a cry echoed through the clearing above the crackling of the fire.

"You!" The initiates turned to face each other, whilst Chase stared at them, faltering. They had all shouted at the same time. A multitude of questions floated through Chase's head, but he could not make words come out of his mouth. Suddenly, everyone was focused on the bonfire. The first of the scraps of paper fell into the heart of the flames and the fire exploded outwards. There was a blinding flash as a column of flame shot skywards. The four initiates fell backwards in their compass directions, a quartet of directional chaos. Chase was rooted to the ground as the flames blasted outwards. The last thing anyone heard was the tortured scream of the young man as he was engulfed by the raging fire. If the four had been conscious, they would have noticed that the fire died out long before the screams did.

Chapter 12 - Aftermath

It was at least twenty minutes before Matt Blake regained consciousness. He kept his eyes firmly pressed shut, not wanting to see what had happened. He was still asleep, having a nightmare and he didn't want to wake up, didn't want to know the truth. An odd smell was making the air thick, forcing itself into his nostrils and pressing dangerously against his lips. He knew what the smell was, it was burnt flesh, a cross between the smell of blood and roast dinner. He hadn't expected Chase to turn up like that, and he definitely hadn't expected the fire to explode. Suddenly, a rustling sound broke the silence of the clearing. Someone else was moving wildly about, breathing rapidly.

"Oh my god! What are we gonna do?" came Rich's panicked voice. "Did you see that? What are we gonna do?" The rustling sound doubled as more people started to wake up.

"What happened?" This was Scott. He sounded scared more than anything else, the disbelief evident in his voice. *'It must be particularly hard on him,'* thought Matt, as all of the carefully laid plans that his studious counterpart had spent hours perfecting had seemingly been ruined. "Is everyone all right?" asked Scott.

"What kind of question is that?" shouted Rich hysterically. "It... it exploded!"

"You know what I mean!"

"Where's Matt?" They immediately stopped bickering and Matt could envision them looking around frantically for him. *'Well Rich would be anyway...'* he thought shrewdly. He doubted if Scott had fully forgiven him for showing him up both at the meeting and then in their fight.

He opened his eyes. He was lying on his back a short way away from the bonfire, which had now been reduced to a few glowing embers, red eyes in the black face of the soil. Rich was standing stock still, staring at the remains of the fire, his eyes wide. It looked to be all too much for the poor guy, as if he would collapse again at any moment. Scott was frantically hurrying around the clearing, collecting as many of the oils and candles as he could find. He obviously didn't want to leave any evidence of what had been going on. With a swift ducking motion, Scott scooped a Book of Shadows into his rucksack, and then tossed a second one to Rich. It took Matt a moment to spot Josh in the gloom. He was standing at the edge of the clearing, with his back to everyone and was staring intently at something on the ground. Matt shook his head groggily before announcing his awakening.

"I'm here." Despite speaking quietly, the others heard him. Scott froze briefly then carried on his collection, avoiding his eyes. Rich turned to face him, but Josh remained focused on the edge of the clearing. "I'm not hurt," he added as an afterthought. He could still hear Scott bustling about the clearing muttering as he tried to collect anything incriminating. Dwelling on this sentiment, Matt casually felt his pockets. Empty. The contents must have spilled out when he was thrown to the ground. He rolled onto his front, wildly now, casting his hands in large circles, trailing fingers through the dirt. *Where was it?* There was so much ashen debris now littering the clearing that perhaps nobody would ever find it. But could he take that risk?

"Looking for this?" Rich was standing over him hand outstretched, the smooth red form of Matt's mobile phone in his palm. Matt released the breath he had been unconsciously holding.

"Err…yeah. Thanks," he muttered as he pocketed the phone. With a final roving look across the soot covered clearing he scrambled to his feet, and was immediately struck by the urge to retch. The stench of incineration was overpowering, as if the atmosphere itself was scorched, yet it hung palpably above the floor. He had not smelt its full aroma when he was lying down. With difficulty, he forced his gorge back into his stomach and began to squint around the clearing, already knowing what he must see. There were only four people. "What happened to Chase?" he asked slowly. Scott stopped rummaging around on the ground and stood up so fast that it looked as if he had just stung himself. Rich spun around wildly, but again Josh did not move a muscle. Matt looked at Scott worriedly, seeing his own expression of curiosity and fear on the other's face. The two of them started to walk towards their companion.

Josh Thomas had no idea what was going on behind him, had not heard a word since the explosion. He had been nearest to Chase when the fire had erupted, and he alone had seen the conflagration of the human body. He stood now, staring down at what used to be Chase Rivers. The jacket the young man had been wearing had burned away completely. Burned or melted, Josh couldn't be sure. Either way, the younger man's chest and face was now a mottled pattern of scorched black and blasted red raw skin. There was a shining patch of silver where a necklace the young man had been wearing had fused itself into his skin, the form now unrecognisable. His expression was unreadable, but his immaculately crafted spiky hair was unmistakable, even if it was now blackened and ragged. Chase's mobile was lying next to his limp hand, singed from the flames but still whole. Without thinking, Josh knelt next to the stricken form and scooped the aged phone into one of the pouches in his belt. Chase wouldn't need it anymore.

Josh stared down solemnly at the body, still unable to comprehend what was going on. He didn't even register as the others arrived either side of him.

Matt stepped in front of his friend and looked down. The sickening smell filled his very soul, and this time he could not hold it back. He turned away and retched into the nearest bush, unable to force it back this time. Scott stared solemnly but Matt wasn't ashamed of being sick, after all it wasn't every day that you saw the charred remains of someone you knew. He looked up again, wiping his mouth. Rich was finally making his way towards the others, the last to see the horrific exhibition of death. As he expected, his shaken companion took one glance at the body and jumped back wildly, staring around at the others, eyes popping.

"Oh God, oh Christ, oh shit!" he blurted, as he started to shake uncontrollably. "What are we gonna do? He's dead… and we killed him! It's our fault!" The Air Elemental raised the book he was still holding, flicking frantically through the pages, his hands shaking as he did so. "There has to be something…" he muttered. Matt caught his meaning and gently shook his head.

"It's too late man," he said consolingly. "He's long gone." Rich took another look at Chase's prone form and let the Book of Shadows fall into the soft leaves. He looked at Scott, trembling more and more. Dependable Scott would have the answer - wouldn't he?

For the first time in his life, Scott could not say anything to help. He stared blankly at Rich, wishing he could do something to ease his friend's pain, but there was no answer. How could he have even begun to prepare for something like this? The worst he was expecting was that they would get stopped by the police for starting a fire in a public place, and that would have been easy to solve. The signpost warning against fires had long since been stolen, so who could have accused them of doing it on purpose?

He shook his head slightly. If the situation had not been so serious, he would have smiled to himself as he envisioned the hypothetical conversation with the police officers. Instead, he tried to look sympathetically at Rich, as if he would be comforted knowing that he himself wasn't freaking out. Rich, however, did not seem to notice as he turned to the others. Neither of them said anything. He was going to have to do something himself, everyone else was too stunned to act. Scott could already see Rich working things over in his mind, could tell what he was going to do. In fact, he could pretty much predict the complete downward spiral from here, as if things could get any worse.

Rich shakily reached into his pocket and fumbled around until he pulled out his mobile phone. The yellow plastic cover stood out shockingly in the gloom of the clearing, harshly out of place in the world of darkness into which they had all been so irretrievably plunged. Breathing deeply, trying to steady himself, he began dialling. Suddenly, Matt sprang forwards and grabbed Rich's wrist as if he had just been electrocuted into action. Rich yelped and twisted his arm in vain, trying to break Matt's grip.

"What the hell are you doing?" Matt demanded loudly. Rich began to twist more frantically.

"Let me go!" he shouted, his voice rising in pitch. "We have to call the police!"

"Are you crazy?" yelled Matt before taking a deep breath and lowering his voice. The last thing he wanted was someone to hear them and come to investigate. That sort of thing had already caused them enough trouble. "We'll go down for this," he continued. "There's no way we can make this look like an accident! Fires don't just explode randomly you know."

"We could say that a stone cracked, or he tripped or something?" The young man's fingers were poised just above the rubber-coated numbers.

"No good," countered Matt. They'd ask why we didn't help him. We'd still go down." Rich started to hit him wildly in the chest, but still he would not release the phone.

"We deserve to go down!" the distraught young man screamed as he continued to pummel. "We killed him!"

"Hey!" shouted Matt, and with a sudden surge of force, he punched his companion squarely in the jaw. Rich fell backwards, and Matt released him as he slumped onto the ground. "Will you keep your bloody voice down?" he hissed.

Josh rushed forwards and grabbed Matt's arm. "Don't hurt him, man," he pleaded as Matt shrugged his hand off. Instead, he turned to Scott.

"Will you help me?" Matt whispered indignantly. Scott gave a frightened shake of his head, but still kept silent. He was obviously shocked that Matt had punched their hysterical friend. Matt sighed and turned back to Rich, who was kneeling now, massaging his jaw and trying to hold back tears. "Ok, Rich. Look, I'm sorry all right?" He held out his hand but Rich didn't take it. "I over-reacted. But we really don't have to call the police because… because-" Matt faltered. What could he possibly say to make Rich change his mind? They probably should call the police, but he was responsible for this too, and there was no way that he was ruining his life in jail over one small hitch. Of course there was also no way that he was telling anyone that either, that would make him out to be some sort of heartless monster.

"Because we didn't do anything wrong." Scott had finally come to his senses and interjected. "It was an accident Rich, just a terrible accident." At this, Rich slumped against Matt's legs as if his bones had all been broken. He wrapped his arms tightly around Matt's waist, crying freely now.

"We didn't do anything wrong," he sobbed. "Just an accident." Scott stepped forward and put a hand consolingly on Rich's trembling shoulder. It was amazing how awkward Matt looked as he tried to prise himself out of the embrace. When he was eventually free, they walked over to where Josh was hovering cautiously. He was watching Rich, evidently checking that the poor guy wasn't going to do anything stupid again, but it seemed that he had limited himself to crying pitifully into the ground.

"Hey Josh," Matt said. "You Ok?" Josh turned slowly to face the others. He still had a glazed look in his eyes.

"Yeah," he muttered, shaking his head and regaining his normal expression. "Sorry. Yeah, I'm fine." Matt nodded and all was silent. Nobody knew what to say. First Chase, and then Rich losing it. How should they go about sorting this mess out? Josh decided to get straight to the point. "What are we gonna do about... you know, the body?" As if to emphasise himself, he nodded pointedly in the direction of the corpse.

Scott scowled. "He's still a person," he muttered.

"I didn't mean-" Josh began, but Scott cut him off with an apologetic wave of his hand. Emotions were all running high, and the last thing anyone wanted was for a rash comment to escalate things.

"We could take him to a hospital?" Scott suggested hopefully. If they said that they found Chase like that, then they could just let the doctors deal with him. Matt was already shaking his head.

"Yeah good idea!" he snapped sarcastically. "That's

just the same as calling the police, you idiot! And it's not like any doctor could fix that, is it?"

Josh let his mind wander as the two of them starting arguing about how to solve their immense problems. Matt did have a point, as the hospital was bound to get the police involved. And of course they would want to question the people who brought the body in. As he considered the various possibilities, an idea formed in his mind, the pieces falling together in perfect symmetry. They needed someone to blame for this whole thing, someone who was more responsible than the others, but who could they use?

"What do you want me to do?" shrieked Scott, as another one of his suggestions was obviously shot down. Before he could stop himself, Josh opened his mouth, damning words spilling out into existence.

"You've done everything else…" The other two froze. Scott looked thunderstruck, but Matt was staring at him with an intrigued twist in his mouth. Josh would never have accused one of his friends like this, but a blinding desire to end this had taken hold of him, and the more he thought about it, the more his reasoning made sense. Scott gulped, looking deeply hurt. "You were the one that wanted to do this rubbish!" Josh continued, more conviction creeping into his voice as he spoke. "You were the one that brought us here. You were the one who said it would work. Now Chase is dead, and you're the one that should deal with it."

Josh turned his back and walked out of the clearing as Scott looked on in disbelief. Moments ago, he had stopped himself from losing his temper with a sharp word, and now Josh had done just that. How could all this be blamed on one person? And why did that person have to be him? Josh had entered the circle, just as he had. Josh also drank the blood and threw his paper into the flames. How were those actions innocent when his own same actions were guilty? He turned to Matt, who was staring at him intently. Any second now, his friend would forget their rivalry and would say something that would condemn Josh, they would help Rich up and the three of them would sort this whole thing out. To his horror, Matt shrugged.

"Your idea, your book that started it all, your rules," he echoed Scott's phrase as he followed Josh out of the clearing. A double betrayal. Within moments, Scott was standing alone with only Rich's quiet sobs to listen to. In those few seconds, he had lost everything. He sniffed, also close to tears as he looked mournfully after his two former companions.

Rage bubbled in his core. He could not believe that he was being blamed for all of this. He turned to Rich, who was still cowering on the ground. Instead of being consoled by his suffering, Scott was only angered further. Rich had no right to be so weak. They all had to deal with this and he, Matt and Josh weren't just lying on the ground crying their eyes out. His head pounded as he thought of Josh's treachery and Matt's abandonment. Before he knew what he was doing, he heaved a rock out of the ground and threw it with all his might into the trees.

"It's not my fault!" he screamed, the tears finally rolling down his cheeks. The wail seemed to linger in the air and he was taken aback. A group of birds squawked, and panicking flew from their roosts in the branches. But they weren't the only things that were moving…

Rich heard Scott shout something. The others had left, and his remaining companion was furious about something. He felt drained, as if it would kill him to move. He thought he was imagining the low rumbling sound that had just started, but Scott had heard it too. He was standing frozen in the centre of the clearing. There was no mistaking it - beneath Rich's head, the ground was trembling. Faintly at first, but becoming stronger, the forest was actually shaking. The ruins of the village trembled and mortar reduced to dust as the historical stones moved for the first time in centuries. Rich sat up, just as large cracks began to appear all around the clearing. Like angular snakes, they started to inch their way toward the spot where Chase lay. Rich watched as a crack ran under Scott's legs, knocking him to the ground, panting with confusion. It looked as if the body was caught in the centre of a monstrous spider's web as the cracks encircled him. Rich clamped his hands over his head and screamed as the body began to sink into the ground. It was as if the soil had turned to water, and the corpse was vanishing as easily as if it had been thrown into a lake. Within a minute, Chase Rivers was nowhere to be seen. The rumbling softened and the ground stopped shaking, leaving the forest silent once more. Rich gingerly lowered his hands, and looked wide-eyed at Scott. He was still lying where he had fallen and was staring at the space where Chase had been just seconds ago. All that remained was a patch of uneven soil, as if someone had driven over it with a truck. Scott turned to him, as he searched for something to say.

"You... did you... you did..." he stuttered, awestruck. His companion seemed petrified as he scrambled to his feet, snatched up his rucksack and ran out of the clearing. Rich stared after him, and then turned back to the churned ground. He didn't want to stay here alone. He stood up and ran after his friend, just as he always had done.

Chapter 13 – The First Detriment

The rumbling of the ground filled Scott's head as he sat on the sofa in his attic, trembling slightly in awe of what had just happened. In a way, he was glad that he was home alone, as he didn't want to explain to his mother why he had stormed in at some ridiculous hour, frantically emotional. As it was, he had retreated to his sanctuary with a bottle of whiskey "borrowed" from his mother's cabinet, the warm liquid steadying his nerves and seeping into his core.

It was only now that the true depth of the night dawned on him. He had caused the soil to swallow the body of the young man that he and his friends had inadvertently killed. It would hang over him for the rest of his life, the knowledge that they had killed Chase Rivers. Every time he thought of "them", Josh's face flashed in his mind, replaying that scathing remark that somehow placed all of the blame on Scott's fragile shoulders. He was suddenly Atlas to a world of fault.

The whiskey began to do its job and Scott's eyes started to droop, his friend's poisonous words echoing over and over in his mind.

Josh blamed him for Chase's death, and then he and Matt left. Scott was standing frozen in the centre of the clearing. There was no mistaking it. The ground was trembling.

Scott's eyes snapped open. He had no idea how long he had been asleep, but he had a pounding headache. He stared blearily around the room, the bright light glaring at him, and then he felt it. The ground *was* trembling. The whole room shook furiously, the various trinkets rattling loudly as they jumped and fell. It immediately flashed into his mind that he was causing this, but he discarded that concept almost as quickly as it had sprung into being. After all, his mind was clear now, unclouded by anger and pain. He was in full control and this was nothing to do with him. It must just be a normal earthquake then, he thought. Still a rarity, but not completely beyond belief.

Across town, Josh was woken by the shouts and cheers of his flatmates. They had still been up and partying when he had stormed in, but they obviously knew better than to talk to him, or at least were too drunk to try. He had jammed his pillow firmly over his head to drown out the cheesy Halloween music, but the new shouts were too loud even for the pillow. He rolled out of bed and immediately felt the violent rocking beneath the carpet. It was as if the halls themselves were trying to creep away from the frivolity. The other students however seemed to think that the earthquake was the funniest thing they had seen for ages, turning it into another excuse to drink more vodka.

The other half of the fateful four were similarly disturbed, Matt's Crystal Homicide CD jumping and scratching as he sat at his desk, mulling over the night's events solemnly, whilst Rich's cat had woken him up, deathly afraid and twitching just before the earthquake had actually started. And then it was over. Less than a minute of tremors were gone as suddenly as they had begun. All over the town, people returned to their slumber, their dreams and nightmares, musings and memories, none the wiser.

Scott stood, arms still held out for balance even after the trembling had stopped. The only sign that the earthquake had struck was the shelf of Dr Who figures that now lay on their backs, a legion of plastic warriors flattened by Earth's wrath. Before he could move, his bedroom door flew open and his mother rushed in, dressed in her nightclothes. She hurried over and wrapped her arms around her son.

Sarah Fielding always had a soft spot for Scott. Her eldest son had long since left, having completed his degree and started his own life in London, but Scott had stuck around, letting her mother him for a few years longer. She loved her job, jetting to exotic countries, but she loved coming home even more when she could spend time with her fine young man and still feel needed by him.

"I wasn't sure you were in or not," she said, a hint of relief in her voice. "Did you feel that earthquake?" Scott squirmed out of her grip. At nineteen, it was embarrassing to see his mother in her nightdress. She held him at arm's length and began to sniff the air. "Oh, Scotty you've been at the Vat 69 again? You know I keep that for special occasions." Scott shrugged apologetically before letting his face fall. He had been briefly distracted from the tragedy that had tarred his soul, but now everything had come crashing back into his consciousness. Ever attentive, Sarah immediately pulled him back into the hug. "What's up, champ?"

Scott smiled to himself, listening to his mother try and talk "cool". He always told her not to bother, but he was glad that she was approachable enough to talk to whenever he needed to even if she did try to spice up her vocabulary with words like 'champ'.

"I've just ruined my entire life," he stated dramatically. "I'm never going to speak to the others ever again." His mother sighed as she guided him over to the sofa.

"You and those boys! There's always something going on with you lot. Is it a girl?" The young man shook his head as Sarah narrowed her eyes playfully. "Is it a guy?"

"Shut up, no!"

"Well it can't be that bad then can it?" the woman
reasoned. "Relationships are the most complex thing in this
world, so if it's nothing to do with that then I reckon your
life is pretty much intact."

"What if you did something," Scott began
tentatively. "And somebody else got hurt by what you did
but you were sure that you couldn't make it right again."

"Well it's not as if you knew that something would
go wrong or you wouldn't have done it." Scott grimaced at
his mother's words. *Of course, the magpies should have warned
him off the whole thing.*

"No," he murmured quietly.

"There's nothing that can't be made right again," his
mother consoled. "If you've got the ability to hurt
someone, then you've got the ability to undo that, through
words or actions. Now there are plenty of examples I could
give you, like the time you told Matthew about his surprise
birthday party, or when you laughed at Richard's A Level
results, and of course the time when Josh dyed his hair blue
because you said it would be a good idea." As his mother
paused, Scott imagined she was reading out his list of
convictions in court. "But there's one thing in particular I
want you to remember. Do you know what you said to me
after your first day of Primary school?" Scott shook his
head solemnly. "You said 'Mummy, I've made the bestest
friends today. We're gonna be best friends for ever and
ever. Nothing will change that.' So whatever's happened
between you and the others, you'll get through it,
understand?" She leaned over and kissed her son on the
forehead, pretending she hadn't noticed his shining eyes,
before standing up and ruffling his hair. "I'll see you in the
morning. Sleep well," she said before leaving the room.

The traumatised young man continued to sit in
silence, poring over long buried childhood memories. He

couldn't actually picture himself returning home on the day his mother had mentioned, but he did remember that feeling of certainty that he had felt when he thought of his old friends. From the very first days of his education, he had been randomly put in the same class and at the same table as Rich, Josh and Matt. Something had just felt so natural about that arrangement that the four of them had clicked instantly. From then on, they had never spent more than a couple of days apart. They were a team together during their Duke of Edinburgh expedition, and they even went to their Year Eleven prom on identical micro scooters. Even when they had grown up and made different choices regarding University, the connection that had been forged between them was so strong that they still remained friends. It was as if right from the very beginning the four of them were guided by some unknown force, destiny even, to lead them to this point. He just hoped that whatever fate had created them was strong enough to keep them together.

Scott turned his critical eye to the Witchcraft itself. He wasn't going to accept Josh's words and assume sole responsibility, nor was he going to blame his late grandfather who had given him the Book of Shadows in the first place. Thinking about that was a pointless endeavour, but Scott began to wonder where the book had actually come from. He knew that his grandpa hadn't written it but somebody must have. The old man always said that an 'angel' appeared one day and gave the original book to his ancestor, but that just led to the imagination spiralling out of control with notions of alien invaders and otherworldly happenings. Although was that really so far from what had just happened? After all, the ritual had worked hadn't it? Scott had moved the soil in the clearing, he was sure of it. Still, there was an easy way to find out.

He made for his desk and pulled out a sheet of plain paper, clearing a space and laying it down. The Book of Shadows stated that every living thing had an aura that only the Encrafted could sense, a sort of outer layer of spiritual energy that absorbed other energies and protected the physical body. There was a whole section in the book about what various colours could mean, and how auras could be affected by scars and dark spells.

Hesitantly, Scott held his hand over the paper – a pure white background would make this a lot easier. He closed his eyes and concentrated. If the ritual truly had worked, then when he opened his eyes, he should see his own aura. He opened his eyes and gasped. His hand was surrounded by a faint outline of green, reflecting the connection with the forces of Earth that he must now have.

He continued to stare; aware that the immense guilt he was feeling was now tinted with a hint of silvery pride in the achievement that he and the others had managed.

Hours later, Josh sat in his shared living room amongst empty cans of beer and endless reams of streamers. He was in his dressing gown, dark shadows hanging under his eyes like parasites as he strained to make out what the newsreader on breakfast television was saying. Apparently, the epicentre of the night's quake was in Thailand, but the waves had been felt all over the world. *Thailand!* thought Josh. Thousands of miles away, and it had still been enough to rock the foundations of buildings all over the country. *It was no wonder that people had died,* he mused grimly. So far the death toll was around 400, but aid teams were still pulling more bodies from the rubble.

Matt Blake had not slept, the events of the night still fresh. He wondered how the others were coping, and ran through each of his friends in turn. Scott would be putting on a brave face, a coat of shiny paint on the fence that was decaying inside. Josh probably wouldn't care either way. He had passed the buck and could probably live with himself now, and Rich… Rich would be the most traumatised, he reasoned. The Air Elemental was the ever-faithful companion, and now that it looked like the group had split, he would be at a loss. The lifelines that Rich relied on were cut, and Matt wondered with strange fascination, which one of them he would run to first, when the pressure became too much.

As Matt walked pensively to his local shops, he was surprised that the sun was again shining brightly. The world didn't care what had happened last night, there was no life-changing event, it was just another day for humanity. In the small paved area that formed the shopping arcade, an angular fountain stood in the centre, light jets cascading from twelve spouts arranged in a circle. It was an attempt to brighten up the community, a central column with a number of gaping jaws. Usually, each minimalist opening held a large concrete sphere.

Matt remembered that in the olden days, similar things were used on a smaller scale to ascertain the direction of a disaster, but today all of the spheres had fallen to the ground, resting in the deep trough designed to hold the water from the fountain.

A man was standing on one of the decorative concrete spheres. He looked something like a priest, a purple disc with a silver S in the centre hanging from his neck on a thick chain. Matt slowed down curiously as he took in what the man was saying.

"This earthquake is a sign!" he shouted enthusiastically. "The world is full of sinners and the sin has grown too much. Compelled by greed, we have sought to better ourselves endlessly regardless of who suffers. It shall not end here! Those poor souls last night were the first to be punished." *Typical*, thought Matt. All it took was one disaster and everyone picked a religion to herald. Walking into the shop with a sneer of disgust, he picked up a bottle of Coke, ignoring the till girl's flirtatious smile as he paid for it. The preacher was still ranting as Matt left the shop.

"Repent! Repent! No sin will go unpunished. The end is nigh!" By now, the man was practically shrieking with fervour, gaining an increasing amount of dark looks from passers-by. Suddenly the preaching man seemed to look straight at Matt with his piercing brown eyes and his voice lowered to a murmur. "The Gods are coming…" he said threateningly. "And they are vexed."

Matt stepped back from the man's makeshift pedestal, fear lancing into his core for a split second, but the preacher had returned to shouting about sin and repentance as if nothing had happened. For some reason, this seemed to shake Matt more than the terrible events of the night before, but he could not quite understand why. As he walked home, he mused on it briefly before his concrete resolution once more flowed through his mind, covering all emotions and setting solidly in an unreadable countenance.

On the other side of town, Scott was standing awkwardly on a street that stretched off into the distance, the trees that lined the avenue vanishing behind the gasworks at the far end. Before going to sleep, he had looked up where Chase Rivers had lived, and was now dwelling on what his mother had said about fixing his problems. The notion of knocking on the front door and explaining to the boy's parents exactly what had befallen their son had seemed like a good idea last night, but now that he was actually there, he could not bring himself to step down the driveway. What would he actually be able to say to convince them anyway? Perhaps the Rivers' had already reported their son's absence to the Police and an investigation was now under way? In that case it would only be a matter of time before he and his former companions were tracked down and apprehended. Unless… What had his mother said about being able to undo his actions? She had used the word ability, and now Scott had a whole host of abilities that he hadn't possessed earlier. What if he could somehow use the Craft to bring Chase back to life? If he managed that before the Police came knocking, then everything would be back to normal again wouldn't it?

With a final look at the curtained windows of Chase's house, Scott turned and began to jog back to his own street, intent that until he had found a way to undo what the four of them had done, he would not leave his room.

Chapter 14 – Absinthe

It was mid-afternoon and signs of life were finally emerging at UCE Garnsworthy Hall. So far, Josh had seen two of his flatmates amble past the living room door, each looking equally as tousle haired and bleary eyed.

The warmth had amplified the smell of beer dregs, but Josh had only moved to get dressed, swiftly returning to his spot on the sofa, deep in contemplation. The events of last night were swimming repeatedly around his mind, preying piranhas at his resolve. So entangled in his own thoughts was he, that he didn't even notice when his flatmate Eric slumped next to him.

"That was one hell of a party…" he began casually, trying to lure Josh into conversation. When none was forthcoming, he tried again. "Dude, you look rougher than I do. You had a blast of your own last night?" Josh winced at the choice of words.

"Something like that," he shrugged. He took a closer look at Eric, taking in the tangled blonde hair and the greenish eyes haloed with the crimson bloodshot of a heavy night. Eric was on the UCE swim team, and no doubt the coach would reprimand him for his jubilant night. "What were you on anyway, you look rough as?"

"Aha," Eric laughed. "You're not wrong there. I can only remember till about eleven then it's all a bit blurry. The guys said I kissed Tina but…"

"Isn't she, you know, the other way?"

"Not sure, but whatever happened, it's my own fault."

"How do you mean?" Josh asked. Despite his earlier reluctance, it felt refreshing to have a normal conversation that didn't revolve around witchcraft – anything to take his mind off the fire and the screams. Eric chuckled again as he launched himself from the sofa and headed for his room.

"How's your constitution?" he replied with a grin. Josh slouched for a moment until his flatmate returned with a bottle of what looked like luminous green pond water. Josh sighed as he recognised the drink as Absinthe.

"No way," he exclaimed. "That's one night at the union I'm glad I can't remember. Been there, done that."

"Not this you haven't," Eric smirked with a shake of the bottle causing the viridian liquid to slosh and foam in the container. "This is home made. The guys in B5 make it. Originally, Absinthe was banned because it had wormwood in. It's a hallucinogen or something. The commercial stuff doesn't have it but-"

"Let me guess," Josh cut in. "This is wormwood-a-go-go?"

Eric nodded. "Yup, a load of other herbs and a shit load of vodka, just for kick." As he said this, Eric poured himself a cap full and necked it, grimacing as it burned its way down his throat.

"Don't you have training later?" At this Eric shrugged and offered the bottle across. Even from there, Josh could feel the strength of the drink, sending a toxic plume of vapour into the room. He could almost picture his nostril hair curling and wilting as he inhaled. But then if this was strong enough to give him an hour or two of sleep, it was surely worth it?

Decided, he took the bottle, filled the cap and drained it. Before his taste buds could react, he swiftly repeated the process another two times, much to Eric's amusement. As Josh leaned his head back, he saw his flatmate pour himself another cap and knock it back, all concerns about impending swimming training cast out with his inhibitions.

Josh closed his eyes and waited.

The wind blew his hair about mischievously as he flexed his toes, feeling the countless millions of sand grains trickle between them. Seagulls drifted through the sky above him and the water lapped casually at the shore a few feet away.

Josh could not place the exact beach he was standing on, but knew he was safe there. An intense feeling of peace and solitude washed over him, soaking into his skin and filling his entire body with detached contentment.

As he stood gazing across the endless ocean, he became aware of something changing. The azure sky darkened and the birds scattered. The rolling waves that had been caressing the shoreline moments ago were now rushing forwards and biting at the sand viciously.

Accompanied by Polaroid flashes of lightning and the deep rumbling of thunder, a wave rose up and pulsed towards land, frothing and spitting malevolence as it raced forwards. By the time it was a couple of metres away, the wave was a sheer wall of water, striving to sweep over Josh and crush him beneath tons of pressure.

The young man turned and ran, making for the shadows of the trees. As he became enveloped in their cool shelter, he heard the crashing roar as the immense volume of water cascaded onto the land. He increased his pace as he twisted through the palm trees and tropical creepers, jumping fallen trunks and ducking hanging vines. Any minute now the sweeping tidal wave would catch up to him and drag him into its cold and final embrace. Josh pumped his legs harder, faster until they throbbed with burning agony.

A barrier of palm fronds blocked his way up ahead, so he lowered his head and charged, swinging his arms to boost his speed as much as he possibly could. The leaves got closer. Josh leapt as he forced his way through and landed haphazardly onto bare cool soil.

The first thing that hit Josh was that it was now nighttime. The air was a lot cooler, and the towering oaks and beeches confirmed that he had somehow swapped the tropics for something a little more local. He spun around, but of course there was no sign of the tidal wave, or the palm enclosed bay he had just fled from.

Josh's heart sunk as he realised where his thoughts had dragged him. As he turned once more, he saw the lifeless teenager slumped in the centre of the clearing, stony eyes devoid of being, yet boring into the young man's guilty soul. He watched as Chase erupted into a mass of scalding orange tongues, burning with such ferocity that the body was soon reduced to ash - clothes, skin, hair and muscle all combined into a single charcoal dust. A person, a life scorched into nothing. The fire continued to burn relentlessly, and Josh could feel the heat even from where he was standing, like a grazing blow against his face.

The flames flared upwards and a piercing screech, bird-like, tore through the clearing, seeming to come from the heart of the blaze. The inferno split into what looked like a vast wingspan, golden feathers of twisting flame...

Josh sat forwards, breathing heavily, his head pounding inside his skull. The back of his neck was damp with sweat and he wondered how long he had been dreaming. To his surprise, Eric was sitting bolt upright, eying him suspiciously.

"That was some weird voodoo…" he muttered.

Josh gulped, hoping he didn't look too distressed. "What did you see?" he asked casually. Eric stood up and straightened his t-shirt awkwardly. His face was flushed, and he too looked like he had just been through an intense ordeal.

"I saw you," he whispered.

<u>Phoenix's Triumph</u>
<u>November 17</u>

Chapter 15 – Out Of The Ashes

The forest was silent as midnight approached. Phoenix crouched on the ground, surrounded by the five candles that formed his ritual circle. He had already lit his oil burner, and the small clearing was beginning to smell of the rich, peppery mixture of spices that made up the deep red Fire Oil that filled the glass dish. The moonlight outlined everything in silver, and Phoenix was reminded of one of those pictures that children made by scratching a black covering from metallic paper. If only his life was that simple, as if what he was doing could just be scratched out and started again if something went wrong. As it was, there could be no room for mistakes. Phoenix took the leather cord from around his neck and laid it on the ground in front of him. On the cord was one small disc of metal with a single flame etched into it, the elemental symbol for the power of Fire. The young man remembered back a fortnight when Dex had given him it – the cord had held so much promise then. Phoenix's breath hung in the air as he wrapped his cloak tighter around him. He was still cold despite having the hood up over his hair, which was now pushed forwards into curtains across his forehead. He nervously glanced at his watch, the luminous face reflected twice in his deep blue eyes. It was midnight.

"Ina kioymarinatoh firel paroywonelrai oyfia Farinaraiel tohoy firel kiunasarel oyfia firel fioynarai," said Phoenix confidently, his voice ringing loud and commanding through the thickly entwined brambles enclosing him. It was done. He had successfully performed his part of the ritual. Phoenix released the breath he had been unconsciously holding as he sat back, slipping his pendant back over his head. He had followed the plan so far, but one aspect was nagging at him. What was supposed to happen now? He was expecting some sort of sign to show that the ritual had worked, but nothing had happened. Where was the flash of light, the gust of wind or whatever? Phoenix looked around to see if anything had changed at all, but nothing had. Maybe the other parts of the ritual weren't complete yet? But what could be taking so long? One phrase didn't exactly take long to say, and Phoenix certainly hadn't rushed it. He was just about to whisper the incantation a second time when he felt it. He sat bolt upright, his hand clamped over his heart. There was no pain to speak of, but it felt as if something was tugging at his insides. He felt a great sense of urgency, and the face of Dex flashed in his mind's eye. This feeling was nothing to do with the ritual he had just done; Dex must have lit a calling candle. Dex was in trouble and he needed Phoenix's help. For a second, he wondered why Dex had chosen him, but then again perhaps the Earth Elemental had lit all three of his candles and was summoning the group back together. Whatever it was, it must have been important.

Phoenix quickly got to his feet and spun around, trying to get his bearings. Earth was opposite Fire, so Dex would be right on the other side of the forest. Phoenix would have to move fast if he intended to help. He forced himself to breathe deeply and unfocused his eyes, slipping into a kind of meditation. Phoenix was trying to find Dex, and sure enough there was a faint glow far away through the trees. It was as if Phoenix was looking through infrared goggles, and Dex was his target. He remained in this trance-like state until he was sure he was on the right path then began to run, his cloak whipping out behind him as he dodged in and out of the trees.

Phoenix didn't even register as he ran through The Haven, but it would have struck him as strange that only two weeks ago, he had fought one of his closest friends there. Two weeks felt like two years, and so much had changed since then: a raging pole fight seemed innocent compared to now. Something whipped across Phoenix's face, the sharp barbs stinging his cheek. He had lost concentration for just a moment and had run through a veil of brambles. He spun around, his arms flailing as he tried to slow himself down from sprinting speed. His face glowed with the smarting pain that the small thorns had traced across him. Phoenix halted, staring around wildly. He had been so intent on getting to Dex that he hadn't actually taken any notice of where he was. And now, thanks to his stupid pirouette, he had no idea which way he was facing, and which way he should be. Cursing silently under his breath, Phoenix slipped back into his unfocused state, and tried to search for the green glow that would indicate Dex's location. Damn! He had swung too far across, and Dex's resonance was now quite far away to Phoenix's left. He blinked, bringing everything back into the sharp focus of reality, and once more began to move, jogging this time, carefully picking his way through the branches and roots that littered his path. Annoyance crept over his countenance for a brief second as he thought of how Dex would probably have been able to just make the trees move out of his way, but now was not the time for jealousy. Phoenix couldn't change his element; it depended on when he was born, and who could change that? He would be Fire forever, just as Dex would be Earth forever.

To Phoenix's surprise, the forest abruptly ended and he was bathed in the clear, cool air as he paused, surveying the large crop field he was now facing. He idly blew a long strand of hair out of his face as he thought about what he would find in the field, for that was where he had to go. There were no visible trails or trodden down stalks, but Dex was in there somewhere. Without hesitating, Phoenix plunged into the tall plants, again wishing that he had Dex's affinity for not getting repeatedly clubbed and stung as he bumped into practically every plant growing there.

Phoenix emerged into a large clearing, and the first thing he saw was a tangled mass of orange fur that looked like it had once been a fox. Something had literally gutted it and the soil all around was a deep crimson. There was also what looked like a human ear lying in the dirt. Phoenix's gorge rose threateningly, but he managed to suppress the urge to be sick. As he remembered from Halloween, it would take more than that to spill his guts. Instead, he drew a silver blade from his belt, knowing full well that Dex would never have done this to a fox, a creature of Earth. He looked up, and that was when he saw it.

Everything went silent, as if Phoenix had suddenly been forced into a vacuum. Dex was sprawled on his back towards the other side of the clearing, his shirt ripped cruelly open and soaked in blood. He wasn't moving. A red candle was still burning near the body, the same candle that Dex must have lit, frantically needing Phoenix's help. Lying next to it were broken fragments of blue and yellow candles. *It seemed like it was just him who would have to witness this tragedy,* he surmised.

The grass all around the clearing was bowed inwards, as if to show respect for the fallen Earth Elemental. It seemed like time itself had slowed down as Phoenix ran over to the body. In reality he ran, but in his mind it seemed like he could not get there fast enough, as if he was moving through tar. Previous enmity stripped away as he crouched, lowering his ear to Dex's mouth, the faint hope that he might hear a breath. There was none. Phoenix looked up, sorrow welling up inside as he looked into Dex's open eyes. The usual shining blue had been replaced by icy, lifeless cobalt. This was not a person; this was an empty shell, devoid of all personality. Scott Fielding was dead. Phoenix was vaguely aware that he had broken some law or other about only referring to brothers by their spiritual names when performing rituals, but Dex was only half of who this body used to be, and the Scott half had also been brutally stabbed. One half could not live without the other, and if one was harmed, then both suffered. Things had gone wrong ever since Halloween. It had been completely different to how Matt had planned it. The whole thing with Chase was unexpected, and now Scott was dead, but how could Phoenix have known it would go this way?

Phoenix thought back to when this had all started. It was towards the end of their A Levels, and their intellectual friend, who had probably finished all of his revision, had arrived with an amazing prospect to give the others a break from theirs. He remembered the barriers he had put up even then, arguing on the side of science, when Scott had convinced him that this *was* a branch of science when you thought about it. It was all about manipulation of particles and energy, just like a physicist would do, but on a grander scale. 'It's not magic, there's no such thing as magic,' ran the now familiar Fielding quote. Never to be heard again. Phoenix shook his head, casting away his thoughts. There was still the problem of who - or whatever did this still being around. Of course, Phoenix knew it had to have been Chase, but was he still classed as a person after what happened to him? The others might be in danger - *he* might be in danger. He looked down at Dex one last time, actually taking in the fatal wound. There was a hole in his left side, below the rib cage. It looked as if the blade had been angled upwards, slicing through the diaphragm and puncturing his left lung. Phoenix was stunned. Nothing seemed to penetrate his emptiness. He could not move, could not feel, could not cry, nothing would reach him.

There was a slip of paper left in the centre of Dex's chest, which the blood had encircled but not touched. Curious, Phoenix picked up the paper, careful not to touch Dex's marble skin. The paper was old and torn at the top, as if it had been ripped from the page of a book. There was only one simple line written in black; "The willing fifth, you must sacrifice to gain true power." Phoenix's emotions flooded in like a river bursting its banks. Whereas seconds ago he had been unable to feel anything, now he was blinded, incapacitated with rage. He closed his fist, crunching the paper so hard that his fingernails cut into his palm. Chase had left this on purpose, as if he knew that Phoenix would see it. Not only was the Spirit Elemental hunting them, but he was playing mind games with Phoenix, taunting him. Even now, Chase could be torturing Dylan or Altair - maybe they were dead already. He had no idea how long it had been since Dex had been murdered. He looked at the body again. One of Dex's arms was outstretched, as if he had tried to claw at something before the end. Now the arm was pointing behind his head. Phoenix followed the direction of Dex's arm and saw that the grass had been trampled. At least he knew which way Chase had gone, and from the look of it, he had headed back towards the forest. Towards the others. Phoenix knelt down and gently closed Dex's eyes. Scott Fielding would never see anything again.

"I'm so sorry…" he whispered as he stood up again and ran after his target, blade drawn.

Chapter 16 – Fire With Fire

"Nobody has power limited only to good or bad, light or dark. Just like everyday life, we can act on either side. Anybody with the power to bless also retains the power to curse. This is the law of equals."

The Book Of Shadows

Phoenix had stormed through the field and back into the forest, not paying any attention to where he was heading. He was driven by blind fury, fuelled by anger. He knew he was on the right path, he could feel it. It was as if Chase had somehow poisoned the ground he walked on, tainted it somehow. No living thing made a sound, no birds or even insects. The whole world cowered from this new threat. Phoenix was on a crooked path, deep in the darkness of the forest. The trees barely paid any heed to the edges of the path, ready to invade at any moment. The forest could easily reclaim its territory; after all, it owed no allegiance to mankind. It was only the good graces of a few that kept the paths clear for the many. The trees hunched over the path, blotting out the moonlight above. It was as if the moon was too dignified to see what was going on in the mortal plane - if Chase was even mortal any more. The trees seemed to know what was going to happen, could sense the conflict that was brewing and didn't want the rest of the world to see it. Phoenix mused for a second, wondering if the trees could actually sense things like that. Dex would have been able to tell him, if he hadn't been mercilessly cut down. Thinking of his spiritual brother only enraged Phoenix further as he quickened his pace.

The sickness emanating from Chase was growing thicker, so Phoenix knew he must have been gaining on his prey. Perhaps the monster was not hurrying, was walking with the satisfied swagger that always followed a predator's kill. Suddenly, the path began to slope upwards, heading up one of the many hidden hills that were concealed within the immense woods. Phoenix froze suddenly, his anger stuck in a pause, flickering like a candle in a light breeze, unsure if it should continue to burn or not. Chase was standing at the top of the slope. He had his back to Phoenix, and was slightly bent over, his cloak wrapped around him and the hood up in a twisted parody of someone afraid and needy. The path must have led right to the top of the hill, as the moon was suddenly visible, giving the young man an eerie backlit quality. He was just a silhouette, so menacing that not even the moonlight dared to pass him. The air was rank with his pollution, and Phoenix's rage ignited once more, brighter than before. Chase's very presence was enough to destroy the atmosphere around him and he had no right. Phoenix considered his options, wondering why Chase was just standing there. Was there another one of the four lying helpless in the mud in front of the monster? The young man's body was charged, but apprehension held him back. Contrary to what others might have thought, he wasn't a fighter. He had never been in a real fight before, usually choosing stinging words as his weapons, but now he was faced with the ultimate encounter – his baptism by fire, as it were.

He thought of his favourite film, wishing he could strap himself into a giant robotic suit and storm forwards screaming "Get away from them, you bitch!" or something similar – he had no doubt that this confrontation would be of equal proportion, but it felt different in real life. Phoenix was suddenly aware of his own fragile body, about how easily it could tear and break just like Scott's had done. *Scott.* That was the crux of it all. No matter what had gone

on between them in the past, he had to avenge his
companion. He would live or die to honour the fallen.
Before he could stop himself, before he had a chance to
come up with even the smallest of battle plans, Phoenix
found himself charging towards his enemy. Chase still
made no sign that he even knew that anybody was behind
him, his arrogance only fuelling Phoenix's anger further.
The Fire Elemental raised his knife as he approached, the
silver blade catching in a stray patch of moonlight and
glinting in the darkness. Suddenly, Chase wheeled around
and pressed his hands together. As if they were made of
flint, sparks flew as he grated his wrists, shooting out a
blast of flame, which hurtled towards the awestruck
attacker. Only just in time did he raise his own hand and
screw his face up with concentration. The blast of fire hit
his outstretched palm and split into two smaller streams of
flame, one flowing either side of him. Phoenix had
successfully deflected the attack, but it had been close. He
had only just managed to focus his energy before the fire
reached him. He realised that if he was to stand a chance,
he needed some sort of protection or risk upping Chase's
body count.

He sheathed his blade and tried to concentrate again,
knowing that Chase was probably already executing his
next attack. Phoenix tried to block this negative thought
out of his mind as he felt an intense heat flowing down his
arms and into his hands. He knew what he wanted to do,
but would he have the power? There was no time to
consider his capability, as another blast of fire was thrown
his way. This time however, the attacker's aim was off, and
the burning jet flew past Phoenix's head, setting fire to the
tree directly behind him. The smell of singed hair rose up
through the smoke, and Phoenix noticed that a part of his
fringe had curled like steel wool. Still concentrating,

Phoenix focused on transforming his own body heat. Sure enough, two streams of molten flame sprung from his fingertips and he rapidly traced a ring around him on the ground, surrounding himself with a wall of flames.

Phoenix finished his circle, his fingers tingling from the heat he had created. He could relax a little now and think properly about what he was going to do next. Or not. Chase strode unharmed through the flames as easily as if he often went for a relaxing stroll through the fires of Hell. He stopped to laugh maniacally and Phoenix took the opportunity to get a better look at his adversary. The Spirit Elemental was a lot paler than he had been when he was alive, almost completely white, with no sign of the horrific burns that he had suffered on Halloween. His left ear was missing, but he seemed unaffected by its absence, judging by the way he was grinning sadistically. Phoenix remembered the ear he had seen earlier. *At least the fox got a hit in before it died,* he thought consolingly.

"What's the matter Matthew?" Chase taunted, mistaking Phoenix's silence for apprehension. His voice cut into the Fire Elemental like a razor. "Afraid of what you created?" Phoenix tried to look as blank as he could. The last thing he wanted to do was provoke this insane fiend more than he had to.

"I don't know what you mean," he said through gritted teeth. Chase smiled and shrugged, the fire reflecting in his colourless eyes, making them glow with burning hatred.

"Your little Earth Boy acted all defiant too, and you probably saw what I did to him," he went on. Phoenix grimaced at the mention of his former brother.

"How did you find out?" Phoenix asked as Chase rolled his eyes.

"Broken record!" Chase snorted. "It doesn't bother me really. I was planning on killing you guys anyway. You four – sorry, three – are my only competition. Too many cooks spoil the broth, apparently. So I have to kill some cooks." He chuckled at his own joke before striding forwards and punching Phoenix straight in the face. Phoenix felt his nose break and blood poured into his mouth. He spat onto the ground before retaliating with two punches and a kick of his own. Chase's reason had obviously been replaced with arrogance, as he was caught by surprise, thrown backwards, falling through the wall of flame, arms flailing. It was a cheap flurry of blows that Chase had been too confident to expect, but Phoenix would not be able to repeat his luck. He instantly stuck his hand into his pocket, desperate to find something that would help him. He pulled out the only thing that was in there, a box of matches, and tipped the whole drawer into his hand. He glanced at his attacker, who was still sprawled on the ground and threw the matches into the air as high as he could. Both men stared into the night sky as the matches vanished against the blackness, Chase smirking at the seemingly pointless action. Phoenix however, was focusing his mind on every one of the matches he had thrown. They were reaching their apex, and now was the time.

One of the matches ignited and expanded into a fireball the size of a football as it hung in the air. It looked as if one of the many stars had suddenly exploded, then more of these stars started to appear as the rest of the matches burst into flames and began to fall. Phoenix pointed towards his target, who had now climbed to his feet, an anxious look creeping across his deathly face. He yelled, more out of frustration than fear, as the first of the fireballs slammed into the ground a few feet away from him. Phoenix jumped out of the circle of flame and ran to the cover of the trees as a second fireball crashed even closer. Soon, the apocalyptic spheres were raining down, causing the sky to glow a brilliant orange, as if sunrise had come six hours early. Chase jumped and twisted, avoiding the incendiary projectiles as the whole world turned to flame. Trees and ground alike burned with a ferocity that mirrored the hatred between the two men. Suddenly, one of the fireballs hit Chase directly in the chest, knocking him back up the path towards the summit of the hill. He crashed into the ground painfully, his cloak and black t-shirt burning viciously into tatters.

The last of the matches fell to the ground and Phoenix dodged out from the shadow of the trees. Chase was writhing on the ground some way up the path, trying to extinguish the fire that was burning on his chest. It was as if he was destined to be torched again just as he was on Halloween. In the end, he wriggled out of his shirt and cast off his cloak, red blotches standing out against his colourless flesh. As he was untangling himself from the last shreds of smouldering fabric, Phoenix noticed that Chase had a tattoo of some sort on his shoulder. *Didn't think he was the type,* Phoenix thought as he watched Chase pat the tattoo tentatively as if checking it was still intact. The Fire Elemental seized his chance and charged once more. The attack was expected, however, and the downed man slipped Dex's athame into his hand at the last moment. As Phoenix lunged at him, he flicked his hand out, catching the charging Elemental across the chest. Phoenix cried in pain as a thin line of blood appeared on the front of his shirt. It was a shallow cut, but it had bought Chase the time he needed to climb to his feet. Phoenix reeled. The wound was almost identical to the one Scott had given him in their impromptu sword fight, a memory of youthful rivalry now burned over with the ashes of genuine hatred.

"These knives are cool…" Chase exclaimed, smiling again. "I must remember to thank Scott for it. Forgot to clean it though…" Phoenix felt sick as he thought of what the murderer was talking about. That was the knife that had slain his friend, and now it was threatening to kill him too. Chase advanced, slashing the blade in front of him, hoping to catch Phoenix with another cheap shot. Instead, Phoenix jammed his forearm outwards, sending his attacker's arm reeling to the side and leaving his bare chest completely exposed. Before he could bring his arm back down in defence, Phoenix had thrust his own athame deep into Chase's ribs. Phoenix screamed with rage as the monster dropped the stolen athame in surprise, the pure shock of being stabbed overwhelming even to him.

It was as if a veil had been lifted from Phoenix's mind. Everything seemed so much clearer now. Any moment, Chase would crumble, the pain of the blade embedded between his ribs and piercing his heart too much for him regardless of how spiritually super charged he thought he was. There would be no need to carry out the rest of the ritual, Phoenix was sure of it. Chase stopped struggling and Phoenix looked up, expecting to see the peaceful mask of eternal slumber on his face. Instead he fell right into the deep grey pits of his enemy's eyes as they stared straight at him. They burned with an ancient fire, burned with glory and passion, and Phoenix felt himself sinking inexorably beyond reach. His brain was no longer transmitting to his limbs, and he couldn't even let go of the sliver of metal he had forced into the other's flesh. Chase was grinning smugly, the smile growing even wider as Phoenix gasped, fighting for control of his own body.

"Think back to any film or story you've ever heard of," Chase taunted. "Since when have you been able to just stab the villain to death?" He laughed as he tilted his head

downwards to scan the knife hilt sticking out of his chest, a
knowing smirk crawling across his face as his gaze flowed
from the pommel and along Phoenix's arm. The Fire
Elemental still could not release himself, as a voice
whispered constantly in the back of his mind. *Hold on, hold
on, hold on.* It felt that if he let go of the knife, the wound
would be undone somehow. Suddenly the blade began to
glow, first a deep red, but becoming rapidly brighter until it
shone like a brilliant white star, bleaching everything in the
clearing to simple monochrome. With a loud roar, an
intense heat flowed out of Chase, through the athame and
into Phoenix. His sleeve flashed into flames as he jumped
backwards leaving the blade embedded where it was. The
whispering voice ended abruptly as the contact between the
two men was severed. Scrambling for Dex's discarded
blade, Phoenix waved his arm frantically.

He tried to dredge up the most severe spell he could
remember from his Book of Shadows, as the Spirit
Elemental casually tapped the glowing hilt of the knife in
his own ribs. Phoenix had no hope of remembering the
Theban Locte, so he thrust out his palm and roared in
English.

"Chase, fall victim to hybrid onslaught,
May your emotions erupt in self-destruction,
So mote it be."

With a jolt, he felt a rush of energy shoot from his hand
and fly towards his nemesis intent on ripping the fiend's
emotions into frenzied chaos. Phoenix's face fell as the
Spirit Elemental swatted the shimmering orb of light out of
the air as if it were no more threat than piece of dust.

"That won't work either," he taunted. "My emotions
aren't the same as yours, idiot." Chase stepped forwards
with a malicious laugh and grabbed his shirt roughly. With
what seemed like no effort at all, he lifted Phoenix off the

ground as if he was made of cloth. In less than a second, the Fire Elemental's feet were dangling uselessly a couple of feet from the mud. Phoenix closed his eyes, waiting for the inevitable. Chase was right, he was afraid of what he had created, and now it was going to kill him. He thought back to when he was still at school and reading Frankenstein. The professor lived in constant fear that his creation would ruin his life, and the only way he could escape the torment was to die. Phoenix was faced with the same curse, and any minute now, the man who held his life in his hands would give a small twist and snap him in two. It didn't come. Instead, Chase threw Phoenix as hard as he could towards the edge of the trees. Phoenix felt the brief sense of weightlessness as he flew through the air. It was as if he was a puppet being pulled along on strings. A sickening crack echoed through the forest as his spine connected with a large tree trunk, sending jolts of pain through Phoenix's nerves and flakes of bark flying into the air.

Phoenix fell to the ground and slumped in the mud. He had landed on his front, his face crinkled with pain, tears flowing freely down his cheeks. He didn't dare try and move his legs: he had hit the tree so hard that he may have broken his back. They say that despair is the lowest of human feelings, and that once you give up hope then life is not worth living. Like sparks drifting onto kindling, despair crept up to Phoenix and planted itself firmly in his mind. His nose was shattered, his arm was burnt, his back was severely injured and even at full health he couldn't hold Chase off. What chance did he have now? What it would be to just close his eyes and let sleep take him. He could forget everything and join the peaceful procession of the countless souls making their way to the next step. Chase had not advanced again - he was obviously watching from a distance the damage he had caused. The Spirit Elemental was certain that he had finished the fight, so why wouldn't Phoenix accept it? Because he kept seeing his friends in his mind. Altair had not given up when Chase had tortured him, Dylan had not just sat and waited to drown and Phoenix was sure that Dex would have fought with all his strength before letting Chase stab him. All had been tested, would Phoenix be the one who failed? No. After all, what was pain really but just a state of mind? Dex was always quoting the Book of Shadows and hadn't that once said that magic was all in the mind too? If he could turn matches into fireballs just by thinking it then he could conquer his pain and carry on.

Phoenix weakly looked upwards and saw that the fight had taken him almost to the top of the slope the path climbed. Just over the ridge, he could make out a large clearing where the ground had been burned and turfed up. A pair of aged stonework pillars formed an inviting archway, beckoning Phoenix forwards, as if urging him to complete his goal. It was the clearing of the Halloween Initiation and the perfect place for Chase to be. If Phoenix could just lead him to that clearing, then providing that the others had performed their parts of the ritual, their tormenting creation would be stopped.

It was time for Phoenix to test the extent of his spinal damage. Slowly, he concentrated on moving his left leg. A sharp flash of pain dominated his body for a brief second but his leg moved exactly as it was supposed to. It was safe to say that Phoenix had not been paralysed by his collision. *Well that's one thing,* he thought as he slowly and arduously began to crawl up the rest of the slope, Chase laughing cruelly at his efforts.

With the inhuman fiend watching in amusement all the way, Phoenix finally managed to claw his way into the clearing. Something was supposed to happen now. He hadn't understood the exact details of the ritual they were supposed to be doing but now that Chase was here, something should definitely be happening. Phoenix continued to crawl towards the centre of the clearing, but his time was up. Chase had lost his patience and was looking to end this encounter. As Phoenix edged through the dirt, he heard the sound of footsteps approaching steadily from behind him. Before he could turn around, his back crunched once more as a heavy boot stamped down on it. Phoenix writhed, the pain in his already brutalised spine now utterly crippling. With a powerful kick, Chase flipped him onto his back, curling and twisting desperately trying to protect himself. Chase walked forward until he was standing straddling his fallen victim. As Phoenix looked up in terror, Chase finally pulled the athame out of his own chest and stretched out his arms in the classic crucifixion pose.

"Let there be light," he smirked as lightning flashed, temporarily blinding Phoenix as he lay looking up at his killer. Chase smiled briefly, and then the expression was gone, lost to the overwhelming malice and hatred that took over his face. He put his hands together then raised his arms above his head, brandishing the knife threateningly over Phoenix's face. Phoenix screamed as he heard the blade slice through the air, split seconds away from driving between his eyes and into his brain. The cracking and tearing of flesh never came as suddenly, four streams of energy shot out of the trees at each compass direction. One green, one blue, one yellow and one red, the four bursts of energy slammed into Chase as the knife was less than an inch away from Phoenix's forehead. The next few seconds passed in a haze as Phoenix thought about how close he was to death.

As he was lifted into the air, Chase viciously flung the knife to the ground, aiming for Phoenix's face. The blade veered at the final moment, tracing a razor fine streak of crimson as it glanced against his cheek before plunging to the hilt into the embracing mud. Chase spat in disgust, the four ribbons of colour swirling almost playfully around him. There was a flash, and the four beams combined into one purple band of energy that swiftly encircled their prisoner until he was contained in a sphere of pure violet power. Phoenix watched as Chase pounded against the force field to no avail. He could not break free. An unearthly scream filled the air as, wearily, Phoenix sat up, pulled his blue and yellow calling candles out of his belt, set them on the ground and lit them with a click of his fingers.

<u>Eric's Connection</u>
<u>November 1</u>

Chapter 17 – Contagion

The whistle blew and Eric Levy channelled all of his energy into his legs, knees bent like pistons ready to surge forwards. He stretched his arms in front of his head and launched himself into the air, a spearhead of rippling muscle and sinew. For a second he was weightless, the tiled horizon that separated the side of the pool from the churning water tilting wildly as his body curved gracefully towards the steaming liquid.

Bubbles crackled in his ears as he plunged beneath the surface, pulling his chest up so that he began to glide fluidly along the waterline. By the time he broke for air, he would be almost halfway across the pool, and hopefully his teammates who he was practicing with would still be a couple of metres behind. He kicked upwards, his head bursting into the cool air for a quick breath before sinking below the tumultuous waves once more. Eric began pumping his arms and tilting his head rhythmically, preparing to crawl the rest of the way to the far side of the pool.

There was Eric's flatmate Josh standing in a clearing, tall trees looming from all directions. Another boy was lying in the dirt, cold and unmoving. He watched as this boy erupted into a mass of scalding orange tongues, burning with such ferocity that the body was soon reduced to ash, clothes, skin, hair and muscle all combined into a single charcoal dust. A person, a life scorched into nothing. The fire continued to burn relentlessly, and Eric could feel the heat like a grazing blow against his face.

Eric opened his eyes, instantly closing them again against the glare of the high powered ceiling lights. Taking a moment to adjust, he opened them once more and assessed his situation. He was lying on his back, the coolness against his skin suggesting that he was on the tiles of the pool. His skin was still wet, so it couldn't have been that long since the race, but why was he lying here instead of hitting the showers and getting changed?

He propped himself up on his elbows, and immediately felt his head throbbing. His tongue felt swollen and he could taste blood – perhaps he'd bitten it? The rest of the team were standing against the wall, eyeing him awkwardly before turning back to their own conversations and pretending they hadn't been looking. Only the coach was kneeling next to him, a concerned look in his eyes. It was odd to see the man who always shouted and gave them a hard time looking like he cared.

"What happened?" Eric asked thickly, brushing a strand of wet hair out of his face.

"You had some sort of fit," Coach began. "I had to pull you out; you gave me quite a scare." Eric only then noticed that the Coach's t-shirt was clinging to his skin. He felt a sudden swell of gratitude for the man, and wondered if he had any children of his own.

"Thanks, I guess I owe you one." He tried to laugh it off, like this sort of thing happened all the time and that nobody should be worried but he could already tell by the look on the other man's face that he hadn't succeeded.

"You have anything like this before?" Eric shook his head before Coach continued. "I was about to call an ambulance, you still want?"

"No, I'm good," he said, feeling anything but.

"Well you should definitely go see your doctor in your own time. For now, take it easy and don't worry about practicing for the next couple of days, ok?" Eric nodded and climbed shakily to his feet, using the Coach's arm for support. As he walked slowly into the changing rooms, he could feel the eyes of his teammates watching him go. He straightened up, as if to say *hey I'm not bothered* and went for his locker.

Ten minutes later, Eric was striding across the quad of UCE, intending to head back to halls and sleep. He would see the doctor tomorrow if anything else happened. The breeze was pleasantly chilled against his damp hair and the sun was out, making the November day seem unusually bright. A number of students were crossing the wide space, and Eric watched them calmly, focusing on a particularly attractive girl with dyed red hair tied up in dreads. He had always gone for the punky girls; the ones that would make his dad wince if he ever brought them home.

His eyes followed her as she moved from the Saunders Block towards the John Terrence building, then he froze with confusion. One of the lecturers, Mr Adams was outside John Terrence, talking to… *what exactly?* It was basically human shaped, but all Eric could make out was a dark silhouette that seemed to be bathed in violet flames. The silhouette looked as if it was wearing armour or padding of some sort, and holding a spear or javelin, but nobody else gave him a second look. Mr Adams continued to talk, enthusiastically waving his hands, and the girl Eric had been watching walked past without even turning her head.

It was as if he was hallucinating. *Of course!* He thought, the idea exploding inside his brain. It had to be something to do with the absinthe he was drinking at the party. He suddenly wondered if Josh was experiencing something similar, although he didn't dare ask him. What if

Josh blamed him? That would make living together awkward to say the least.

Tearing his eyes away from the purple apparition, Eric turned on his heels and headed for the gates, a hundred different conversations buzzing through his mind as he desperately tried to find a plausible way of explaining this to his doctor.

Eric's GP just happened to be in an office attached to the actual hospital, and on the few occasions that Eric had needed to go, he always felt guilty walking through the waiting room that was shared by all the people with serious hospital injuries, when all he needed was a repeat prescription of his hay fever pills. Today though, the waiting room was empty of any major incidents and Eric walked casually through to the smaller reception desk that served as the GP's service point.

A middle-aged woman was sitting at the desk, idly flicking through a copy of *Heat*. When she saw Eric, her eyes lit up and he guessed it had been a slow day all round. She closed her magazine and turned over a new leaf in her medical report pad, pen poised eagerly.

"Do you have an appointment?" she asked.

"Um, no. Sorry." This only made the woman's smile even wider, obviously adding a whole new element of excitement to the task of taking his details.

"Not to worry," she beamed. "What's the name?"

"Eric Levy." He could see her lips move, sounding out the letters as she wrote them down.

"And what's the trouble?" At this, she looked him up and down as if trying to spot the trouble herself. Eric was glad that he didn't have any outward symptoms like a lazy eye or something.

"I had a fit earlier, and then I've been seeing weird stuff, like hazes around people." He did his best to keep his tone even, so as not to make it sound too weird, but the woman remained professional throughout.

"I see," she said, writing the words *fit/ hallucination* on the form. "Well there's nobody in at the moment, so you might as well go right through." She tilted her head to the left, indicating the door to the doctor's office. She tore the form from the pad and handed it to him. "Just pass that to Doctor Turner and he'll be able to sort you out I'm sure." She smiled as he headed for the door.

Once in the office and faced with the actual doctor, Eric felt more relaxed and was able to tell the whole story, including the homemade absinthe and exactly what he had seen in the UCE quad. He had expected the doctor to laugh once he had finished, but like his receptionist, he kept a straight face regardless of what he might have been thinking on the inside.

"Well it certainly seems to me that it's a mild case of drug abuse." Eric opened his mouth to disagree, but Doctor Turner cut him off. "Unfortunately, that's what the wormwood counts as, Mr Levy, whether you count it or not." Eric nodded solemnly, feeling suitably chastised. "However, based on what you've described, the things you saw, I would feel a lot more comfortable if I could call one of my colleagues. A specialist, you might say. Is that all right?"

"Feel free, anything to sort this out." Eric wondered what sort of doctor could be a specialist in absinthe hallucinations, but sat patiently as Turner spoke into his phone. After a few moments, there was a knock at the door and Doctor Turner got up.

"I'll leave you to talk in private." As he opened the door, he exchanged a glance with the suited man that now entered the room. He walked with confidence, like he was used to wearing the finest outfits and he came across as more of a businessman than a doctor. He looked to be in his early fifties, his hair beginning to show silver streaks, but this only improved the impression of success rather than hindering it. He was wearing a purple lapel pin with a silver S on it, but Eric didn't recognise the symbol.

"Mr Levy," he began in a toneless voice. "I'm an associate with the Spyrus Company. Sometimes we offer our assistance with certain medical… situations. Wormwood is a very powerful substance, as I'm sure you're now aware. Please tell me about what happened."

Eric took an instant dislike to the man, but explained everything again regardless. When he had finished, the suited man asked an unexpected question.

"What was the name of the other boy you shared the drink with?" At this, he noticed Eric's confused expression. "Just in case he starts to experience similar effects?"

"Josh Thomas – he's my flatmate."

"Ah yes, Josh. One of the four."

"Excuse me?"

"Nothing," the man muttered. "Just an expression. Well I think that's everything I need to know." He got up to leave.

"Wait," Eric interjected. "Aren't you going to give me anything?"

"Here," the man added almost as an afterthought. "Take my card. If the problem persists, then come directly to Spyrus." He offered a small rectangle of card with a phone number and the same purple and silver logo. As soon as Eric had taken the card, the man swept out of the room without another word. It was only as Eric was walking bemusedly back to halls that he realised the man hadn't given his name.

Fifteen minutes later, the young man was marching purposefully down the corridor of his flat. He strode past the door to his own room and headed straight for the end of the corridor – Josh's room. He had decided on the way home that he really should warn his flatmate about the possible effects of his stupid drink. He just hoped that Josh wouldn't be too angry. He was quiet and usually spent most of his time with other friends, but Eric still got on with him.

He knocked loudly on the uniform "halls door", blue and featureless. No answer and no sounds from within. Perhaps Josh was in there, fitting out and helpless? Eric grabbed the handle, took a breath and opened the door, half expecting to see his flatmate writhing on the floor. The room was empty, and the young man sighed with relief, glad that the potentially awkward conversation would have to be put on hold.

He looked around the room, casually running a finger along the bedside table. It had always struck Eric as interesting to see other students' rooms, as everyone was given the same blank canvas when they arrived in halls, but after a month there was a diverse selection of styles. On his many visits to other flats and halls, he had always tried to take a look at the bedrooms, trying to suss the type of person that might live in them. As a result, he had seen so many variations of the bed, wardrobe, sink, table combo that he was beginning to think there was a science to it. He had seen fairy lights, art deco chairs, *Topman* window posters and even a shop dummy, so he liked to think he was fairly well versed in the art of student room decoration.

As it was, Josh's room was fairly standard. The walls were blue and mainly adorned with comic book posters. Along the windowsill was a line of empty bottles of various shapes and sizes – an exhibition to binge drinking. The bottle taking pride of place in the centre was something called *Barcelo,* which boasted 70% alcohol, and Eric found himself wondering how anybody could survive drinking it.

Eric turned to leave when a small shelf caught his eye. It was a roughly cut piece of chipboard with an elaborate design painted onto it – lots of circles and twisting symbols. There were a number of candles and miniature bottles, along with a stack of cards and a notebook. It was the cards that drew Eric the most, as he recognised the design on the back as a Tarot deck. He had no idea that Josh was into that sort of stuff, but then again, he didn't really know that much about the guy. He was a hardcore X-Men fan - that much was obvious but there were few other clues.

The young man casually turned over the top card, a picture of some swords falling from the sky, and a man waiting to catch them. *Swords are cool,* Eric thought. *I can live with that…* At least it wasn't Death. Eric took a final look at the design on the card, then placed it back on top of the pile and left the room, vowing that next time he saw Josh; he would explain everything about the absinthe.

Dylan's Plan
November 16

Chapter 18 – Rude Awakening

Josh Thomas carefully adjusted his hat as he walked across the University quad. It wasn't cold or anything, it was just that a couple of years ago, Scott had convinced him to dye his hair blue for a party they were going to. He had deemed his patchy blue/black hair unworthy to see the light of day, and had worn the bucket hat ever since.

He was alone, which was unusual, and he missed having other people to talk to. In a lame attempt to break the silence, he tried whistling a tune but it came out as the scary kind of haunted house music rather than the cheery uplifting melody he had been aiming for. Remind me never to play music for weddings, he thought to himself with a grin.

With no forewarning, there was an extremely loud bang and the ground shook as a column of flame and smoke blossomed into the sky. Josh stared at the explosion, which looked as if it was coming from the United Kingdom Nursing College, which had its campus a few streets away from UCE. He flung his bag to the ground, spilling computing textbooks onto the grass, and ran to the main gates in the corner of the quad. As he suspected, the main building of UKNC was ablaze and a crowd of worried looking girls were gathered in the street. Nobody else was around, so Josh ran towards the girls. As he approached, they saw him and turned to meet him.

"It looks like the college has been completely destroyed," said one of the girls as she twirled a finger through her long hazel hair. All of the girls were still dressed in their nurse's uniforms and were staring intently at him.

"Are you ladies all right?" said Josh calmly. The girls were obviously in shock and he needed to keep his cool so they could respond to him. A beautiful girl stepped forwards in her short nurse's skirt

and looked innocently at him, batting her eyelids.

"We aren't injured. It's just that our dormitories were caught in the explosion and we have nowhere to sleep tonight. Do you know somewhere we can go?" Josh thought for a second, then smiled.

"Well, there is one place you could stay. Here, let me show you...."

Josh opened his eyes suddenly, his room slowly coming into focus. That was shaping up to be an interesting dream and he was annoyed at being woken up. He rolled over and glared at the ringing phone on his bedside table. The clock next to the phone showed that it was 2:36 in the morning. Who the hell would be phoning at such a stupid hour? He lay back, hoping that the caller would just get bored and hang up, but the high-pitched beeping continued. Josh didn't want to wake Eric and the others up but if he wasn't careful, he would be in for some very evil looks in the morning. Twelve rings. Thirteen rings. Fourteen rings. Growling with annoyance, Josh answered.

"Err, hello?" he said drowsily.

"It's Rich." Josh paused before replying. He was seriously considering hanging up then leaving his phone off the hook, but something told him that his former friend wouldn't call unless it was something important. He compromised. He would talk but he would be purposefully blunt.

"Oh," he said negatively. "What do you want?" On the other end, there was a sigh.

"I tried phoning Scott but he didn't answer." *Great,* thought Josh. Not only was it past two in the morning but he wasn't even the first choice. Just two weeks ago, he would have been the first and only person that his friend would have turned to if he needed help. Even if Rich just wanted to share some joke he would have called, and Josh

would have called him too. He became even more annoyed
as he thought about the friendship they had shared before
the accident. Against his best efforts, he couldn't keep the
harsh edge from creeping into his voice.

"Good for him. Rich, it's late and I'm not in the
mood to chat, so just get on with it, ok?" The other end
was silent for a second. Josh shook his head in disbelief but
to his surprise, Rich began to explain in an
uncharacteristically forward manner.

"Fine. I think something is going on. I went to
Campus Security and she said that Chase was in his lessons
today." Josh sighed. He should have guessed it would be
about this. Rich had totally freaked out when it had actually
happened so he was probably still caught up about it. Not
that Josh had forgotten for a second the terrible feeling of
helplessness he had felt at the time. But life had to go on;
he couldn't let it take over. "Then I saw him on the way
home," Rich continued. "Only it wasn't him."

"There. It wasn't him. I don't see any problem
here." Already he had dismissed the cautious apprehension
as pointless worrying and he was now anxious to get back
to sleep.

"No! I mean it was him, but when I looked again, it
wasn't!" It sounded like Rich might be losing his temper,
but Josh didn't care. He should try getting woken up in the
middle of the night then see what mood that puts *him* in.
"And what about him turning up at Uni today?"

Josh was quickly losing his patience. "For God's
sake, Rich. Everybody knows lecturers just fake their
registers when they can't be bothered to do them. Chase
wasn't in uni today, and you didn't see him in the street.
The mind plays tricks. Just forget it. Now if you're finished,
I did plan to sleep tonight." As far as he was concerned, the
conversation was over. He had put Rich in his place, case

closed.

"But the nosebleeds!" Rich shouted. Josh froze. How could Rich know about the nosebleed he had had earlier today? It was roughly half past six in the morning when he had woken up, slowly covering his pillow with blood and he now cast a nervous glance over at the corner where a crimson stained shirt lay crumpled against the wall. "Me and Matt had nosebleeds!" Rich continued. "It made the exact same pattern. It can't be coincidence… Josh?" Josh knew what pattern he was talking about. His nosebleed had made three slashes across his chest, and they looked so real. He became lost in thought. Nothing could be wrong could it? It had to be coincidence. Rich was just feeling guilty about Chase and was obviously getting paranoid about it. And as for the nosebleeds, well the weather was hot; it was probably something to do with air pressure or something. *Yeah that was it,* thought Josh. Nothing to worry about.

"It's nothing. Goodnight Rich." Josh hung up and lay back against his pillow, staring up at his blue ceiling. The moonlight was shining through a gap in his curtains and was casting a strange fragmented shimmer on the opposite wall thanks to the row of empty alcohol bottles that he kept on his windowsill. As he had hoped, his eyelids began to droop as sleep tried to lovingly ensnare him once more. However, he was to be denied again. Just as his eyes finally closed, a loud bang echoed from outside. Outside the room, but inside the flat. Josh's eyes snapped open once more, this time fully alert. His breathing quickened as the noise came again, louder.

The young man slowly slipped out of bed and shivered as the cool air hit his bare chest. He edged towards the door, his toes sinking into the carpet, and stuck his head out into the corridor. His bedroom joined onto a long hallway with many other doors leading from it. There were two bathrooms and his three friends' bedrooms. Josh smiled as he noticed that he was the only one that slept with his door open. He and his course mates had been sharing this flat for long enough, yet still they did not trust each other. *I bet they all still lock them at night too,* he thought with a scowl. The only other door that was open led into the kitchen and after listening for a moment, it became apparent that the noise was coming from inside. The light switch was at the far end of the corridor, so he kept one hand trailing along the wall as he slowly crept towards the kitchen. As he approached the door, the banging came again and he halted, considering what he should do. Their flat was on the ground floor, what if it was a burglar? Even worse, what if it was some crazy killer or rapist? Josh considered heading back down the corridor and hiding under his bed cover like he used to do in thunder storms when he was small. *Yeah, and end up not being alive in the morning.* He even toyed with the idea of waking Eric or one of the others up, but nothing said 'I'm a big girl' more than that would. He braced himself for facing the mysterious noise alone.

Josh shot around the corner suddenly and raced into the kitchen, fists raised. The room was empty, but he could immediately see what was making the sound. The window had been left open and a loose cupboard door was banging in the breeze. He couldn't help smiling to himself. It was funny what the mind invented when something was unknown. He was also thankful that he hadn't woken Eric, as he would surely be getting beats about now. Shaking his head, he walked over to the window, closed it and then headed back into the corridor. As he returned to his bedroom, Josh stared at the phone for a second, still smiling to himself. He had just been on edge because of what Rich had said, that was all. He spun around to turn the light off and jumped back in shock. Chase Rivers was standing in his bedroom. He was dressed completely in black, with a long cloak that was billowing out behind him despite there being no wind to move it. He looked pale but very much alive, not at all how he had looked when Josh had last seen him. Chase watched him for a moment, and then smiled.

"Hello Joshua," he said calmly. As Josh watched, frozen with confusion, Chase cast his eyes over the room and tutted loudly. "Oh dear," he said as he inclined his head towards the small shelf where Josh kept his Wiccan things. One of his Tarot cards had been overturned. "Ten of Swords? That's the worst card in the deck! Ruin…"

Dazed, Josh shook his head. "It's not my card." Suddenly, Chase's face contorted into a silent scream and all of the bottles on the windowsill shattered, raining shards of glass down to the floor. Josh shouted as he fell backwards and sat on his bed, one arm raised over his face. He was still only in his night shorts and the cascade of glittering razors was threatening to cut his bare skin.

"What the hell?" Josh spluttered, unable to comprehend what was going on. "I don't… what do you want?" Chase frowned, looking generally taken aback by the question.

"You mean you don't know?" he exclaimed. "You're telling me you have absolutely no idea why I might be here?" Josh stared blankly, shaking with fear. He could already tell that Chase was worse than burglar, killer and rapist combined. An expression of mock sympathy crossed the intruder's face as he continued. "Aww, never mind," he cooed. "Allow me to fill you in. You killed me! You and your stupid friends! I get some message telling me to go to the forest, so I do and I get fucking scorched. Only I bet you regret it now don't you! Your little ritual got me too! There's just one thing. I'm like a wild card, more powerful than any of you pathetic losers. I am Fire. I am Earth. I am Air and Water. I am Spirit and you're not going to steal that from me like you did my pathetic shell. I even thought of a cool name. Deus. Means God, don't you know." Chase paused triumphantly after his big speech, but Josh was still taking it all in.

"What do you mean, the ritual got you too?" he said slowly.

Chase rolled his eyes. "God, could you be any more stupid? I'm talking about the power of the Elements. You have one, I have five. Get it?" he said patronisingly. Just like on Halloween, various components of consciousness seemed to lock into place as another moment of realisation dawned in Josh's mind. He had always assumed that because of the accident, the initiation ritual had failed. He hadn't even bothered to try anything to see if his powers had worked. Chase must be lying. But how was he here now? How could he have broken all the bottles? More importantly, how could he not look all burnt and disfigured? Josh had to be sure, so he asked the most obvious question he could think of.

"You mean the ritual worked?"

"Whatever. I'm bored now. I wanted to be part of the group, but instead I surpassed it. No matter. It's simple. You killed me, so I kill you. It's that easy. Only you don't get a second chance like I did. Killed in sin and all that…. I would say give my love to the others, but I think I'll be visiting them in person, if you know what I mean. Goodnight, Josh." Chase was obviously expecting him to say something, but he was dumbstruck by what he had just been told. Whilst he sat on the bed looking confused, Chase shook his head, giving a casual wave of his hand.

The door immediately closed and locked. Next, he closed his eyes in concentration and raised his arms, fingers outstretched. The air in the room began to swirl around Chase's fingertips as small clouds started to form. The air was condensing, turning to water before Josh's eyes. Within seconds it was as if there was a storm inside the bedroom, and water was running in rivulets from the ceiling down the walls. The carpet was already sodden as Chase turned and smiled maliciously at Josh, who was staring around wildly, his eyes wide. With another little wave, the young man vanished, popping into nothingness and leaving Josh alone in his room as it slowly filled with water.

Chapter 19 – The Third Test

Less than twenty minutes had passed, and Josh's room was
now almost completely filled with water. It seemed like no
time at all had passed, the amount of rain coming from the
ceiling falling at an alarming rate. There was only a couple
of feet left between the surface and the ceiling and it felt
like he had done nothing but watch it rise. He hadn't, of
course. The first thing he had done was run to the door. He
pulled as hard as he could but it would not move. Chase
had locked it but the worst thing was that it was one of
these new fire safety doors, completely airtight. The water
could not escape, even under the door. Frustrated, he had
spent a few moments swearing about how everyone was so
bothered about not letting fire escape that they didn't care
about people, then noticed that the water was now lapping
against the top of his bed. He desperately sloshed through
the knee deep pool, trying to find some clothes that weren't
soaked through but it was too late. In typical student
fashion, all of his clothes had been conveniently on the
floor and were now as wet as he was. After this, he had
rather futilely started to gather some of his possessions and
placed them on top of his wardrobe, the highest point in
his room. This had taken him to where he was now,
treading water in the middle of his bedroom, which had
quickly become a two metre deep pool.

Josh shivered and looked desolately down into the
water. Like a bizarre aquarium, all of his belongings were
floating eerily around the room. It was like one of those
films where everything comes to life when the owner isn't
around. He moaned as one of his X-Men comics drifted by
like a ghost. The collection he had was his most prized
possession and was the first thing he'd placed on the
relative safety of the wardrobe top. That was now under an

inch of water, and the comics were quickly turning to an inky mush. Life just wasn't worth living without his X-Men comics and the young man was beginning to lose hope. The ceiling was getting forever closer, and he was running out of energy. Treading water was harder than it looked, and still used up a lot of power. He could always hold his breath for as long as possible, and maybe the window would give way under the pressure. *The window! God, I'm retarded!* thought Josh. How could he have been so stupid? He had tried the door but hadn't given a moment's thought to the window. He looked around to get his bearings, and then saw the faint glow of the moonlight still shining into the room. After a brief pause, he took a big gulp of air and dived downwards.

Josh's senses were sent into chaos. Everything went muffled, but every bubble, every ripple sounded louder than a gun shot. The water was full of bits of broken bottle, and he swam with his eyes closed; only opening them briefly to see where he was. It was amazing how a relatively normal sized room could seem like the Pacific Ocean, but if he didn't hurry up, it would become the Dead Sea. A soft texture brushed against Josh's face, forcing him to open his eyes. Something was staring straight at him. The submerged man fought with all his might not to scream. That would be the end of him. If he opened his mouth, the water would rush into his lungs and he would drown. Instead, he flailed his arm in front of his face and pushed the thing out of his face. As it drifted further away, he could see that it was only a teddy bear, but up close it had looked like something far scarier. Josh reached the window, but before he even started pounding it with all his remaining strength, he could tell he was wasting his time. Just like his door, it was sealed tight. The window was the height of security, there was no way he could break it with his fists. Rapidly running out of energy, he allowed himself to float to the surface and broke through, feeling the pure oxygen wash over him. The ceiling was now just a few inches above his head and in about five minutes, he would have no more room to breathe. He had to smash the glass, and soon.

Josh took another frantic gulp of air before plunging back into the gloom, casting frequent blinks, trying to spot something he could use. Moments later, he was treading water in the centre of his aquarium, wielding his office chair which was now miraculously light. The young man hefted the chair as hard as he could, but without bracing against a solid surface, he found himself propelled backwards as much as the chair was thrown forwards. As it was, the piece of furniture drifted almost gracefully into the wall, ineffectually sinking to the floor. As his brain screamed for oxygen, he pushed himself into the sliver of air that remained, gasping wildly.

Josh didn't feel sad about his imminent death, but a wave of anger swept through him. He felt cheated. It was not as if he had been beaten in a fair fight. Chase had used magic to kill him, and there wasn't even the chance to defend himself. He swore again, cursing himself for being so narrow minded. Magic was the answer! Chase had said that the ritual had worked. It must have done, otherwise he would not have been able to condense the air then vanish without a trace. That meant that Josh must have some sort of power too. He racked his brains, trying desperately to think of how he should go about this. He needed to break the window so that the water would drain out. He was the Water Elemental so his powers were limited to the use of water. *Got plenty of that!* he thought angrily. He looked down to see another X-Men comic floating eerily beneath him. Iceman was on the cover, blasting a wave of ice at some unseen enemy. Of course! Finally an idea stuck in his mind, he just hoped he could concentrate hard enough. What did Scott always used to say? Something about the mind. Magic was in the mind. All Josh had to do was think about it and it would happen.

Josh held out his hand, palm down in the water, and screwed up his face with concentration. After a moment, the water seemed to shimmer but then stopped. The shock of actually seeing something happen had made him break his concentration. He slapped the surface of the water angrily as he forced his mind to focus again. The water had now risen so high that he had to tilt his head to stop it flowing into his mouth. Holding out his hand once more, Josh's mind repeated over and over what he wanted to happen. Sure enough, the water began to shimmer again, but this time it started to freeze. Again, he lost his train of thought, but he was getting there. He opened his palm to reveal a handful of small ice crystals.

"Yes!" he shouted triumphantly. The water began to lap against his nose, cutting the celebration short. An image of pure panic crossed his face as he took what may turn out to be his last ever breath. He plunged once more into the icy pool. Waving one arm to hold his position, he held out his hand again. Quicker and more definite than before, the water began to shimmer and freeze immediately. Josh had a large lump of ice before he decided to stop. A huge block wouldn't do any good; he needed something that could direct the pressure onto one spot of the window. He rose again, hoping to catch one final breath, but it was too late. The water was now touching the ceiling, and Josh did the worst thing he could. He gave in to panic. Before he knew it he was frantically pushing against the ceiling as if he could move it upwards and give himself a couple more inches of oxygen. It was a hopeless cause, and his brain started screaming for air. He had maybe enough breath for one last attempt, and then it would be all over. His flatmates would wake up in the morning, maybe they would open his door and find him floating in his liquid tomb, or maybe they would just go to their lessons and forget about him. Either way he would die if he couldn't break that window. With a fresh surge of determination, Josh dropped back down to the centre of the room, his brain beginning to pound against the sides of his head in protest. He held out his hand for the last time and watched as the water around began to freeze. However, instead of letting it form a useless block, he used his other hand to sculpt the ice crystals before they hardened. Within seconds, he was holding a long spear-like shaft of ice that tapered off at one end. The Water Elemental could feel the force of the water against his lips like a pair of fatal hands trying to prise them apart. His brain was demanding oxygen but his mind was denying it, and a fight between the conscious and the subconscious was raging inside the human shell. The subconscious was stronger and before he could stop it, a small stream of water broke through the corner of his mouth and snaked down his throat. In a last ditch effort, Josh hurled his crystalline needle towards the window as hard as he could just before his mouth gave way and his whole life became liquid.

The spear sliced through the water and collided with the window before it shattered into tiny crystals that rapidly dissolved. The weapon was no more, but it had served its purpose. In the centre of the window pane a crack was blossoming, rapidly spidering outwards towards the edges of the frame. With such structural damage, the integrity of the glass was compromised and it did not take long for the whole window to blow outwards, a cascade of murky water blasting out into the street. What had been a deathly still pool became a raging torrent as the room swiftly drained, sending all of Josh's belongings surging through the broken window. Josh was being clubbed by a steady stream of books and videos, and only just narrowly missed being knocked unconscious against his desk before he himself was sucked out of the room and deposited on the grass outside. If his flat had been even one floor up, he would have broken his legs as he fell. He lay on his back as gallons of water poured out of the window. He coughed a small fountain of his own, and then started reliving his ordeal. He had been so close to death, the water had actually been in his lungs. Seconds later and he would have lost consciousness.

After about ten minutes, the water slowed to a trickle, snaking its way down the bricks onto the now sodden lawn. Josh sat up and looked around, thinking about how bizarre this must look. He was sitting on the grass, his black shorts clinging to him and his hair plastered over his forehead, surrounded by clothes and sludge that had once been paper. His room was now only filled to the level of the windowsill, a waist deep pool littered with the sunken treasure of his furniture. His mind was racing; the events of the last hour flashing past his eyes like a film in fast forward. Except one image kept recurring. Chase Rivers smiling just before he evaporated. Only then did it dawn on Josh that his best friend had been right. Up until now, he had been too concerned with trying not to drown that he hadn't actually considered the serious ramifications of Chase's words. Even now, the undead one, or whatever he was, could be hurting one of his friends, maybe it was already too late. He climbed stiffly to his feet and shook his head, sending droplets of water raining down as his hair flicked around. Shivering, Josh wrapped his arms around himself and began to run down the street. He was slightly puzzled as to how nobody had heard or seen the destruction of his room, but at the same time, he didn't exactly have any explanation prepared as to how his room had become a human fish tank.

Twenty minutes later, Josh was standing outside Rich Benson's front door, his naked skin rapidly purpling from the cold. Luckily, he had encountered nobody else as he ran to his friend's. He could not have begun to explain why he was soaking wet and only wearing a pair of boxers. Mr Benson's car was not in the driveway, so he had knocked as loud as he could. He would much rather face off with an annoyed Rich than his annoyed father. There was no answer so Josh stepped forwards and squinted through the mottled glass of the door. The house was dark inside, which was no surprise considering it was almost four in the morning. He knocked again, beginning to get worried. Surely nobody could sleep through a knock that loud. Rich must not be there either. Or maybe he was inside, but hurt, or even dead. What if Chase had come here after he had tried to kill Josh? What if he had been here *before* Josh's? It hadn't been that long since they had spoken on the phone had it? But the Spirit Elemental could move fast... His best friend could have been dead even as Josh spoke to Chase. It was lucky that Josh could get into the house another way. Heart pounding, he ran round the side of the house and into the back garden where the flowers slept in their immaculate beds, a tribute to Rich's mother who had died eight years ago.

When he was fourteen, Josh had accidentally broken a vase in Rich's living room. This had resulted in Rich's dad banning him from the house and giving his son lectures about how Josh was a bad influence on him. This hadn't stopped the two best friends, however. Within hours of the trouble, Josh had already discovered that he could climb up the trellis on the side of the house, onto the roof of the conservatory and then into Rich's bedroom. He still remembered the look of shock on his partner in crime's face as he tumbled through the window, then the two of them had snuck downstairs and stolen Mr Benson's cigars. He smiled to himself as he remembered his rebellious teenage years and looked up at the flimsy wooden structure. It seemed a lot smaller than it had all those years ago, and he doubted if it could hold his weight, but he had to try. Tentatively, he put a foot onto the first wooden slat. The trellis shook alarmingly, but did not come away from the wall. Taking this as a good sign, Josh began to climb. Soon, he was crouched catlike on the conservatory roof, almost frustrated at how predictable Rich was. He had always slept with his window open, mainly so his dad wouldn't smell his cigarette smoke, and sure enough, it was now open wide enough for Josh to slip through.

To the untrained eye, it would have looked as if Rich had been burgled but Josh knew better. The piles of clothes and papers littered around the floor were all part of his friend's natural habitat. The only thing missing was the man himself. Josh quickly scanned the room, desperately searching for any clue as to what had happened. The door was closed and the mess around it undisturbed, indicating that Rich had at least left of his own accord, he hadn't been dragged away, but where had he gone at this time of night? Could he have gone to one of the others? Doubtful. Scott hadn't answered his phone when Rich had tried to call him, and Matt had abandoned them on Halloween. A sudden stab of remorse hit Josh when he thought about that night. Matt wasn't the only one to have walked off, Josh had led the way, leaving Rich when he had needed his friend's help. Josh subconsciously vowed that it wouldn't happen again. Friendship is too strong to sacrifice over an argument.

As he was dejectedly turning to leave, something

caught his eye. There was a yellow shirt lying crumpled on the carpet near the bed, and underneath it, he could see the corner of a book. The book was old and bound in purple tinted leather; however it had been recently picked up, judging from the dusty hand print on the cover. Curious, he bent down and fished the book from underneath the shirt. The title of the book was *Back To The Beginning*, but the pages were blank, exuding a musty unused scent. Josh ran his finger over the embossed words on the cover, closing his eyes. He could sense moisture on the deepest level: Rich had also run his fingers over the title, he had been enervated by this book, Josh was sure of it. Instantly, he knew where the Air Elemental had gone. The beginning of all this, the source of the raging river that was threatening to sweep away everything they knew. Halloween and the clearing in the forest.

Josh snatched up the baggiest pair of jeans he could find and pulled a hoodie over his head, before searching the room for some shoes. Eventually, he managed to unearth a pair of musty trainers that looked as if they were a couple of sizes too small. He squeezed his feet into them, ignoring the pain as his toes were forced together. As an afterthought, he snatched a beanie hat from the floor and took one last glance at the room. Rich always used to call it organized chaos, the very thing they were up against now. He sighed as he stuck his legs out of the window and dropped down onto the conservatory.

Soon, Josh was in the looming shadows of the forest. The first of the early morning dew was forming, and he could sense every drop. Since he had discovered his power just over an hour ago, the young Elemental was in a constant state of awakening. It was as if his acknowledgement of the forces he could manipulate had been the trigger, and now the element of Water was desperate to show him the extent of these forces and their abilities. Josh wondered if the others were feeling as overwhelmed as he was. Could Scott feel what every creature was feeling? Could Rich see every change in the wind and would Matt be able to sense every pair of opposite particles waiting eagerly to collide and ignite? He hurried through the twisting paths, aware that the borrowed shoes were probably doing a lot more damage to his feet than he realised. He emerged into the smaller space of The Haven, meaning that the ritual clearing was just a few more meters up the next path. The feeling of unease grew as he approached the clearing. What would he find there? Maybe nothing at all, maybe everything he feared in the world, compressed into the shape of an eighteen year old boy. Suddenly spurred on by his misgivings, he began to run, the desire to know for sure conquering the potential bliss of ignorance. He burst into the clearing sooner than he anticipated.

Squinting in the half light, Josh surveyed the clearing. Towards the far side, the ground was shifted into great mounds around a small, roughly rectangular hole. It was like a travesty of a funeral service, and he could only imagine what the guests would look like. He didn't have to guess what had been in the hole, and it had only just occurred to him that he had not once even considered how Chase had come back from the dead and what the others had done with the body after he and Matt had left. From what he saw now, he assumed they must have buried it. The rest of the soil in the clearing seemed to have been disturbed also. There were deep impact marks and great trenches that looked as if they had been gouged into the soil with a giant rake. In between two of these immense gorges lay Rich. Josh ran over to his friend and knelt down beside him. He wasn't moving. His face was covered in blood, his nose probably broken. There was no question about his right arm however, as it lay uselessly slumped in the mud where he had fallen, each finger contorted unnaturally, fragments of bone jutting out at awkward angles.

Josh grabbed the wounded man's other wrist and dropped it suddenly. As soon as he touched his skin, he could feel the fallen man's pulse pumping so loud that it seemed to shake every inch of Josh's body. Blood had high water content, and he could feel every cell fighting to keep his friend alive. Relieved but furious, he carefully hoisted the limp frame onto his back and walked as quickly as he could out of the clearing as the sky turned from black to morning blue.

Chapter 20 – Caput Mortum

"Magic is an exchange of energies. When something is taken, something must be given and vice versa. When a spell is cast, attempts should be made to restore the balance consciously, because, if they are not, the exchange will still take place, but there will simply be no control over what is taken or given."

The Book Of Shadows

The sun was shining weakly through the pale yellow curtains of Rich's bedroom, bathing him in gold as he lay safely in his own home once more. Josh had carried him to the hospital where the doctors had reset his fingers, put his arm in a sling, and wired his broken nose. Josh had managed to fend off most of the curious questions by explaining that Rich had been the victim of a terrible gang beating and the broken man was now sleeping, after having a powerful cocktail of drugs. Whilst waiting in the hospital, Josh had been overcome with anxiety, but now that they were home again, fury once more took hold. He boiled with rage every time he thought of Chase, that he would actually *dare* to pursue his vendetta.

The first thing he had done after putting Rich to bed was to grab a packet of salt from the kitchen and sprinkle a fine layer around every door and window. He remembered reading in his Book Of Shadows that salt was the soul of the Earth or something, and evil could not cross it. Josh hadn't really taken in the background story, as long as the process worked when the time came. The last thing he wanted was Chase appearing here and wreaking more havoc.

Now he was back in the bedroom, reliving his ordeal and imagining Rich's with a grimace. *Enough is enough*, he thought as he turned to the shelf where his friend kept his Wiccan equipment. He took down the Book Of Shadows and frowned. The writing inside was far too neat to belong to Rich. Flicking back to the front cover, he looked at the bottom left corner for the initials he knew would be there. SF – Scott Fielding. It was another sign of the intellectual's attention to detail and order that he initialled all of his belongings. Each of the four had their own Book of Shadows, copied from Scott's master version, *which was this one,* Josh reminded himself. *So Scott probably had Rich's book.* For a brief second, he pictured his friend's face when he noticed the untidy scrawl and half hearted diagrams that Rich's book would comprise of, then cast his eyes over the meticulously laid out profiles that Scott had done, which included birthdays, starsigns and traits for each of them. As if to emphasise this, there was another box which just had their birthdays in.

Rich – October 10
Josh – March 3
Matt – April 1
Scott – May 7

He told himself that he would ask Scott about that next time, and began to scan through the pages, searching for a particular one.

After a few moments, Josh had found what he was looking for, *Caput Mortum – The Death's Head.* Scott's perfect joined handwriting told him this was one of the worst rituals in Wiccan Lore – something called a Tainting, but Josh was beyond reason. Both of them could have been killed earlier: Chase deserved pain; he was owed pain for what he had done, for what he could still be doing to the other half of the group. He read the page carefully, taking

in everything he needed to perform the ritual. Scott had
decorated the ritual with a skull wreathed in spidery black
lines, as if evil itself was coursing through the veins of the
paper. Josh shuddered as he tried to shake off the image,
but instead he became entranced even deeper into his
thoughts about the Wiccan craft and how they had gotten
into it. Nobody knew exactly where the Book Of Shadows
came from, though Scott always said it was given to him by
his grandfather. It looked a lot older than just two
generations however, and Josh suspected that even though
Scott's book was a copy of the original, it had still been in
the Fielding family for a very long time. Scott always used
to tell the story that his ancestor had once said that "an
angel" gave him the book, but Josh was certain that the tale
was simply an old Fielding anecdote.

The book had sat gathering dust in the bottom of
one of Scott's cupboards for years until his grandfather had
died. Whilst clearing out the old man's flat, his grandson
had found a bag of runes, etched onto a set of smooth
stone tablets. As far as Josh knew, his friend had done
some research about the runes, and found that they were
linked to the contents of the mysterious book he had now
inherited. For a couple of years, Scott had read through the
book and added his own research before finally introducing
the idea to his friends. He had said at the time that it
seemed like the natural thing to do, and the Water
Elemental could see his reasoning. Who better to share this
new found knowledge with than the three people you had
spent most of your life playing with. It was the next logical
step.

Josh recalled the scepticism he had displayed at first,
and how his friend had gradually fed them information.
Scott had begun with a lot of theory, then some herbal
properties and remedies, a simple Book of Shadows

blessing with some candles and then wham! Full blown initiation ritual, death, torment, and now here he was, about to perform one of the darkest rituals in the book. He gave Rich an apologetic glance and then headed downstairs and out into the garden.

A quick search through the shed led to Josh standing at the end of the garden brandishing a shovel. He was staring at a tiny stone sticking out of the soil with the word *Adonai* scratched onto it in a childish scrawl. Adonai had been Rich's cat since he was twelve, but it had died a few years ago. Rich had got a new cat since, but had been devastated when Adonai had gone. He paused for a second. Was he really prepared to go this far? He was about to throw down the spade when he saw the image of his friend in his mind. Rich might never be able to use his right hand properly again, Chase definitely deserved the Caput Mortum. His face set, he plunged the shovel into the soft ground and began to dig.

It didn't take long for Josh to find the tattered box that contained the bones of Adonai. He grimaced as he pulled the container out of the ground, strips of cardboard rotted to little more than translucent lace crumbling away as he moved it. As he lifted the box, the bottom collapsed, spilling the remains of the cat onto the immaculately cropped lawn. He gagged as the bones tumbled onto the ground, a broken jigsaw that had once contained life. Thankfully, Adonai had been dead long enough to be almost completely decomposed, but the Water Elemental still held a sleeve over his mouth as he poked at the bones with a stick, trying to untangle the skull. As it came free, he wrapped it up in a tea towel, hastily stuffed the rest of the bones into the soil and buried them once more. Satisfied that the flowerbed looked relatively similar to the way it had before, he went back inside the house.

Rich lay exactly as Josh had left him as the Water Elemental set up the altar for the ritual. He carefully placed the cat's skull in the centre of the altar and then lit a tall black candle. Taking a deep breath, he re-read the ritual and tried to clear his mind. This would be the hard part. He had to be absolutely sure in his mind that Chase was owed this, otherwise it would not happen. Magic was not something that anybody could just do by saying a little poem - the higher forces had to be convinced that the spell must be done. If the intent of the caster was not completely pure, then the spell would not work. The Elements will not bow to anyone but the most devoted, so a clear mind is one of the most important tools of magic.

Josh took one last look at his prone charge, as if to cement his decision and, sure enough, his temper began to rise. He held his right hand over the skull and closed his eyes. Forcing his mind to focus, he replayed everything that had happened since Chase had appeared in his bedroom. With each image of the flooding, the laughter, the vanishing, the escape and the sight of Rich's body lying bloody and broken, Josh's anger became more intense. He could actually visualize the hatred pouring out of his hand and into the cat's skull. His head began to pound, the intensity of the anger causing his blood to boil. He had poured his need for vengeance into the skull and now was the time to finish the ritual.

"Make way for darkness,
There shall be no end.
The Death's Head calls for Chase Rivers.
Aman ye shall feed tonight,
And ever gorge until mine enemy is destroyed."

Whilst Josh was reciting the incantation, the flow of energy between his palm and the skull seemed to change. There was an ethereal jolt, like a river that had suddenly started flowing backwards and his hand began to shake. Suddenly, it felt as if he had been branded across the wrists. The shock was enough to make him jump and he turned his arms over to see what was wrong. Blood splattered into the cream carpet as his eyes went wide with shock. His wrists had been cut, vertically along the artery and blood was rapidly spurting out. *It has to be a test*, Josh thought, trying not to panic. The elements probably wanted to see if he was devoted enough to continue the ritual. The blood was burning the skin as it seeped out, and as he watched, it started to smoke and bubble where it lay, soaking into the carpet. He hissed, gritting his teeth against the pain, but would not give up. He grabbed the black candle and held it over the skull. His wrists scorching, he began to pour wax into the eyes, nose and mouth of Adonai. Just as the skull began to cry tears of black, Josh broke, the agony too much. Tears were falling freely into the pool of blood that he was kneeling in, but still he would not stop.

"Caput Mortum," he whispered. "Caput Mortum. Caput Mortum!" On the third call, Josh's body was completely taken, penetrated by a force beyond his control. He threw his head back and his arms out as he seemed to erupt into a force of raw energy. He was on his knees, cross-like and wreathed in purple mist, his eyes glowing deepest violet. It felt like he was swimming in the purest form of pleasure, as if for that brief moment, nothing else in the world mattered except for his gratification.

"So mote it b-" Josh was cut off as Rich moaned. Suddenly, he came crashing back to earth, torn from the glimpse of infinity. The cuts on his wrists had sealed themselves and he knelt on the stained carpet, panting as if he had just run across town to get here. He looked across at Rich, who was shaking and thrashing about on the bed despite still being unconscious. Josh forgot all ideas of vengeance and power as he looked across at his helpless friend. He reached out his hand and tentatively placed it on Rich's bare chest. Once again, he could sense his friend's pulse, except this time it was pounding so fast that it felt as if his ribs would shatter outwards. Josh stared as the unconscious young man began to convulse violently, his face twisted in silent pain. Josh started to move, to run to the phone to call an ambulance but then stopped. *He won't make it in time,* he thought. If Rich was going to pull out of this, then Josh would have to help him directly.

Without knowing why, Josh grabbed Rich's undamaged hand and pressed it firmly against his own chest. Now they were connected, a loop of rhythm. He could feel the alarmingly fast heartbeat, and through Rich's hand, he could feel his own steady pumping. He screwed up his face, and pressed the limp hand even tighter into his chest.

"Come on Rich!" Josh shouted, exasperated. "Feel this! Feel my heart and copy me. Come on mate! Copy me." As he closed his eyes, he seemed to disappear. He, Rich and the room all vanished, and all that was left was black. Suddenly, two swirling shapes appeared in the darkness, one blue and one yellow. The blue one was throbbing steadily, with a constant rhythm, whereas the yellow one was flailing about erratically. In his mind, Josh forced the two together, until they overlapped. With him concentrating as hard as he could, the yellow beat started to emulate the blue one, slowing down and becoming more stable until it was matching the blue one completely. Through his hand, he could feel Rich's heartbeat slow back down to a normal rate, and the unconscious man began to calm down once more. Suddenly, he woke up.

Josh hastily lifted his hand from Rich's chest as his friend sat up, blinking in the pale yellow morning. Rich stared for a moment, waiting for his eyes to focus and then looked at Josh, who tried to give what he hoped was an encouraging smile.

"How're you doing?" he asked. Rich looked blankly at his broken arm. It was obvious that the drugs he had been given were still having some sort of effect, as everything he did looked as if it took a great deal of concentration and deliberation. Josh thought it was a miracle that Rich wasn't screaming in pain. Eventually, the wounded man seemed to remember the question and looked back up at his saviour.

"I had strange dreams," he said bluntly, his broken nose distorting his voice as if he was talking through glass. He noticed the change, and gingerly reached up with his good hand to feel the bandages on his face. "Great," he sighed sarcastically. "I got my nose broke again." Josh grinned to himself as he looked down at his bandaged friend.

"Yep. 'Fraid so mate," he said apologetically. He thought back to the first time Rich's nose had been broken. The two of them had been about thirteen, playing on the swings at the local playground. A group of fifteen year-olds had turned up asking for cigarettes, and of course Rich was in the typical cocky and invincible mindset of the early teen. He had told them to sod right off and they had beaten him up. Josh himself hadn't escaped either, and now his hand automatically went to his right temple, where there was a small scar that looked as if someone had shaved his eyebrow while he was asleep. That was his battle scar, and even though the two of them had lost the fight, they still felt like heroes. Josh's face hardened as once more he thought of the terrible wounds Chase had inflicted on his best friend. Did he feel like a hero this time? This wasn't a fight you could just laugh about afterwards; this was literally life or death.

Lost in thought, Josh hadn't noticed that Rich was now watching him. He turned to his friend, but all he saw was a broken soul, he could not see past the blood and the bandages. A tear started to form in the corner of his eye, and he sniffed, trying to hold it in.

"Josh, please don't," Rich said, but Josh couldn't help it. Like sinking into oil, guilt had swept over him and he had to release his feelings.

"I should have believed you from the start," he began. "If I had just listened, then this might not have happened." Before he knew it, he was crying freely. He was dimly aware of Rich's hand holding his wrist, but he did not open his eyes, did not want to look into the bruised face he had created through neglect. "Chase almost killed us, and it would have been my fault. If anyone else gets hurt, I'll never forgive myself I swear." Josh paused and breathed deeply. He had finally said what he had been feeling deep down inside.

"I didn't even see Chase," Rich said softly. "He did all this with his mind or something so even if you had believed me, it wouldn't have made any difference." Josh looked up. He had just got exactly what he needed. Forgiveness. Rich didn't see it as his fault, and in his heart, Josh knew that he wouldn't have, but he had still needed to hear it.

"I was so angry after we got you sorted out," Josh admitted. "All I wanted to do was kill him. We owe him pain. He tried to beat you to death and drown me in my own room. He deserves to die."

Rich thought for a second. "I suppose... but what if we deserve *him?*" Josh frowned as his wounded friend articulated his words. "Think about all the stuff in the book about balance. What if Chase is somehow the price we have to pay for our powers, like a trade?"

"That doesn't make sense," Josh began. "It's not balanced now, it's just five people with power. To equalise it out, someone would have to die or something."

"Someone *did* die."

"Exactly. If Chase dying was the balance, then him coming back upsets that balance again."

"Look at it this way," reasoned the Air Elemental. "We get our powers and Chase dying was an accident. That still makes it four people with power to be better than the rest of the world. What if Chase was sent back with more power than us as a countermeasure, to keep us in check?"

"No, Rich. He's not keeping us in check; he's trying to kill us. To cancel us out!" Josh's temper was rising at the thought of something higher regulating the use of their skills. "It's my power and I'm keeping it! He deserves the worst." Josh could see the thoughts going through Rich's mind - his eyes always flickered slightly when he was working something out.

"The worst?" asked Rich. "Josh, what did you do?" Josh shrugged vaguely as Rich's eyes swept over to the bloodstained carpet and the wax-covered skull. He frowned and then looked imploringly over at his friend. Josh looked away as Rich grabbed his hands and turned them over, undoubtedly seeing the razor cuts that had been bleeding only minutes before. "Caput Mortum…" Rich whispered. Did Josh just imagine the hint of curiosity in his voice?

"I didn't get to finish it," he admitted. "You st-… something distracted me."

Rich looked relieved. "Good!" he exclaimed. "Haven't you ever heard the phrase 'Evil begets evil'? Why do you think Scott warned us about even having Caput Mortum in our books?"

"He gets to have everything, so I copied everything too," Josh said obstinately.

"It's bad news, Josh. Supposedly people who do it get tainted with darkness; they're never the same again. It's like Scott said before, power corrupts." Rich finished, breathing deeply. He obviously still wasn't back to full strength. Josh quickly snatched his hands back and hid them in his sleeves.

"Well it doesn't matter now, does it?" Josh snapped. "I didn't do the ritual, no harm no foul. You should try and get some more rest. I'll try and find a way to stop Chase that doesn't involve me selling my soul to the bastard devil." Rich nodded amiably and settled back down into his pillow, leaving Josh to his thoughts. He was right, of course, but something was still burning away at Josh's mind. It definitely didn't feel like evil at the time. He knew what he had felt, and it was the most pure form of pleasure he had ever experienced, that probably ever existed, even. He would never forget that feeling. He sighed as he picked up the Book of Shadows and started to look for an alternative.

Chapter 21 – The Lost Souls

Only a few hours had passed, but Josh was already utterly
bored of scanning through Rich's books. He found his
mind wandering back through town and onto the UCE
campus. His room had probably stopped seeping onto the
surrounding plant life by now, and he began to have grand
ideas about being able to salvage some of his belongings.
Surely some of his stuff would be alright once it had dried
out a little? He knew that his most personal items were
probably ruined, his photo albums for instance. There was
absolutely no way he was ever going to have those
memories again, especially considering his digital copies
were all saved on his now waterlogged hard drive. But it
couldn't hurt to look could it?

    After checking that Rich was sleeping soundly, Josh
once more squeezed himself into the ill-fitting shoes and let
himself out. He had warmed up a little since his impromptu
swim and the air was no longer as biting as it had been. The
walk didn't take too long, and he soon found himself
peering carefully at his building from across the road. He
could make out a number of items strewn across the grass:
his desk, an upturned chair and several small piles of what
looked like sludge – obviously his comics and paperwork.

    The building had been cordoned off, and a number
of campus security guards were standing outside, poking
through the debris and muttering quietly to themselves.
Thankfully, there was no sign of the police.

    Josh's flatmates were standing in a huddle,
gesticulating wildly as a campus guard explained something.
This obviously wasn't going down too well, and it looked
as if Eric and the others were not allowed back into
Garnsworthy Hall. After another few minutes, in which
Josh kept himself out of sight, the three students were

escorted along the road, probably to spend the night in one of the other blocks.

The campus officials had probably seen all manner of stunts in their time, and this was going to be just one more on a very long list for them. Josh himself remembered some of the things he had seen in his tenure at UCE. There was the occasion when some guys in a top floor flat had made waterbombs first out of condoms, but then had rapidly progressed onto bin bags. Also, Josh noted the time he had returned from a lecture to find a perfect recreation of somebody's room assembled in the centre of the quad. Unlike his own room, where the possessions had been destroyed and scattered, this one had been immaculately set up just as it had been inside the building, everything in a specific place.

Adopting what he hoped to be a casual expression; Josh stepped across the tarmac and joined the security guards, assuming the role of the curious bystander. One of the campus security workers, a large lady with an impatient demeanour, turned to face him, a disgusted look on her face.

"Come to survey your work, have you?" she scalded.

Josh raised his eyebrows. "What makes you think I've got anything to do with this?"

"Well it's bound to be one of you lot isn't it? The first one to the scene of the crime is usually the guilty party."

"You learn that at police school did you?" Josh muttered before he could clamp his mouth shut.

The woman scowled. "This is more than my job's worth!" she exclaimed with exasperation. She continued to rant as she moved along the pavement. "Burning trees, broken windows, Chase Rivers, flooded bedrooms!" Josh hared after her, suddenly alert.

"What did you say?"

"Flooded," the woman said, turning. "The room was flooded, though God knows how. There was so much pressure it blew the window out."

"No, not that," Josh replied, flustered. "You mentioned Chase Rivers. What about him?" The woman sighed, obviously desperate to get back to her office and get the paperwork out of the way as soon as she could.

"Someone came in a day or two ago," she began. "Had some wind up story about Chase being killed by wizards or something." *Rich,* Josh thought to himself, remembering what his friend had said during their phone call. "Don't worry," the security guard went on, mistaking his pensive look for one of concern. "Chase is fine. One of the lecturers saw him not long ago." The woman considered him for a brief second before realising he wasn't going to say anything else, so she walked off muttering blasphemies against the student generation.

Josh stood staring bleakly at the pulp of his comic collection. It was obvious, now that he was here, that he couldn't save any of it. What was dry was also broken, but that had slipped from his mind. He couldn't help thinking about what the security guard had said. A small portion of his consciousness was also reserved for Rich, lying at home in such a fragile state. Perhaps he should return to his friend, after all, anything could happen in his absence. He began to curse himself for leaving in the first place, but he had needed a break from all that research. *Pointless research,* he corrected himself.

He kicked at a heap of mush, lumps of congealed paper and ink flying up before landing with a sickening squelch. The stub of a candle rolled onto the pavement and skittered into the drain, and Josh was suddenly struck with a mortifying thought. All of his Wiccan equipment was in this mess somewhere, and the security woman had already mentioned 'wizards'. Candles and incense he could explain, but if somebody found his Book of Shadows, that would definitely raise some suspicions. He glanced around cautiously, double-checking that the campus security guards were not paying attention before tiptoeing onto the sodden grass next to his fragmented window. Rooting around his possessions brought a lump to his throat as he was forced to cast aside some of his most treasured items. The teddy bear that had given him such a fright under the water now lay stained and ragged, the sentimental gift from his first girlfriend twisted into a grim and haunting wreck. Finally, he caught sight of the incriminating document and shoved it unceremoniously up his borrowed hoodie, the moist slimy paper causing his chest hair to stand on end.

"I saw you, you know." Josh turned around to see Eric standing on the pavement, arms wrapped around himself against the cold. "Were you trying to hide from us?"

"I didn't want… I didn't know what you would think," Josh said sheepishly, trying to avoid the other man's questioning glance.

"That woman told us it was a burst pipe, but I could see she didn't know what she was talking about." Josh smiled, thinking back to his own encounter with the Campus Security Jobsworth. There was a moment of silence.

"So what are you doing back here? I thought you were taken somewhere else for the night?"

"I wanted to ask you a question," Eric said nervously. "About the absinthe." Josh immediately thought back to the disturbing and fiery dream he had had after drinking the hallucinogenic liquid. "It's just that I've been seeing things. Like now, all your stuff is glowing, and even you look different. Kind of blue."

The Water Elemental tried to keep his face neutral, despite his insides reeling with shock. It sounded like Eric could see his aura, and also the after effect of Chase's destruction – something that wasn't possible for a normal person. Even with his newfound skills, Josh couldn't see the trails left by power, so how could Eric?

Of all the feelings, Josh felt jealousy rise up within. He had been through fire and pain to get his affinity with the craft, and now here was Eric, able to do something that he couldn't.

"It's nothing," he snapped. "I can't see anything. You probably just had too much wormwood."

"Who was the boy that caught fire?"

"I don't know what you mean," Josh said hurriedly. "Go home Eric." He stared so hard, that he felt the other man shrinking beneath his glare.

"Fine," Eric said nonchalantly, as if he didn't really care about the whole thing anyway. "Where are you going to stay?"

"I'm at Rich's."

"Well I'll see you when this is all sorted then." Eric turned and jogged down the street, disappearing into the shadows as soon as he passed out of the halo of the streetlamps.

Josh kicked angrily at another lump of sodden paper. On one hand, Eric seemed to have some sort of vision, which wasn't fair, but on the other hand, he also appeared to know about Chase and his dream. What if Eric worked it out and went to the police? That was a chance they would have to take, but still didn't explain how Eric had seen the same thing that he had under the thrall of the absinthe. Perhaps Josh had subconsciously used his gift to radiate it somehow, and Eric being next to him at the time had absorbed it somehow? Josh didn't remember reading anything in the Book of Shadows about something like this, but then again, there was a lot the book hadn't mentioned.

"You! You know Chase." Josh jumped slightly before whirling round. *Who the hell is it now?* he thought angrily. A man was standing by his side, tall and thin but obscured by shadow. It looked as if he had bandages wrapped tightly around his chest. Instead of playing the fool, Josh answered truthfully.

"Yes." The silhouetted figure stepped forwards, and Josh recognised him as one of the guys who worked on The Rag. Ed something or other.

"I know you do," Ed began. "I've seen you lot together. Do you know where he is?" Josh shook his head. He didn't have the heart to explain everything that he knew about the death and now *undeath* of Mr Rivers. It seemed that he would have to play the fool to some extent after all. He couldn't risk anybody else getting involved in this disaster.

"What happened to you?" Josh asked, changing the subject with a nod towards the other man's injuries.

"Chase broke my ribs," Ed stated as he gingerly touched his bandages. Josh's mind snapped to attention, the idle small talk turning deadly serious. He thought about whether this incident happened before or after their own involvement with Chase, but he doubted that the withdrawn young man they had murdered would have acted so violently before his untimely demise. "He wasn't himself," added Ed, confirming Josh's fears.

"Yeah, I've noticed that too," the Water Elemental muttered dejectedly. "So why do you want to find him?"

Ed swallowed hard before continuing. "I need to apologise." Josh looked visibly stunned. Shouldn't Ed be angry or something? The other man noticed his expression. "I think it was my fault," he continued.

"What do you mean?" Josh said. Did Ed really have something to do with this? Maybe he was finally about to find out why Chase had returned and why the ritual hadn't worked in the first place. Ed faltered, obviously considering what to say.

"He was normal one minute," he continued. "Then he just lashed out, like he was a completely different person. I think I somehow turned him into something bad." Josh was shaking his head doubtfully. As expositional plot reveals went, this was a disappointment.

"What did you say to him?" he asked.

Ed paused briefly. "It doesn't matter." Josh nodded sympathetically, although in his head, he doubted that Ed was the reason for Chase's temperament. The other man hadn't even mentioned the mess they were standing by, and probably didn't know anything about the magical element of their predicament.

"Well you've just got to put it behind you." It seemed like Ed was just another poor guy that had got in Chase's way. "I'm sure he will be back to normal soon, then you two can sort it out and make up or whatever," Josh said, half lying. After all, he was still unsure as to what his ultimate goal should be. Was he out to stop the Spirit Elemental or kill him?

"You don't understand," Ed said awkwardly. "I looked into his eyes and... I've got to find him. I can't stop thinking about him. Do you know where he is?" There was that question again, the desperation creeping into the other man's voice. Josh shook his head, seeing Ed's face fall. "I'll find him. I have to know what he did to me. It's like he took something, stole my heart. I'm not complete without him..." Ed's voice petered out as he turned, downcast.

Josh stepped forwards and grabbed his arm, a sudden desire to protect this man from any further harm boiling within him. Perhaps it was the guilt rising once more for not being able to prevent Rich's assault, but Josh was tired of seeing suffering. If there was a chance that he could stop any more then he would try.

"Look, Ed?" he began. "Promise me something?" Ed watched him curiously as he continued. "Promise you won't go looking for Chase. When he's ready, he'll come and find you, I'm sure of it. But for now, he's done some things that… well, you're not the only person he's hurt, and people might be after him."

"To hurt him?" Ed said wide-eyed. "To hurt Chase? No, they can't, I need him."

Josh grabbed the bandaged man harder. "Ok, you are freaking me out now. Whatever Chase said to you, whatever he did to you, *he wasn't himself.* You have to remember that. Now go home and cool off. Do anything but don't get mixed up in this."

Ed broke his grip. "That look, you have it too." Josh opened his mouth to protest before the other man continued. "Not as much as Chase, but it's there. Like something boiling away behind your eyes." The Water Elemental gulped, but before he could reply, Ed's face contorted uncontrollably. "The Gods are coming, and they are vexed!" he spat, before gasping. It looked as if he had no idea what he was saying. Ed looked down at his own hands, expecting them to rise up and act without his consent as his mouth had done, but they remained still. With a final horrified glance at Josh, he turned and ran.

Josh was stunned. It was like Ed was somehow obsessed with the spirit. Perhaps that was what happened to normal people when they came into contact with Chase? Was the power of the Elements the only thing that saved him and Rich from dementia? And what about the similarity that Ed had noticed between the two of them? What if Josh had done to Eric what Chase had done to Ed? If only the Caput Mortum had worked – all of this could have been solved by now.

As if on cue, Josh shuddered with the remnants of the ritual. It was only a few hours ago, but the intense feeling of guilty pleasure was still lingering in the back of his mind, tangible but inaccessible. He shook his head, trying to dislodge the emotion, but like a cork bobbing in water, it kept resurfacing, tantalisingly out of reach. He had touched something for a brief second, an infinite energy, much more immense than the elemental power he had only just acquired. He had to find it; he couldn't stop thinking about it… *No!* The panicked young man had given him a harsh jolt with his morbid comparison. The last thing Josh wanted was to become like the man they were trying to vanquish.

He forced the notion to the back of his mind and looked around, panic on his face for a split second. He was beginning to obsess himself, and there were much more important matters at hand. Standing where he was, crying over the proverbial spilt milk wasn't going to help anybody. With a worried sigh, he pivoted on his heels and headed back to Rich's to continue with the research.

Chapter 22 – Haematite Undetection

The sun had long since reached its apex, and it was now beginning to sink once more behind the line of trees that bordered Rich's garden. Rich himself was asleep again, a slight frown on his face but otherwise untroubled. Josh was sitting at the desk, surrounded by open books and staring bleakly at the computer screen. He rubbed his eyes wearily and sighed. For hours he had been flicking through the pages of Rich's books and clicking the mouse, scrolling through an infinite number of useless websites and directories. They all promised the same thing, these websites. On the homepage they would boast about being the most extensive occult resource on the net, but when Josh actually clicked on any of the links, he found that they were filled with mind numbing theory and no actual measures for action. *These people wouldn't know true power if it smacked them in the face,* the exasperated young man thought. The books were similarly disappointing. So far, he had learnt the various different properties of daffodils and also what you could do with a pendulum. Since neither daffodils nor pendulums had "destroying evil wraith beings created by disastrous initiation rituals" listed as one of their uses, the young man was becoming more and more frustrated. Of course, what had he expected? Scott had already told them that for all intents and purposes, the Witchcraft that they thought they knew of was nothing more than a knowledge of plants and stones, a dose of mystery and a truck load of imagination. All that *could* exist online and in these published books was information about herbs and general speculation, because that's all everyone else actually knew. If others had the access to the Book of Shadows that Scott had, then there would be tons of idiots running around firing spells at each other all over the place. It stood to reason that Josh and his friends were unique, or if they weren't, then other true Wiccans were very well hidden. Josh turned away from the monitor for a second and glanced down at the open Book Of Shadows in front of him. The page was entitled "The Initiation" and he frowned. Had he not just been thinking about that night? This was the ritual that had killed Chase, and Josh was pretty certain that it had somehow brought him back too. Had they done it wrong? Was there something they didn't do that they were supposed to? He scanned the page quickly, checking off each step in his mind as he read them. Suddenly, Josh was in the clearing on Halloween, watching himself and his friends perform the ritual. It felt strange, looking at his past self, the nerves showing in his furrowed brow.

As one Josh stared, the other one took a deep breath as Scott began to cast the circle. Josh could still feel his finger running down the page slowly, although the room and the book had vanished. Surely enough, they all were confirmed at knife point, and then they drank the blood just as they had done two weeks ago. Trembling, Josh watched as the four men in front of him held up their scraps of paper. He knew what was coming, who was seconds away from bursting in to the clearing. He jolted around and peered into the gloomy undergrowth. If he could just find Chase before he interrupted the ritual, then maybe he could stop all of this from happening. He tried to creep away, but his legs were rooted to the ground. No matter how hard he fought with his own mind, he could not take even the smallest of steps, and even if he could, he realized that it wouldn't change anything. He had not travelled through time, this was all in his mind, and so whatever he did now would just be wishful thinking.

Whilst he was struggling with himself, there was a

disturbance in the centre of the clearing. Their unexpected guest had just appeared. Josh took a closer look at everybody's faces, and from his vantage point outside the circle, he could gauge each person's emotions a lot more clearly. Scott looked shocked and scared to the extent of appearing slightly ill, Matt looked typically stone-faced although Josh noticed that his mouth was curling strangely at one corner, Rich was shaking minutely and Josh himself looked surprised with a hint of curiosity. To his surprise, Chase seemed to be the most frightened and speechless although when it had actually happened, all Josh had noticed was his determined jaw line. For the first time since the accident, he actually found himself seriously thinking about Chase Rivers. Had the young man known what he would find when he arrived at the clearing? What was he going to do if the fire had not exploded? He had never really spoken to Chase properly. The monster's rant before he had flooded Josh's room was probably the longest time the two of them had ever spent together, but was that really the mild mannered and shy lad that he had sometimes seen rushing into the Print Room at uni? Josh could not help wondering what his hobbies were, what his favourite colour was and what he liked to eat. Was he good at sports, and did he listen to dance music? There was so much that Josh did not know about his inadvertent victim, and as he turned to look at the five bodies lying on the ground around the smoking fire, a tear rolled down his cheek.

Josh was awoken from his daydream when his finger brushed against something odd. He had reached the bottom of the page, but the edge felt different and frayed somehow. He opened his eyes, the hazel orbs quickly becoming accustomed to the brightness of artificial light after the gloom of Halloween. Looking down, he could see that this page was about a centimetre shorter than all the rest. One line had been carefully ripped from the bottom of the page, though if the line said anything, he could not even begin to guess what it could have been.

Suddenly struck by a flash of inspiration, Josh grabbed his own Book of Shadows from where he had jammed it on top of the radiator. The inks from the blue cover had run a crooked river down the front surface of the heater. Hopefully, the book would still be usable. He carefully peeled the pages apart until he found the Initiation. The majority of the page was a smeared collage of blue roses where the ink had blossomed and spread in the water but two things at least were clear. Firstly, the page was intact all the way to the bottom, and secondly, there was nothing extra written on the final line. Unsure whether to feel relieved, the young man considered the options. Either Scott's book was just ripped, and they all had the full version of the ritual, or there *was* a line missing from the original but it had gone before the others had copied it. However, Josh reasoned, that was a mystery that he would have to solve later, as right now, stopping Chase was the number one priority.

Dejectedly taking a sip of his cold coffee, Josh turned over, to where another page of herbal properties stared out at him from the book, explaining how to use petunias to make you better at cooking. Just as he was thinking that if he saw any more herbal properties he would explode, he turned the page once more and stopped, intensely scanning this new page. It was titled "The Blocking Ritual", and described how they could contain a certain subject by surrounding it at the four compass directions and using their elemental pendants along with an incantation.

The Blocking Ritual would ensure that Chase would be contained; now Josh just needed to find a ritual that would blast the crap out of him once he was there, an "Expulsion of Malevolence." Josh wasn't sure if such a thing existed, but the name he'd given it sounded cool enough. Giving up on the internet completely, he slowly scanned through the Book of Shadows, hoping that something would catch his attention, although surely if it was as easy as that, one of the others might have spotted it first.

As he suspected, Josh soon reached the end of the book, the brightly coloured and immaculately scripted rituals giving way to pristine blank pages. Blank pages waiting to be written on. A plan was beginning to form in the young man's mind. Somebody had to have written all this originally, somebody with power. Now he had power so why couldn't he write his own ritual tailored to what he needed? Maybe that's how you developed your power? *It was all about the power,* Josh thought hungrily. Inspired, the Water Elemental snatched a pen from the desk and wrote the title "Expulsion of Malevolence" with a grin. He wasn't sure if Scott would forgive him for writing in his book, but desperate times called for desperate measures. As a guilty afterthought, Josh underlined the title in a vain attempt to make his page look the same as all the rest.

After half an hour, Josh had crudely crafted a ritual, albeit in his own style of language. He had tried to keep everything official sounding, but the odd colloquialism had crept into his writing. *At least he had managed to keep on the lines,* he thought with a smirk. Basically, he had written a glorified cleansing ritual with an awesome sounding name. In theory, the four of them would use the essence of their Elements to purge Chase of his evil. Josh had even written an incantation that sounded suitable, asking the Elements to help their cause. A lot of the other rituals seemed to have those, so he reasoned it couldn't do any harm to

include one. Once again he considered Scott's reaction to
his cavalier attitude. He would probably veto the idea
because it was untested, but what alternative did they have?
And anyway, Josh realised, nobody had ever tried out the
Initiation before them, and his creation couldn't turn out
any worse than *that*.

Suddenly, Josh found himself remembering the
conversation the four of them had had on the evening of
the Initiation, about true names. Scott had said it was the
second law of names, or something. That would be a sure-
fire way to keep Scott happy, use some of his own spiel in
this new ritual.

Josh hastily scribbled a line away and wrote a new
one, including the use of the name Deus, which was what
Chase was now calling himself. *That should seal the deal,* he
thought triumphantly.

Once Chase was contained, they would use this new
ritual to put an end to his power. It sounded simple
enough, but it could easily become more complex. What if
the Spirit Elemental wasn't affected by the blocking ritual?
Which element was strongest? How would they lure Chase
into the target area? What if the others wouldn't cooperate?
As soon as Josh considered his friends, he was struck by a
terrible thought. He had been researching for nearly seven
hours, when really the first thing he should have done was
called the others. In seven hours, Chase could have easily
disposed of both of them. He shook his head, checking
himself guiltily. How could he have such a low opinion of
his brothers? If he could escape from the supposed all
powerful one using his powers for the first time, then
surely they would be able to fend him off. However, Josh
had only narrowly escaped. Battling with his conscience
once more, he rushed to the phone and dialled Scott's
number. He waited with bated breath as the phone rang

once, twice, three times.

"Fielding house. This is Scott speaking." Josh grinned; He had never been more relieved to hear his friend's fake upper class phone voice.

"It's me," Josh said, trusting his friend's ability to recognize him. Immediately, Scott's accent returned to its usual yet unusual blend of northern and cockney.

"Oh, hi." Scott did not sound too happy to hear him, and the Water Elemental wondered why for a second before remembering that the last time they had spoken was when Josh had blamed him for Chase's death completely. Relieved that the phone had even been answered, he could not stop himself from blurting all of his questions at once.

"Are you all right? Have you seen Matt at all? It's good to hear you; you've not had any trouble or anything?"

"Hold on a minute!" Scott interrupted. "What's going on? What's happened?" Josh swallowed. Could the Earth Elemental really have no idea about any of this? Chase had definitely said he was going to kill them all, but if Scott was telling the truth, then the madman had not been anywhere near him. A glimmer of hope shone in Josh's mind briefly. What if Chase had tried to attack Matt, who had somehow heroically killed him? Obviously their unreadable friend probably wouldn't have told them, but it couldn't have been that easy could it? "Josh?" The voice sounded worried. Josh snapped back to his senses.

"Sorry," he said. "Um… We have a problem. A big problem."

"We killed someone… I haven't forgotten."

"A different problem. But it's ok, I have a plan." He could visualize the look of disbelief and surprise on Scott's face as he said this.

"You have a plan?" the intellectual said, trying to keep his voice as neutral as possible.

"Yeah, I knew you'd like that," Josh said. "I'm at Rich's. Can you get hold of Matt and come round as soon as you can?" Scott was silent for a moment, obviously thinking it through. After all, Josh had explained nothing, saving the impact for when they were all face to face. Eventually, his friend reached a decision.

"Alright," he began. "Leave Matt to me. We'll be less than an hour." The line went silent, leaving Josh thoughtful. He was glad that Scott had decided there was nothing to lose from hearing the plan, but also slightly annoyed that the Earth Elemental didn't even know that Chase was back. Not that he wanted either of them to have been hurt like Rich was, but it still bugged him that the man they had all burned should have so adamantly tried to kill half of the group, but left the others untouched. He shook the thoughts out of his head as he turned to Rich, gently calling his name until he woke up, bleary eyed but rested.

Forty minutes later, the three spiritual brothers were all standing facing Josh, together again as a foursome for the first time since the accident, and it felt good. It was like recapturing a lost memory, like seeing an old photograph after many years.

He had just explained pretty much everything he knew about Chase's return, which admittedly was not very much. Scott had immediately suggested using salt and burning the body to destroy the angry spirit, but Rich had shot him down by reminding everyone that they were dealing with Chase himself, not his ghost.

"What about a binding spell?" Matt said casually.

"Too simple," replied Scott. "If he's as powerful as you say, he'll be able to undo it. We need something he won't be expecting. Josh?" Josh had then continued to go over his plan to stop the menace of Deus, and was now waiting for the others to say something. He had left out

Caput Mortum, not wanting to incite the curiosity of the others. Thankfully, Rich had not said anything either. The Air Elemental was still bandaged up, but from the look of determination on his face, he wanted to see this plan through more than anyone. After all, he was the only one who had been systematically tortured by their twisted progeny. Matt was looking typically emotionless, and Josh was not going to even try to work out what he was thinking, although it might have been Josh's imagination, but he could have sworn that the Fire Elemental was deliberately avoiding Rich's gaze. Perhaps he was feeling guilty for punching him on Halloween, Josh wasn't sure.

When Scott had first arrived, he had complimented Josh on his use of salt then had immediately fussed over Rich, horrified by his injuries, giving a visible shudder when he saw them. He returned the Air Elemental's Book of Shadows, apologising profusely for picking up the wrong one after the tragedy, as if Rich having his own book might have saved him somehow. Scott had accepted the severity of the situation without question. Josh supposed he had no choice, as what else could have done that to Rich except for a crazed maniac? But now the Earth Elemental was staring at Josh with an impressed look on his face.

"So, you get it?" Josh asked. "It was what Chase said about us not taking his power away. I know I would hate that. He must be afraid of that subconsciously or it wouldn't have slipped out." He paused for a breath and looked at the others watching him with varying degrees of admiration. It wasn't often that he came up with a worthwhile idea, let alone backed it up with sound reasoning. "You understand we have to do it tonight, before Chase does any more damage. It's just…" He didn't want to admit that he was worried for the others. He had just come up with a plan all by himself, not to mention rescuing Rich from certain death. Quite frankly, he had been a bit of a hero lately, and heroes didn't get soppy over their friends. To his surprise, Scott walked forward and smiled.

"Josh, it's fine," he said, not knowing how much his approval meant. Scott was always the one who organised everything and guided the others, so for Josh to hear him say that he, Josh, had done a good job was overwhelming. "Although I don't remember that expulsion ritual from my book?"

Josh looked down guiltily. "I kind of made it up."

The intellectual looked pensive for a second before smiling. "It's strange," he began. "I've spent the last fortnight shut in my room trying to find a way to undo what we did to Chase, but I never thought of creating something myself."

"I just figured somebody must have made the rest, why couldn't I make one? I'm powerful too."

"It's worth a try," Scott said with a nod. "I kept hoping Chase would come back, for absolution, but it seems it happened anyway." Josh looked at him curiously.

"You didn't find anything to help?" he asked, knowing that if Scott's research had been anything like his, he would have been unsuccessful.

"No. There's nothing in the Book of Shadows about necromancy, except a small passage. To try it is to taint your soul, a bit like the Caput Mortum."

"What's the deal with those anyway?" the Water Elemental asked, trying to sound only vaguely curious.

"The Taintings? They are also called 'Soul Destroyers' because they ruin a part of your soul."

"How many parts are there?"

"Five," the Earth Elemental stated. "One for each Element. Once all five parts are gone, then you die, supposedly. Not worth the risk if you ask me." Josh flushed, changing the subject hurriedly as the wanton desire for power flared up once more.

"So Chase's return was nothing to do with you?"

"Not as far as I can tell. I certainly didn't do any rituals, because there weren't any. And I happen to want my soul as intact as possible. My guess is that it's some side effect of interrupting a ritual accidentally. All that power coming through must have hit Chase as well. Maybe it didn't kick in right away because of the extent of his injuries?"

"Makes sense," Josh nodded. "He did say the ritual *got* him too. But enough of that, what's important now is how we stop him, not how we made him, and there's still some problems that need sorting with my plan." Scott looked at him questioningly. "I need you to translate my incantation into Theban Locte, and more importantly, I'm not really sure how we can get Chase where we want him, without him suspecting anything." As Josh spoke, Scott's brow furrowed and Josh could almost see the ideas running through his mind as he listened. After a moment, he sighed thoughtfully.

"He may already know," Scott began, noticing the look of confusion on Josh's face. "Think about it," he continued. "If Chase managed to attack Rich without actually being anywhere near him, then he must have extremely powerful psychic abilities. Who can say that he hasn't been listening in to this whole conversation?" Josh looked around warily, seeking the simple visual reassurance that the man who was trying to kill them was in fact not in the room. Heart sinking, he knew it had been too good to be true. Whilst Scott had liked his plan, it was typical that he would now pick holes in it. It seemed that Scott was thinking along the same lines, and his next words sounded to Josh like he was trying to make him feel better. "That doesn't mean he definitely knows. All I'm saying is that it's a possibility we should be ready for." Josh searched through his memory, scanning the infinite amount of useless pages of books and websites he had seen earlier, hoping to catch a hint of something they could use.

"We need something that can tell Chase where we are and when, but not what we plan to do," he said, looking across the room to where the other two were now sitting awkwardly next to each other on the bed. Suddenly, Scott clicked his fingers loudly.

"Haematite!" he exclaimed, a grin forming on his face. Josh had never heard of Haematite, and had no idea how it could help them, but Scott appeared to be excited about it. "Rich, Haematite?" Scott asked the blank-looking Air Elemental. He rolled his eyes as Rich shrugged. "Bloodstone!" Scott gesticulated impatiently.

Rich suddenly realised what he was talking about. "Oh!" he said, smirking through his bruised face. "Why didn't you say so? It should be on the shelf." Josh watched as Scott hurried over to the altar and found what he was looking for. Turning to the others, he opened his palm and revealed a lump of stone about the size of a small fist. To Josh, it looked as if his friend was holding a stone heart, the blood red tint of the rock shifting and glinting as he tilted his hand in the sunlight. Josh, however, still had absolutely no idea what his Earth brother planned to do with the stone, and from the looks on the other's faces, neither did they. He mused for a second, wondering if he would even be able to tell if Matt did really know what the Haematite was for, his face was so unreadable. He again turned to Scott, who was looking excitedly down at the stone. It was as if for that one moment, he had forgotten all of the danger that they were in and was as gleeful as a child opening his first Christmas present. After a few moments, Scott finally noticed that the others were not sharing his excitement. His enjoyment faded and he regained his usual superior manner.

"I can see you have no idea what I'm suggesting," he said, almost piteously. Josh and Rich looked blankly at him, but Matt turned away. He wasn't sure if he was sniggering or growling, but it was clear that the Fire Elemental was not a fan of Scott's tone. The Earth Elemental became resigned, giving up on the idea of explaining his plan. "Look," he began. "Just play along, ok?" Josh nodded as Scott picked up a square of black cloth and laid it on the floor, sitting cross legged next to it. He picked up the Haematite in his right hand and began to whisper.

"I call upon the Elements,
To make this stone a sanctuary.
A place of safety and privacy for our craft.
May it keep our secrets safe,
And protect us from the curiosity of others."

Josh was slightly taken aback that Scott had said the incantation in English; for he knew full well that the Earth Elemental could have said it all in Theban Locte without hesitating. He supposed that Scott had done it for their benefit. Rich in particular had always had difficulty in switching between the two languages. He watched curiously as Scott placed the stone back onto the cloth and took a deep breath. "Chase is too powerful!" he said, an element of panic playing in his voice. "There's no way we can stop him on our own." Josh looked confused as the other paused. Just a moment ago, he was filled with confidence, but now he was seemingly giving up hope. As Josh stared, Scott widened his eyes and inclined his head slightly towards the onlooking Water Elemental, as if wanting him to do something. Eventually, Scott continued, but slower this time, more obvious. "If only there was something we could do. Some place we could go." Suddenly, Josh was struck with a flood of jealousy. Scott always knew what was going on before anybody else. Did he get more power than the others in the ritual? Scott had the original Book of Shadows somewhere, maybe there was a whole load of knowledge that he wasn't sharing? What if Scott had tried the Caput Mortum too and also accessed the immense power that seemed to lie beyond? In an instant, Josh was convinced that was the reason for his friend's aptitude.

"We don't really know how Chase managed to survive," said Rich, Scott smiling slightly as they began to understand. "Perhaps we should go to the clearing as soon as possible, see if we can find some clues." Josh turned to the others. Matt only shook his head but Rich was nodding in encouragement. It seemed that they wanted him to play along with the conversation. With the others staring at him, he rapidly felt the tide of envy ebb away. Rich's face shone with resolute trust in the Earth Elemental's actions, but surely he would have known if Scott had misled them? If the Air Elemental trusted the intellectual, then it was good enough, and Josh was himself again, all notions of power and the Caput Mortum quelled for the time being. Cursing the new bipolarity the forsaken ritual had inflicted on him; Josh began to go along with the Earth Elemental's show.

"Um… what time should we go?" he asked. Scott was about to answer but Matt interjected, barely keeping the boredom out of his voice.

"Oh I dunno, how about tonight at, let's say midnight?" he said casually. As Josh looked on, Scott appeared to notice that the performance was not exactly Oscar-winning, and hastily began to bring the conversation to a close.

"Ok, it's a deal!" he exclaimed happily. Josh turned

away as Scott snatched the Haematite, shooting a scowl towards the Fire Elemental. As Josh began to fuss over Rich once more, Scott retreated to the corner of the room where he began whispering into his cupped hand. Josh assumed it was just another part of the Haematite ritual and after a few moments, Scott returned to the group, holding the stone in his left hand this time. He looked pale and drawn as he began to whisper once more.

"Seal this stone.

Make it a place of concealment only I can access.

Seal it securely from the eyes, ears and minds of all.

Bury your secrets in the keeping of the Earth"
Once he had finished, he wrapped the stone in the black cloth and set it gently back on Rich's shelf. To Josh's annoyance, Matt was glowering sceptically.

"Are you going to tell us what that was all about then?" Scott turned to look at his friend's disparaging features, a slight grin on his face. Josh could tell that he was enjoying knowing something that his rival didn't. It was probably making up for that fight that they had.

"Nope!" Scott said almost happily. Matt scowled as he continued. "Just in case Chase is somehow listening in. I wouldn't want to spoil it." Matt turned away, a confused frown on his face, whilst Scott addressed the others. "We should get everything we need and then head up to the forest as soon as possible. The more time we have to run things through the better. Timing is going to be pretty important." Never forgetting his manners, Scott turned to Rich. "Can you make it to The Haven in an hour?" he asked his wounded friend. Rich nodded and he smiled once more. "Good."

"Great." Matt mimicked sarcastically as he walked out of the room. Josh saw Scott frown slightly as the Fire Elemental left, but he knew it would be alright. Despite

Matt's cold front, he was generally good on his word and would not let them down. Things between Matt and Scott had always been the most strained, but they had never once let their differences get in the way of serious things like this. Scott also turned to leave, causing Josh's heart to jump. Before they started working on what could be the final showdown, he had to clear his conscience. Taking a deep breath, he jumped forwards, catching his friend's arm just as he was in the doorway. Scott turned to look at him curiously, and suddenly Josh was lost for words. He had always prided himself on being relatively reserved, yet here he was, about to get all tearful with one of his best friends. He could see Scott's mouth curving into a frown of uncertainty and threw all of his reservations out of the proverbial window. For a split second, he imagined all of the other things that had been thrown out of this window of infinite dimensions, all of them equally important to their owners but completely irrelevant to any onlookers. He finally spoke.

"Hey, um-" Josh began, mentally cursing himself for this fantastic start. "I'm sorry about blaming you for all this." Wow. All of the immensely poetic musings of the human mind, and that was the best he could do. Where were the confessions of imperfection? Where was the inevitable plea to make things better somehow? Instead, he had settled on the rudimentary schoolboy form of conversation. To the point, but relatively meaningless in hindsight. To his surprise, Scott's expression softened.

"Don't worry about it," he said, matching Josh's example of briefness. Scott began to turn again, but Josh had to make one last effort to get his feelings out. With a stutter, he began to elaborate.

"I realise now," he began. "We have to stick together. We were all there. You can't ever blame just one person for something like that."

"I said don't worry about it," Scott replied, his sapphire eyes widening with sincerity. "You just concentrate on getting ready for later. Chase *will* show up." Scott paused for a second, looking thoughtfully down to the floor. "One way or another." Without warning, he grabbed Josh and pulled him forwards, hugging him hard. "I'll see you…" Josh was stunned as Scott released him and walked out of the door. After a moment's pause, Josh turned back to where Rich was sitting blankly on the bed.

"Did that seem weird to you?" he asked. Rich shrugged and lay back down on the bed. After a wistful pause, Josh busied himself with cleaning up the salt ring as Rich closed his eyes.

Chase's Vengeance
November 14

Chapter 23 – Rebirth

Screaming filled the air. Screaming and fire, then blackness.
For an indeterminate amount of time, Chase Rivers was
nothing. Nothing floating in nothing.

Then noise. Incredible noise, screaming and tearing
at his mind. It was as if he was suffocating in sound,
everything cascading in on him at once. Panic spread
through him like a raincloud on a summer's day,
unwelcome yet unavoidable. He could not move at all, yet
at the same time he felt like he could move the whole world
if he wanted to. It was the same for each of his senses, not
feeling anything in particular but being a part of something
much grander. It was as if he was suspended in space, black
and empty, yet unable to twist and spiral in the freedom.
He could feel everything around him, in his mind but not
yet on his skin.

Fear finally took hold, and Chase began to thrash
mentally, unaware that his impulses were finally
transmitting to his limbs. Dirt and soil churned as he
fought through a tomb of mud until the cool air of the
woodland night caressed his face. He had no idea of how
long he had been buried, or of the amount of time that it
had taken him to claw his way to the surface, but now that
he was free, Chase was barraged with emotion. Every tree,
every creature, every stone seemed to have a voice, piercing
his soul with a unique cry. He could feel every change in
the breeze, could tell the temperature of the ground he lay
on, could even know that it would not rain for two days,
but more importantly, he could sense four pulses that
emanated with an energy that was not like the sounds and

feelings he could detect in the forest. Deep down, Chase knew that this was immense power beyond the normal human threshold, and somehow he knew that the owners of these pulses had done this to him. Whatever it was, when he stumbled into that clearing however long ago, he could tell that they were responsible. Matt Blake, Scott Fielding, Josh Thomas and Rich Benson would pay for what they had done, consciously or otherwise.

As fear turned into anger, Chase got to his feet and took the opportunity to look down at himself. The skin on his chest was pink and raw, yet it did not hurt, and he suspected that his face was in the same condition. That would have been the fire that engulfed him, he thought. There was no sign of his shirt, and his trousers were ragged at the knee, the edges melted into tough curls of hardened nylon. There was a splodge of encrusted silver right over the top of his ribcage, and he raised a finger to scratch it curiously. The blasted skin seemed to have fused with the metal, which was now imbedded into his chest. It took him a few seconds to realise that it was the silver cross that he wore around his neck - now it seemed he would wear it forever.

As he wrapped his arms around himself pitifully, Chase felt a ridged patch on his shoulder and craned his neck round to see a small round tattoo – a purple circle with what looked like a small figure standing in it. The skin around the circle was blackened just like the rest of him, but the tattoo itself was pink and seemed to shine with life. As he prodded the image, he felt an underlying surge of *something* force its way to the surface – something that was in him but not him, and he was overwhelmed with feelings of grandeur, somehow knowing that he was now a lot more than simply Chase Rivers, but his entombment seemed to have dulled his mind and he couldn't recall exactly what the feelings meant.

All around the clearing, the ground was cracked and uneven, as if a great earthquake had stricken the land but had somehow left all of the trees and plants untouched. There was the evidence of a fire, and Chase could sense from the heat residues in the soil that it had not burnt for quite a while. So he had been dead for almost two weeks? For a second, he wondered if his mother had even come home yet and noticed that her only son had vanished.

Debris littered the clearing, candles and oddly shaped stones strewn about the place as if they had fallen from the sky. *These were tools*, Chase thought. All of these items had contributed to the situation that had left him dead. Next to where he stood, a thin curl of paper poked out of the ground, a mock sapling forcing its way out of the ashes of murder. Crouching, he gently lifted the paper out of the ravaged soil and unwound it. Squinting in the dark, he could make out one line of elegant handwriting. "The willing fifth, you must sacrifice to gain true power." Was he *meant* to see this? Somehow, he knew this line was important, it was the reason he had died, and it would be the reason he got his revenge.

Tiredness pulled Chase away from his thoughts. What he really needed was rest, a chance to recharge himself - after all, he had been buried underground for a fortnight. The scorched man turned and headed into the trees, the feelings of the world already sinking into the back of his mind, becoming a sixth sense rather than a hindrance.

Twenty minutes later, Chase had forced his front door open and was rooting through his kitchen cupboard. He had inevitably lost his house keys when he was burned to death so he had resorted to kicking the door as hard as he could a few times in order to gain entry. Typically, the dog just lay there eying him curiously rather than barking. The useless thing didn't even get up.

It was only now that the hunger hit him. He had been without food or water for almost two weeks, and for a moment he wondered how his body had survived that long until he remembered that it hadn't. Technically he had been dead, and the sickening thing about it was that nobody seemed to care. There was no police crime scene when he woke up, and the people who did this to him had not even given him a proper burial.

Chase was soon sitting at the kitchen table, greedily reaching into a box for endless handfuls of Cheerios, when he heard keys rattling in the door. The sound stopped when the owner of the keys realised that the door had been forced. As Chase watched, his mother cautiously entered the room, her look of apprehension turning to one of relief as she saw who it was in her kitchen.

"Have you seen this door?" she said, her voice rising in exasperation. "Anything could have gotten in-" Mrs Rivers seemed to halt as if the air had been snatched from her mouth. She brushed her long hazel hair away from her face as if to get a better look at her son, taking in the raw skin, cracked and peeling, the way his hair was burnt and ragged and the fact that he was only wearing what looked like a tattered pair of shorts. Deep motherly instincts rose up within her as she took a step forward. "Are you all right?" she spluttered. "What happened to you? Your face…"

Chase did not look up. "Anything got in," he replied, knowing that the answer would confuse the poor woman. He wasn't entirely sure what he meant either, but it seemed an appropriate way to describe what was happening to him. His perception had changed since his awakening, and he did not see this woman as his mother. Chase Rivers, the pathetic eighteen-year-old loser was dead, and all this being saw was a healthy body standing by the door, harshly regarding his own damaged shell.

Chase's mother started to hurry around the kitchen, frantically opening cupboard doors and slamming them again when she realised they did not have what she was looking for inside. It was clear that the burns were far beyond the capability of a normal household bandage, but she had to feel like she was doing *something*.

Chase stood up, eyeing the helpless creature as she flapped about the room. She was futile like a moth, and he would be the flame that destroyed her. Like knowing he was dead, he knew what he was going to do next. He didn't have to learn it from a book; everything was in his mind, ready to be called upon whenever it was needed. As he approached, she stopped and looked at him, her eyes shining with compassion. Chase smiled, thinking that when he was alive, she had not seemed to care about him at all, yet only now, when it was already too late, was she acting like she should have done for the past nine years. The woman would soon be making up for her shortfalls in parenting.

"I need you to do something for me…. Mother," Chase began, in what he hoped was something like he used to sound. The woman looked at him nervously. It was clear that she was becoming afraid of him, of the way he looked more dead than alive.

"Yes?" she said in a timid half whisper.

"Take off your coat." She did so, and as Chase had hoped, she was wearing a low cut top that was much too young for her. Chase remembered how before, his mother would often dress up like this and drag herself around the town's pubs and clubs, places that he himself would have gone to if he had any friends to go with. Suddenly, the young man shot his hand forwards, his thumb, index and middle fingers jutting out. He felt warmth as his nails broke the skin of her chest. He was impressed that she did not cry out. She obviously had more strength than he gave her credit for. With his free hand, Chase grabbed his mother's hand and forced it towards his own chest, prying her fingers open with his own. There was a crack as his mother's middle finger snapped under the strain, yet still she did nothing more than whimper quietly. With one final breath, Chase jammed her fingers into his skin, the two of them connected in a sick chain of eternity.

Heather Rivers was aware only of a dull pain in her chest, and a throbbing in her hand, as if she was plugged into a power source. She knew that what was happening should be unbearable, but something was numbing her mind, whispering that everything would be alright, that she needed to do this for her son. Tears were rolling down her cheeks, but they were tears of joy, ecstasy that she was finally doing her duty as a mother. Chase looked at her solemnly.

"I claim your heart for my own,
May it serve me as it has served you."
And then another voice, coming from nowhere yet everywhere at once. It was whispering a poem of some sort. It was clear that the voice wanted Heather to repeat those words, but why? It was supposed to help Chase, but how? For a moment, she regained control of her mind, the pain she should have been feeling flashing across her consciousness. Chase noticed her trying to break free and concentrated harder on repeating the incantation in her mind. "Say it!" he shouted, letting anger take hold. His words were wasted however, as his mother was already under his control once more. She straightened up and

began to speak.

"I sacrifice my heart,
And in completing the link,
Take yours in its stead.
We live as each other."

Chase smiled as he released the woman from his grip, and himself from hers. The transference of heart was complete, and soon her energy would serve to recharge his corpse. He opened his arms, drawing his mother in for one last hug. He had been kind to her whilst she gave him what he needed, but now he wanted this woman to die knowing what a worthless bitch she had been. He stopped playing with her mind and pushed her away so he could watch, his eyes glinting with malicious curiosity.

All at once, Heather exploded into an overload of torture. Her finger was broken and her chest was bleeding, staining her green top into a murky brown. She looked helplessly at her son leaning back, a casual observer.

"What have you done to me?" she cried, the pain increasing, threatening to smother her in a wave of razors and needles. Chase held his finger to his lips, and then grinned as he looked down at his body. The boy's chest was rippling and swirling, the burnt patches turning pink and then becoming new flesh. As her son's skin healed, Heather herself screamed, her own skin peeling away like paper, an invisible inferno clawing her away strip by strip, and all through the pain, the voice was back, whispering the same cruel message endlessly. That Heather Rivers deserved to die.

Chase put a hand across his eyes as the person in front of him burst into flames, a shriek vanishing with the flesh and bone that had once been his mother. Not even he had been expecting it to be quite so spectacular, but she had at last served her purpose. She had truly given him life.

Chapter 24 – The Trials Of Retribution

Chase stepped over the blackened remains of his mother
and headed for the stairs. Healing himself had taken up a
lot of energy, and he was feeling slightly drained. *No…* he
corrected himself. Tiring was a weakness, and he was above
that now. He had to remind himself that he had surpassed
the boundaries of humanity; he was higher even than those
Wiccans who created him. He was the most advanced
being on the planet, and advanced beings did not need to
rest.

Chase turned his mind to what was most important
to him, something he had felt since he had woken up in his
suffocating tomb. An undeniable desire for self-
preservation was burning deep within him, probably where
his soul would have been if he had still had one. It was this
that drove him to kill his mother, and now it was telling
him that he had to kill Matt and the others. If they gave
him this power, they could probably take it away again, and
Chase could not allow that to happen. Without this
immense gift, he would have been stuck as that hopeless,
pathetic creature he had been for eighteen years.

Snapping back to reality, dragging himself away from
his insecurity, Chase found himself in his bedroom. He
surveyed the peeling violet walls and the frayed posters
with a look of pity on his face. How could he have lived
like this before? This was no place for a God to reside, for
that was what he had decided he was. Anger surged
through his fresh new body as he leaped forwards and
began clawing the posters from the walls.

Moments later, Chase was crouching in the centre of
a pile of tattered paper and flakes of paint, a sinister
creature in a nest of destruction. His fingertips were
bleeding, but he did not feel it. Instead he held his hands

up and watched with a smirk as the blood trickled across his palms. Surveying his new room, he began to look around at the rest of his possessions, what few they were. A television on a crooked chest of drawers, a wardrobe and a bed. Anything of any worth was kept on a small shelf above the bed, and all that amounted to was a couple of old Action Men, a volleyball trophy that he had won back in Secondary school and a camera. Pathetic. Although, the camera could be interesting. What pointless images had he captured before he died? He remembered his life: the lonely existence and the job with the University newspaper that gave him the excuse to wander around campus taking pictures of people whom he wished were his friends.

A piteous smile on his face, Chase stood up and grabbed the camera from the shelf, a cloud of dust rising as he did so. After turning the light off, he sat back down amongst the tatters of his bedroom and paused, weighing the camera in the palm of his hand. He was about to take a trip down memory lane, he mused. This little box was like a window into the past, and he would be able to see just how hopeless he really was when he was alive. He was certain he wouldn't like what he saw, but he figured it would be a learning experience. Seeing the ashes from which he had been born would spur him on to remain as he was now. There was no way that anybody would take his power away and leave him once more as the insignificant Chase Rivers. He snapped out of his reverie and began to focus on the task in hand. Typically, he had not been able to afford a digital camera so he would have to develop the pictures on his own. *No problem*, he thought. It would prove a good test of his ability to control his new gift. Leaning forward, Chase turned over one of the larger shreds of poster so that he had a white surface. Next, he opened the back of the camera and pulled out the film, holding it stretched between his two hands. He found that he barely had to concentrate to heat up the air particles and focus them through the negative he was holding. Within seconds, an image was beginning to burn itself onto the paper on the floor. By the looks of it, it was a butterfly sitting on a brightly coloured flower. *I don't remember being so gay...* Chase scowled as he screwed up the picture and began to develop the next one.

Soon, Chase had what seemed like an endless heap of pointless images. University buildings, lecturers and Chess clubs. Everything you would expect to find in a uni rag, the world of lonely no hopers. And then there they were, in the last picture. Four handsome young men, roughly nineteen years old, plastered with fake smiles to hide the confusion of being confronted by someone they barely knew. As the picture became clearer, he studied the faces of his four fathers. Scott looked annoyed about something, and hadn't even bothered to try and look cheerful, but it was the other three that angered Chase the most. At least Fielding hadn't pretended to care about Chase being there, but the others...they had all posed for the photo, acting like they were his friends, like they cared what happened to him, when the events of the night that followed would obviously show that they didn't. It was then that he made up his mind. He wasn't just going to kill these four liars; he was going to torture them to the very brink of existence before he finally pushed them over the edge.

As Chase stared at the picture, he noticed that he had captured a fifth person in it. The side of someone's face was just visible peeking out from behind one of the oak trees in the quad. It was an unfortunate angle, as if the tree had somehow grown a face and was staring right at him, and as such, he could not make out who the face belonged to. Probably some random caught in the background by accident.

Chase tossed the camera carelessly aside, suddenly no longer interested in what the rest of the photographs contained. The one picture on the floor in front of him seemed to consume his entire being. A drop of blood fell to the lilac carpet after hanging from one of his fingers for a few seconds, and he remembered that he had cut them whilst ripping his walls. A lot things really were just states of mind, he mused. Without the pain, he really had no idea that he had injured himself. He would have healed in a few hours and been none the wiser had he not noticed the blood beforehand. The body was completely capable of doing so, yet it always seemed to insist on letting its owner know when it was damaged. Yet another human weakness that he no longer had to worry about.

Almost playfully, Chase dipped his finger into the spot of blood and smeared it onto the image at his knees. Three thin lines of blood across the chests of his enemies - a suitable sign that the game was on. Satisfied that he had made the first move of his revenge, he turned his mind to matters of less importance, but still pressing. He couldn't be one of the most powerful beings on the planet in a pair of burnt shorts could he? Chase needed to look the part. He needed to instil fear into those that saw him. People needed to be able to tell just by looking that he was a force to be reckoned with, and so he began to remodel himself.

By the time the sun was up, Chase and his bedroom were unrecognisable. The once purple walls were now charred and black like the boy who used to live there, and the whole room was lit by naked flames burning eternally from the furniture that the he no longer needed. The fire made a suitable alternative to the bright sunlight that was kept at bay by heavy curtains, ragged at the edges. Chase was dressed completely in black, with a cloak like the ones he saw shortly before he was murdered. One of the benefits of being able to manipulate Earth, Air, Fire and Water was that he could pretty much create anything he wanted. He had also been thinking about a name for himself - after all, he wasn't really Chase Rivers any more. His reawakening had not only given him the power of the elements, but he had also been granted the subconscious knowledge of how to use it all, and this included an understanding of Theban Locte, the language that his four creators often used for their magical exploits.

He began to run through a number of words in his mind - words that could reflect his status. Super, ultra and mega didn't seem right, but just as he was growing impatient, he felt the familiar sensation that he had experienced when he woke up. It was like a memory forcing itself to the forefront of his consciousness, something that had always been present but was only now being acknowledged. The name "Dielunasar" had imprinted on his mind, and now there was no question of an alternative - Theban Locte for Deus, which in turn meant God.

Now that Deus was confident that he was complete, he set his mind to beginning to avenge his death. It was obvious that his creators had benefited from their ritual, as their presences resonated so much more clearly in Deus' mind, outshining the seemingly dull general populace who milled around in their pointless lives, barren and grey in comparison. The only thing Deus was still unsure of was whether his adversaries were aware of their new-found powers? Not that it mattered. It would be the subtle difference between merely crushing a struggling ant, and having it try to bite you first. Either way, the ant would die. There was only one way to find out how much they had learned whilst Deus had been in his underground recovery, and that was to pick one to play with.

Of the four men responsible, Deus knew the least about Rich. Josh and Scott were at the same university as Chase had been, so he had often seen them walking through the quad together or deep in discussion beneath one of the oaks. Matt was the only one that had actually made an effort to speak to Chase, after one of his gigs. Choking slightly, the unwanted memory crept into Deus' mind. There was a dark pub, lit by the occasional flashing light as it swept across the crowds swathed in black, chains and piercings. Matt's band, Crystal Homicide had just finished playing a set in the local Battle of the Bands. Ironically, this was the first time Chase had ventured out on a social, and had been well and truly stood up by his colleague, Ed. Chase was standing alone at the bar, rooting through his change and unable to afford even a half pint when Matt arrived next to him, bass guitar slung across his back. Matt had only said a one word greeting, but that was the closest thing to a conversation Chase had had for years. He remembered how he had almost begun to idolise the other man, and the sense of longing he felt, even after Matt had press-ganged him into writing an essay on the Renaissance for him.

Deus shook his head. He hated Matt Blake equally, and resented him even more for somehow allowing this memory of humanity seep back into his afterlife. Deus would not be tainted by Chase's weaknesses any longer. He settled on Rich, wondering the exact extent of the fun he could have before his toy finally broke. He would start with the mind, for what good was pain if the mind was strong enough to disregard it? With a grin, Deus moulded his clothing into something slightly more streetwise and headed out of his old home.

Chapter 25 – Malleus Maleficarum

As Deus stalked purposefully across the city, he took great delight in noticing the faces of the people he walked by. Hardly anybody gave him a second glance, and he supposed that he must look quite normal to the average urbanite. What entertained him the most was that they all seemed to be enclosed in their own little bubble, oblivious to anything else around them. There were the cheerful smiles of the contented, the worry worn brows of the troubled, and of course the iPod generation, locked in their music.

Suddenly, the Spirit Elemental's chest burned with a stinging pain. He peeled back his top and stared down at the melted crucifix, which was now glowing white hot. He wheeled around and saw that he was standing in the foreboding shadow of St Jude's Catholic Church. As he still possessed Chase's knowledge, however rudimentary, he was well aware of the threat of organised religion. He also knew their stance on people like him. *I can spare a little time,* he reasoned. Deus grinned as he waltzed up the steps theatrically, hovering in the doorway for a brief moment before stepping across the threshold.

The main chamber of the church was large and airy, and the man's footsteps echoed softly as he padded across the flagstones. He walked along the central aisle, taking in the elaborately carved stonework and the gilded pews. A large crucifix hung from the ceiling, plain and wooden, cracked and warped. As he walked under this beacon of supposed spirituality, his spine tingled, like walking under power lines.

He continued moving through the hall until he reached the altar, a plain covered table surrounded by a hundred dancing candles. A single nun sat at the front pew, swathed in black and head bowed in reverence. When she felt his presence, she looked up, her face etched with years of experience.

"Are you lost, my child?" she uttered quietly.

"What?"

"Saint Jude," she continued, "is the Patron Saint of lost souls. People usually come here for guidance."

"I'm not lost," Deus whispered. "I'm hunting."

"Well The Church's view on blood sports-"

"Not animals," he cut in. "People. Witches." The nun did not even blink, continuing to stare at him blankly. "Does that not surprise you?"

"I know what you are," she said. "I can see that your soul is broken."

"Ah," the Spirit smirked.

"Have you heard of The Malleus Maleficarum?" the woman asked, the devout belief building in her fragile voice. "They called it The Witches' Hammer. It was the definitive guide to destroying evil in the 1400s." Deus scanned the vestiges of Chase's memories until he settled on a piece of information from a long past history lesson.

"The Great Witch Hunts," he began scathingly. "Years spent burning, hanging and torturing a handful of people who may have had my power." The nun nodded emphatically. "And thousands of innocents who definitely didn't."

"What would you know of innocence?" the woman snarled indignantly. "They were all rank with sin regardless of what you call *power*. The world needed to be purged. It still does." Deus ignored her piercing glance.

"Do you have The Hammer?" he asked. If a copy existed, then it might contain some amusing tips for torturing his four creators. The nun narrowed her eyes, her aged features looking as if they were folding in on themselves.

"If I did, I certainly wouldn't give it to you," she snapped. Her voice rose to a tone of command. "It is a sin to use magic, even if you use it to destroy other witches – it will corrupt all men."

"Oh come now," Deus simpered, flashing his perfect teeth. As he did so, he raised his hand and a flock of pearly white doves erupted from his palm. The lofty hall was suddenly awash with the sound of gentle fluttering, and cream snowflakes drifted casually down as feathers were dislodged. "Surely magic isn't all that bad?"

The nun's eyes were wide. "Parlour tricks and temptations!" she exclaimed. "Using Satan's toys, you will lead us into Hell."

"I might just..." Deus remarked with another grin. He stepped forward menacingly, flashing his fang like teeth once more. He had long since decided that the woman should be punished. The nun sensed danger and fumbled with the chains around her neck. She held out her crucifix defensively, hoping to ward him off like some TV vampire.

"Malum corpus esse attero," she uttered hurriedly in unfaltering tongue, eyes blazing ferociously. When Deus did not even flinch, she lowered the cross with a look of confusion and disappointment on her face. The old woman looked as if her faith was being rocked and battered in front of her. Deus lowered his top so that she could see the shinning scar that had once been Chase's crucifix.

"It seems that I'm immune..."

"Please," the nun spluttered. "We can help you – an exorcism would rid you of the devil holding your soul."

"You think I would give this up?" Deus lifted his palm slightly and the nun rose from the ground until she was suspended two feet above the cold flagstones. He leaned in. "What have you got to say now?"

"God will punish you."

"Oh right, one god in charge of everything, that's what you believe isn't it? Well your god, who does everything for a reason, let this cross burn into my chest and protect me from you, his loyal little servant. I wonder why that was?" He lifted her another couple of feet. "Well don't worry Sister, now you get to die for *his* sins."

"I'll scream."

"I hope so."

She shrieked pitifully as he floated her to the oak cross, a flapping crow amongst a backdrop of startled doves. The hanging symbol swung gently as Deus used his mind to hold the frail woman against it, whilst simultaneously pulling nails out of the nearest pew with a grinding sound of splintering wood.

As he levitated the nails, the spirit extended another mental link snaking right to the top of the church tower where the bells hung expectantly. Mind divided in a trinity of malevolence, Deus held the nun in place, whilst at the same time driving the nails into her flesh, all overseen by a joyous symphony of pealing church bells.

He tilted his head back and closed his eyes in pleasure, feeling the warm crimson raindrops fall onto his face and run down his chin. Exalted, he stepped out of the holy building, knowing that whilst he hadn't found any information, he had still had some fun.

After a deep breath and wiping the blood from his face, Deus headed in the direction of the university.

Chapter 26 – Shades Of Grey

"Knowing those around you is key to survival. For though only a select few might be graced with the gifts of the elements, all can wield powerful spiritual weapons. Emotion is stronger than any form of energy manipulation, and those who use it may not be aware. Fear, Anger, Jealousy, Grief and Love form nature's pentagram, enhanced but not overshadowed by the pentagram of supernature, that is Earth, Fire, Air, Water and Spirit. As Wiccans it is possible to master both, but care should be taken around those without the craft for they are beacons of emotion, radiating feeling and affecting everything they come across."

The Book Of Shadows

Deus hovered at the main gates, the quad stretching out before him. It was still early, but there were groups of students already milling about, and sitting under the oak trees that loomed over the grass, guardians of the university. He was wearing a black hoodie with similar jeans, and the only sign that he had changed at all was his skin, which was now almost white. Narrowing his eyes, Deus stepped through the gates and into the world that he used to inhabit. As he suspected, nobody even gave him a second glance, they were all too caught up in their own lives. Perhaps they had exams coming up, or coursework due in. It didn't matter. Deus was just glad that nobody kicked up a fuss, as the fewer people that caused trouble, the fewer people he would have to eventually kill.

Deus was aware that Rich did not actually go to UCE but that was the only place that he had ever seen him, as he was always sneaking in to hang out with his mates. If he wasn't on campus, then at least Deus would be able to find out where he was instead. As he stalked across the grass, ignoring the paths carefully laid out, Deus smirked to himself. He was above the control of the paths, free to roam across concrete and grass as he pleased. Eyes roving, sifting through the ever-increasing number of students, Deus failed to see anybody he recognised. If he did not find one of his betrayers soon, he would have to find a quiet corner and divine Rich's whereabouts.

"Rivers!" A clear voice boomed across the quad, causing Deus to freeze in his tracks. Slowly, he turned to see a balding man striding towards him. It was Mr Adams, the head of the University Paper. As far as Deus knew, Mr Adams was also a lecturer in some obscure subject like Modern Art. The older man's eyes crinkled cheerfully as he approached. "It's good to see you getting some sun boy; you look as white as death!" he chirped. Deus glared at the teacher… if only he knew the truth, he would not be so gleeful. Seeing that Deus was obviously not going to humour him, Mr Adams continued in a more businesslike manner. "I haven't seen you at The Rag lately," he went on. "There's been some layout changes and I think some of your photos might need resizing."

Some of my photos? Deus mused grimly as he thought back to the hopeless pictures he had burned from his camera. They were not his photos - they belonged to a memory. It would be a small mercy to just destroy the print workshop completely rather than bother resizing some pictures. Deus smiled to himself before realising that Mr Adams was waiting for a response.

"Oh…." Deus floundered, trying to shape his voice into something he hoped would sound familiar to the man before him. "Another time maybe, I have to-"

"No time like the present, Chase!" shot Mr Adams, his unbreakable mood seemingly restored. "Don't worry about your lectures; I'll mark you in myself." Grabbing his arm, the man began to lead Deus to the nearest corner of the quad where the John Terrence building sat, glass fronted and sparkling in the sunlight.

"You don't understand!" growled Deus, his anger beginning to build. "This is really important."

Mr Adams sighed, turning his head to look reproachfully at his student. "I know that at your age, everything seems like the most important thing in the world. Everything's life or death with you youngsters." Deus narrowed his eyes. Why was he being led against his will like a small child? He could easily burn this adult, or blast him away, even kill him but then why did Deus already know he wasn't going to? Straining, Deus tried to concentrate harder, once again feeling the rush of energy seep through him, ready to leap out into whatever he wanted it to. "Plus, I happen to know Ed has been asking after you…" added Mr Adams offhandedly. Chase shook the firm grip off and stood motionless in the doorway. It was as if he had been somehow sucked away from the inside, all of his feelings, his rage and power had vanished. A vacuum had opened in his gut, ripping out his desire for vengeance and leaving behind an empty frame, clinging to the second life it had been granted.

"Are you all right, Chase?" asked Mr Adams, his brow furrowing with sudden concern. Chase gulped and nodded his head, regaining some semblance of still being in control.

"Yes Mr Adams, sir." he whispered, afraid to open his mouth in case Deus forced his way out again and distorted his reality. "I can make it from here," he continued. "You must have other stuff to get on with." The teacher's gaze lingered on the student for a moment before he nodded to himself and headed along the corridor.

"Tell Ed I want the new layout by Thursday." With

that, Mr Adams disappeared round the corner, leaving Chase lost in his thoughts. What was happening to him? He was constantly aware that Deus was trying to claw his way back in to his consciousness, each attempt leaving Chase leaning against the nearest wall, fighting for breath. The one thing that he was sure of was that, for now at least, Chase was in control of his body. *No,* he corrected himself. It had stopped being his body when he had been ripped from it in fire and pain. This was Deus' body now and Chase was on borrowed time.

Deus had receded when Ed had been mentioned, but why? Ed was the layout supervisor for The Rag, a year older than Chase had been and had only spoken about three words to him at any one time. Perhaps Ed was also involved in this business? At this very moment was he trying everything he could to undo what had befallen Chase? Hope seemed to sedate Deus enough for Chase to pick his pace up into a jog as he traversed corridors and turned corners along his way to the print workshop where The Rag was made each week.

Eventually Chase reached the blue double doors that led into the print workshop. A faint repeating hum could be heard on the other side as the various machines did their jobs. He did not usually work in the print workshop, preferring to stay in The Rag office where he could sort out his photos in peace. He only ventured this far into the works when there was an issue with the layout of the paper, as Mr Adams had said there was now. With a deep breath, Chase pushed open the doors and stepped inside, unsure of what he would find.

The humming instantly grew louder and a pulsating light emanated from one corner of the room as a photocopier spat out infinite duplicates of an article. So much interest generated from one piece of writing copied a thousand times. Ed was bent over the machine, his back turned and barely visible through the stacks of paper and folders that covered every available surface. He did not look up when the door slammed behind Chase. As he approached, Chase took a moment to actually look at Ed properly. He was tall and thin, but with a sense of strength underneath. His hair was dyed black, cut short with a few strands left long to hang stylishly down his face. It struck Chase that Ed had a similar self-image to Deus, gothic and imposing, except that Ed chose to look this way and worked on it every morning, whereas Deus was created out of malice.

Ed finally turned around, Crystal Homicide emblazoned across his tight black top. Chase stared: it was Matt's band merchandise. One of his killers had helped create something appealing and it just went to prove that humanity was duplicitous. A man could paint a masterpiece with one hand while murdering his companion with the other.

"Where have you been?" Ed said, his expression immediately brightening. "I tried to call you a couple of weeks ago. I thought…" He paused, taking in Chase's reaction. "I figured we could hang out or something, maybe stick on a couple of films. It was Halloween after all." Halloween? So it *was* Ed that had phoned him before.

"I got your text too," snapped Chase, suddenly angry. If Ed was the reason that all of this had happened, he had to know why. Ed looked confused, his eyebrows raised.

"I didn't send a text," he said dejectedly. "I was too annoyed at chickening out again to follow through…" he added as an afterthought, almost to himself. Chase shook his head, the new layers of meaning piling up all too quickly. What did Ed mean?

"Chickening out again?" questioned Chase. "I don't understand." The older guy flushed slightly before he explained himself. It was obviously difficult, but again Chase could not think why. Usually Ed was perfectly happy teasing him about his photos, but now here he was struggling to construct a simple sentence.

"I was going to come and ask you earlier that day, I had the whole conversation planned out, but I saw you talking to your friends, so I hid." Ed looked down at his feet, disheartened.

"You!" Chase shouted furiously. "You were the one hiding behind the tree. Were you spying on me?" He didn't wait for an answer. "I knew it! You're lying about the text, you're part of this!"

As Ed looked at him, suddenly there was a bright flash of rose-coloured light. The pulse of energy was so intense that Chase was forced backwards, knocking a stack of printouts to the carpet. As the light began to fade, Ed shot forwards and grabbed his arm before he collapsed completely. The grip of the other man's fingers seemed to heat the flesh beneath his hoodie, a deep vibrant magenta snaking its way up his arm and across his chest, angling downwards towards his stomach. Wide-eyed, Chase pulled the hand away, expecting to see anger on Ed's part. Instead, it was as if his colleague had not seen the burning wave of energy, or the mysterious glowing power that crept into Chase's veins. If anything, Ed looked hurt and withdrawn as he turned back to the photocopier.

"You're cute when you're angry…" he muttered.

"What are you?" Chase gasped, holding his chest. Ed faced him once more, his fierce brown eyes shining as tears threatened to form, only held in check by the eyeliner he always wore.

"Isn't it obvious?" Ed whispered. His brow

furrowed as he tried to wrestle with his feelings. Chase gulped. He knew it. Ed was a Wiccan just like the others. Ed had the same gift that had killed him and let his body fall prey to the vengeful Deus. Ed took a deep breath. "I like you…" Chase opened his mouth in surprise. "No, it's more than that Chase," continued Ed, growing in confidence. "I feel a lot more for you than a simple like."

"You… you fancy me?" said Chase, the shock reducing him to playground slang.

Ed grinned slyly. "Rather badly, I'm afraid." Chase felt his heart rate quicken as Ed's words sunk in. It was so unexpected that he was lost for words of his own, a million possible sentences flying by just out of his reach.

"Wait a minute…" he began, confusion still clouding his judgement. "How long have you… felt this way?"

Ed paused before answering. "Since not long after we started working on The Rag."

Chase began to fume, his voice rising. "You liked me for all that time?" he challenged. "I spent every night alone for months when I could have been hanging with you if you'd had the guts to come and talk to me?" Ed looked speechless. "If you'd worked hard enough you probably could have turned me, but now you'll never know."

"Weren't you listening?" Ed snapped, his own voice rising. "I've been trying to get near you properly for ages now, but every time I do, I freak out because I don't know how you'll react."

"Here's a hint!" Chase snapped back. "Hey Chase, do you want to come over sometime?"

"It wasn't that easy!" Ed retorted. "If you liked a girl, would you just go right up to her and say so? No you wouldn't! Imagine how hard that is, when it's a conventional pairing. Now imagine it was a guy, a guy that could most probably beat the crap out of you, and see how

hard it is? I didn't even know what you would do. What if
you freaked out and left The Rag? That would be my fault.
Love is like God; it creates and destroys in equal measure."
Chase faltered, his anger once more vanishing, and there
was the reason. The word *Love*. Love was what had hit
Chase when Mr Adams had mentioned Ed, and when his
colleague had first looked at him, Chase had seen the
emotions blasting out of him like a signal. That meant that
it was this powerful feeling that had subdued Deus initially?
Chase smiled grimly. If that was what it took to get rid of
Deus forever, then he would try it. He would have tried
anything to be normal again, and this was pretty far out
there.

Chase looked Ed in the eye, trying his best to look as
if he wanted this to happen. He had never even kissed a girl
before, so wasn't exactly sure what the ideal plan was, but
he figured he ought to get closer. Closing his eyes, he
leaned towards Ed, aware of him as a faint pink haze on
the inside of his eyelid. As Chase got closer, the rosy glow
bloomed into a vibrant vermilion, flashing sparks of red
branching outwards like tender hands searching for smooth
flesh to caress. The energy shone still brighter and brighter
as he got near enough to feel Ed's breath on his cheek,
bated with curiosity and anticipation.

Suddenly, a cry rang out from across the quad. The
initial sound of surprise and excitement was soon joined by
a chorus of jubilant cheers. Chase felt the teasing brush of
Ed's skin against his lips as the other guy turned to see
what was causing the disturbance outside. Dejected, Chase
leaned back and shrugged his shoulders, trying to sink his
head into his body. It felt like Ed had just rejected him, and
he didn't even feel for the guy, so why was it eating at him
so much? Because that kiss could have been his salvation,
he thought. It would be a small price to pay if he got his life

back, and he could always let Ed down gently once he had bought the time to explain himself. Reluctantly opening his eyes, he saw Ed leaning against the window, mouth open in awe. What looked like snow was gently floating to the ground, covering the grass with light flakes. He ran to the window, a waft of sweet scent filtering into his nostrils, the smell of summer six months too soon. To his amazement, the four oak trees that cornered the quad had burst into blossom, the petals falling into the centre of UCE like a sky full of confetti. Chase had done this, subconsciously or whatever, but he had done it, he was sure of it. He still had power, and with a gut wrenching pain, he felt Deus sense it too.

"Ed!" Chase rasped through the feeling of needles being jabbed into his throat. Ed turned towards him, a sudden look of concern on his face. "You have to get out of here, now!" Pain consumed him as Deus fought for control of his body. His skin burned and itched, threatening to drive him insane with torture. The last time he had felt like this was when he had died, except he knew that what was happening to him now was ten times worse.

"But the trees?" Ed faltered. "I've never seen anything like-" Ed was cut off as Chase coughed blood onto the cream carpet of the print workshop. Chase grimaced as he felt Ed's strong arms grab his shoulders just as he was about to collapse. Using every last ounce of his strength, the stricken man lifted his head, a trickle of blood still leaking from the corner of his mouth, as if the artist had slipped when drawing him.

"I said, get out of here!" he shouted, words turning to a growl as he finally buckled beneath the spiritual onslaught and was once again lost to the ether.

Deus' eyes flicked open, rage immeasurable behind the greyness. So Chase thought this idiot was his salvation?

As if a mere human crush could banish a god? As Deus had slept, innumerable romances had flickered and died. Even lifelong marriages were fleeting moments in an existence of eons, and yet here he was feeling the hope sprung from a schoolboy obsession. Ed looked him straight in the eyes helplessly intoxicated as he was struck in the chest. Deus was only vaguely aware of Ed's ribs cracking against his fist, nor did he particularly notice as the young man flew backwards into the window, through the glass and out into the quad. The rest of the student body had no time to react as at the very same instant, the blossom drifting lazily through the air burst into a hundred tiny flashes of fire, raining ash upon all who gathered to witness what was just moments ago a product of Love.

Deus stormed out of the print workshop, the doors buckling in front of him, a path of cracked windows marking his exit from the campus.

Chapter 27 – Laying The Trail

The worm fought its way through the soil with single-minded determination. Driven by instincts rather than thoughts, the worm needed food constantly, and this was why it travelled, endlessly processing the soil it moved through, extracting the nutrients it needed.

With a jolt, the worm changed direction. Unable to comprehend this unnatural movement, the worm writhed as it broke the surface of the ground and began to float into the air. Sparks flickered as the worm experienced its final moments in this world before the instincts that powered it faded to eternal blackness.

Deus sat in the park, leaning against the bandstand, his knees held up close against his chest. The worm he had just pulled out of the ground now lay in bits on top of a small pile of creatures that had helped Deus calm his fury.

It must be easy being a worm, Deus mused. Even sitting above the ground, he had sensed the energy of the creatures living below him, had sensed the simple lives reduced to the bare necessities. A beetle needed to eat and mate, that was all that ran through its pitiful consciousness as Deus honed in on it. Eat and mate, eat and mate, eat and mate. It was life, but without the complications of feelings and choices. Of course, if the beetle had feelings and the ability to decide, it might have saved itself from being ripped out of the ground and torn apart. Then again it might not have. It might have been a suicidal beetle. Deus grinned at his joke and then turned his attention to the people wandering about in the park. Were they any different to the pile of lifeless insects by his side?

People were hurrying about their business, oblivious to everything around them. The Elements had slaved for millennia to build up a world out of darkness, and its inhabitants didn't seem to notice, dropping their coffee cups and rifling through newspapers. Occasionally, one of the drones would flash an intense burst of colour as an emotion was triggered into consciousness, but these were the only signs of them. If Deus could not see these displays of feeling, then the people in the park might as well have been robots.

Deus shook his head, aware that he had allowed himself to drift away for too long. The rage that Ed had inadvertently caused had now been abated in the torture of a dozen invertebrates, and Deus was ready to resume his campaign of revenge, confident that now he was aware of the downfalls of emotion, he would not be overcome by them again. Reaching into his trouser pocket, Deus pulled out the photograph of his murderers, nostrils flaring briefly as he first scanned their features. Clearing his mind, Deus took a deep breath and placed his index finger on Rich's face, above the lines of blood across the bemused guy's chest. Deus did not need to say anything special to accomplish his goal, but he knew that the words would be *sarinagiartoh oyfir maryoh inanartohelnardieldia*. It was just another indication of his superiority, thought Deus. He doubted that the others could make anything happen without saying it first. Once again ridding his mind of all thoughts, Deus closed his eyes.

When Deus opened his eyes a second later, he was walking along a pavement, a quiet road on his right. There was a cool breeze in the air, and the faint scent of pine needles played across his nostrils, mixed with another aroma, one that he could not place. Still, Deus did not sense anything deeply malign about it, so carried on walking. The sun was shining brightly through the railings on his left, casting a striped pattern of light and shadow across the pavement Deus was walking along. A group of teenagers were walking towards Deus. They were on the other side of the road, typically loud and foul-mouthed…

Deus gasped, Rich's vision snapping back to his own like a television skipping channels. Deus recognised those railings that his target was walking past, they were the iron bars that surrounded the park. The park that Deus was sitting in. This was a chance that he could not pass on, he thought as he cast his mind out towards the teenagers that were approaching his target. Now was the time to start! All Deus had to do was give the tiniest hint of his existence, 'to sow the seeds of doubt,' as Iago would say. Once this was done, Rich would not be able to tear himself away from his destruction. Deus took a deep breath.

Suddenly a gust of wind blew straight into Rich's face, forcing him to look up, straight into the eyes of the last teenager. The spiky haired teen was grinning, his eyes shining with malice. Rich's throat seized up and he staggered back against the fence as if recoiling from a blow to the chest, and then it was over, he could breath again, and the mysterious teenager carried on walking as is nothing had happened.

Deus laughed aloud as he heard the pitiful fool running towards him just before he relinquished his hold on the child outside the park. The kid would not know what had happened, would later think he had been daydreaming. Once he had recovered from Rich's shaking, that is. Letting his merriment fade away, Deus snapped into action. He was pretty certain that he had bought some time with his scare tactic, but he wanted to make sure that the next piece of his onslaught was laid before Rich got home. Jumping to his feet, Deus ran out of the park ignoring the cries of the small child that had just discovered the heap of dead animals that had so amused him previously.

Once outside the park, Deus stood for a moment

taking in the air as it blew playfully across his face. A multitude of smells flickered through his senses, but there was one essence that he was particularly searching for. It was instantly recognisable once Deus had found it, the aura of Lynx deodorant, sweat and the faint undertones of cigarettes that was Rich Benson. Of course, that could still have been almost any male between the ages of seventeen and thirty but the fact that Rich was an Elemental gave his essence a sharp, almost tangible edge. Sensing this rough outline, Deus was able to track his quarry's progress from earlier that day, and soon found himself standing outside what must have been the Bensons' house.

The house was a typical suburban building, double-glazed with a well-kept front lawn. It was hardly the fortress of evil, noted Deus as he wandered around the back of the house. Of course, he could simply smash the door in, but he reminded himself that he was aiming for subtle with Rich. He could save mindless violence for one of the others. *Perhaps Matt,* he thought with a grin. Deus stalked through the iron gate and emerged into a similarly manicured back garden, each flowerbed immaculately planned to match in colour and size. As he approached, the flowers seemed to shrink back and close up, shying away from the vengeful being. Deus did not care however, as he had just spotted his way in. The window above the conservatory was wide open, the corner of a yellow curtain poking out invitingly. Within minutes, Deus had scrambled up a rickety trellis and had crept through the open window. He now stood in what was unmistakably his target's bedroom, casting a disdainful eye across the junk that littered the floor. Piles of clothes seemed to inhabit every available corner, whereas the centre of the room seemed to be carpeted in a scattering of loose paper. The only thing that seemed to be in any sort of order was a small shelf bracketed to the yellow wall. On the shelf stood an assortment of candles and other Wiccan tools. An athame shone brightly in the sunshine, the carved silver handle shaped like a billowing cloud. Deus smirked to himself at the thought of Rich wielding the knife. He wondered if the blade had ever pierced flesh? Had it ever scraped against bone as it drained something of life with cold precision? Deus doubted it as he walked over to inspect the altar more closely, idly trailing his fingers through a bag of runes that sat in a leather pouch on the desk.

Next to the altar sat a small pile of books. There was a rather scruffily assembled Book of Shadows and some run-of-the-mill text books about plants, but one book caught Deus' eye. It was a small black notepad with a square of paper taped to the front. Reaching out towards the book, Deus flinched as his finger tips ignited when he touched the stiff card cover. With a gasp, he shook his hand until the minute pin pricks of flame spluttered into nothing and then turned his attention to the spidery runes scrawled on the cover of the notebook. It was a simple spell, so simple that Deus grinned to himself as he read the words.

"May no unprepared eye or hand behold this book of power. May the elements guard its pages. So mote it be."

As simple as the words were, Deus could not break their power, and would not be able to look inside. *So Rich likes books does he?* thought Deus as he continued to casually browse around the room. Perhaps that was the answer, the next clue for his unwilling playmate to follow. Deus resolutely picked up one of the other books and held it in his right hand. Brow furrowing with concentration, he focused on the book at a spiritual level, intent on rearranging its essence. After a few moments, what was once "101 Uses for Daffodils" had now become an

antiqued tome, bound in aged purple leather, the words
"*Back to the Beginning*" written on the front in gilded writing.
Deus could have filled the pages with profound thoughts,
but he knew he didn't have to. His victim would not need
to look past the title, it would send him exactly where Deus
was going to put an end to his torment.

Satisfied with his plan, Deus tucked the book under
a stray shirt lying on the floor, wafted a covering of dust
over it all so it looked like it had been there for years, and
crept back out of the window.

By the time he had returned home, Deus had already
formulated the next phase of his campaign. Whilst he had
begun his torture of his four creators, a new player had
emerged in the form of Ed. Whilst the Spirit Elemental was
certain that the wiry journalist had nothing to do with his
magical birth, he was still a threat. It seemed that he alone
had the power to bring the pitiful Chase back to the
forefront of his consciousness, and that wasn't good
enough. He wasn't about to let Ed be his Kryptonite. *Still,*
he mused darkly. *If it's love the boy wants, who am I to
disappoint? I'll just make him fall in love with Deus rather than
Chase. I'm sure he can be used for something...*

Deus scanned through the immense library of
knowledge that had invaded his brain since his reawakening
and settled on an appropriate ritual. All he needed was a
heart. The Spirit Elemental closed his eyes, intending to
seek out the nearest available donor, but quickly opened
them again. Of course the solution was lying right
downstairs. Deus stepped lightly down the stairs and into
the kitchen, making sure he didn't step in his mother.
Pepper looked up expectantly with large hazel eyes,
obviously thinking that his master was going to feed him.
When Deus smirked mischievously, the creature must have
sensed that something was not right. It has often been said

that animals can sense danger before humans, and now
Pepper rose shakily to his feet and cowered backwards into
the corner between the cupboard and the washing machine.
He began to produce a timid whining sound through
clenched teeth, but the attempt to induce pity in the human
was wasted. Deus advanced, flexing his fingers menacingly.
Moments later, he was holding a jar in which floated a
tender lump of muscle about the size of a child's fist. He
stared at it, remembering how just a minute ago it had been
pumping away furiously, threatening to burst with fear as
the human ripped into the dog's fur. Wiping blood onto
the nearest tea towel, Deus carried the jar upstairs, where
he set it on his windowsill. He set a candle on top of the
jar, lighting it with a click of his fingers.

  "With fire I draw you,
  In flame I steal you.
  Behind glass I store you,
  Through desire I feel you.
  When candle is burnt out,
  Ed's heart is mine,
  So mote it be."

Satisfied that Ed would soon be under his thrall, Deus sat
back and waited for any signs that Rich had picked up the
breadcrumbs that had been left in his bedroom.

Chapter 28 – Liquid Impatience

"Everything in this world, every person, object and animal has a spiritual echo, invisible to the untrained eye. Those of Wiccan empowerment can learn to sense this echo and manipulate it. As an echo is identical to its origin, so must what happens to the echo occur to the original thing. A captured image of something real also holds an imprint of the subject's echo, and as such, echoes can be read from statues and pictures just as easily as if looking at the actual item."

    The Book Of Shadows

It was about half past two in the morning, and Deus had still not felt that Rich had made it to the forest, to the end of his miserable life. At first the waiting had been enough to keep Deus amused, but now he was getting tired of sitting around. It was time to move things forwards a notch. Back at the house, Deus had envisioned the other three finding their brother's ruined body and being inconsolable. He had planned to give them a few days of emotional ruin before he targeted his next victim, but why should he wait? If he attacked another one whilst he was waiting, there would be double the grieving to be had by the remaining two.

    Deus took out the photograph he had of his killers, staring into the faces of the people who had both ended and given him his life. This image was a portrait of camaraderie, the four of them together in unison, but in reality humans were much more complicated. Deus held his hand over the photo and closed his eyes, tapping into the resonance that was captured on the paper. After a couple of moments, Deus had disassembled the picture into a number of intricate ethereal layers, each one mapping a relationship between its subjects. Josh and Rich were the jokers of the group, spending the most time together, whereas there was a strong sense of rivalry between the other two. It was as if Scott had some sort of control over the group, as his imprint was very rigid and structured. The resonance of Matt Blake, however, contained a number of threatening spikes lancing out towards the leader, as if vying for his position of power. It was this conflict that made up Deus' mind. Josh would be the next pawn in his game, because although it would be soul-destroying for the water-boy to see his best friend die, leaving only Matt and Scott alive together for a while would be such a treat. The two of them would never get on, and they would practically kill each other. Deus could simply sit back and watch them tear each other to pieces.

Also, this would give Deus a chance to try something new that he had been itching to do since he had possessed the child at the park. If he could transport his mind into someone else's, then it would only be a small step to transporting his whole body. Plus, that meant he could stay grounded in his room should his plaything finally drag himself to the forest for some fun.

Deus sat himself cross legged in the centre of his gloomy abode and cleared his mind, the tendrils of thought drifting out of his mindscape like wisps of cloud. Only one idea was allowed to echo in his head. *Find Josh Thomas.* Poised with determination and confidence, Deus placed his index finger on the photograph, forcefully jabbing the grinning Josh in the chest. With a quiet popping sound, everything went black for a second, then cut film-like to an entirely different location.

Directly in front of him, the real Josh Thomas spun around, a look of pure shock on his face as the recognition crept up on him. After all, the last time the two of them had seen each other, Deus had been killed. The stunned young man was dressed only in a pair of tight black shorts, obviously about to go to bed. *Well at least the astral projection worked*, thought Deus, and from the other's face, it was clear that he was real enough in the room. Deus smiled to himself, secretly impressed with his own skills. Now it was time to show the cowering man in front of him exactly what he could do.

"Hello Joshua," he said calmly. As Josh watched, frozen with confusion, Chase cast his eyes over the room and tutted loudly. "Oh dear," he said as he inclined his head towards the small shelf where Josh kept his Wiccan things. One his Tarot cards had been overturned. "Ten of Swords? That's the worst card in the deck! Ruin…"

Dazed, Josh shook his head. "It's not my card." Chase shrugged nonchalantly before shattering a row of glass bottles that stood on the windowsill with a mere thought. As glass exploded around the room like razor sharp fireworks, Josh fell backwards onto his bed, trying desperately to protect his face from the rain of needle points.

"What the hell?" he spluttered. "I don't… what do you want?" Deus frowned. Could it be? Was it possible that this fool was oblivious to everything that had happened since Halloween?

"You mean you don't know?" Deus exclaimed, trying to keep the disdain from his voice. "You're telling me you have absolutely no idea why I might be here?" Josh stared blankly back, shaking piteously. "Aww, never mind," Deus taunted. "Allow me to fill you in. You killed me!" Deus was shouting now, not caring if he let his anger get the better of him. This was what he had been truly waiting for, a direct confrontation with one of the hapless idiots that had stumbled across his power and unwittingly released it. "You and your stupid friends!" he continued venomously. "I get some message telling me to go to the forest, so I do and I get fucking scorched. Only I bet you regret it now don't you! Your little ritual got me too! There's just one thing. I'm like a wild card, more powerful than any of you pathetic losers. I am Fire. I am Earth. I am Air and Water. I am Spirit and you're not going to steal that from me like you did my pathetic shell. I even thought of a cool name. Deus. Means God, don't you know." Deus paused, a flicker of doubt crossing his mind. This should have been his triumphant gloat as he basked in the astute summation of the situation, but instead, he couldn't stop going over his words. He had said that *he* had been killed, and the ritual had affected *him,* but technically that wasn't true. All of that had happened to Chase, before Deus had forced his way in. Was the human somehow seeping back into consciousness like he had with the pathetic Ed? Perhaps Deus hadn't mastered projection as sufficiently as he thought? Either way, he was still in control for now. He glared ferociously as Josh began to speak.

"What do you mean, the ritual got you too?" he said slowly. Deus rolled his eyes, starting to get annoyed with how dense Josh was being. He was prepared to put up with a certain amount of late-night sloth, but this was taking the piss.

"God, could you be any more stupid? I'm talking about the power of the elements. You have one, I have five. Get it?" he said patronisingly. *That was it*, thought Deus. The most basic of ways in which he could have explained it. Deus finally understood why the bad guys in the movies always explained themselves before carrying out their dastardly plots. To kill someone is easy, and almost merciful, but if you first explain why they are going to be killed, the emotional significance is there to add extra weights to the sinking of the victim's soul. Snapping out of his reverie, Deus stared impatiently at the mortal, who still seemed to be mulling things over. Deus almost fancied he could hear the fabled cogs clicking around inside the man's mind.

"You mean the ritual worked?" At last! He was finally beginning to understand. Suddenly, something tugged at the back of Deus' consciousness. In his mind's eye, he saw the mottled shadows of trees twisting away into the darkness. Rich must be approaching the forest! Deus had to wrap things up here if he wanted to catch his mouse as he had planned.

"Whatever. I'm bored now," he said, dropping all pretence of understanding. "I wanted to be part of the group, but instead I surpassed it. No matter. It's simple. You killed me, so I kill you. It's that easy. Only you don't get a second chance like I did. Killed in sin and all that…. I would say give my love to the others, but I think I'll be visiting them in person, if you know what I mean. Goodnight Josh." Was the Water Elemental going to offer any defence? No, instead he just sat on his bed looking confused. It was a wonder that Deus had felt even remotely threatened by these four amateurs. Shaking his head, Deus waved his hand at the door, stretching out his spiritual essence and interacting with the essence of the lock. With a clicking sound, the door sealed shut. Next, he closed his eyes in concentration and raised his arms, fingers outstretched. The air in the room began to swirl around Deus' fingertips as small clouds began to form. Within seconds it was as if there was a storm inside the bedroom, and water was running in rivulets from the ceiling down the walls. With one last vengeful grin and a taunting wave, Deus vanished, popping into nothingness and leaving Josh alone in his room as it slowly filled with water.

Deus blinked as he was jolted back to his own room,

the rapid switch of location disorienting him slightly. Any normal human would have overloaded from all the psychic power, thought Deus as he reminded himself that his body had been here, his mind at Josh's and not to mention he had Rich's vision tucked away behind his eyes like a split screen movie, fractioning off with each new character that came into the fray.

Scrambling to his feet, Deus reached for one of the old Action Men that he had not destroyed when revamping his room. Staring at the simple little face for a second, the dull eyes staring uncomprehendingly back at him made Deus smile. As humanity used the small unfeeling figures to act out their imaginations, so did he use humanity in the same way. The human race was his plaything.

Enough musing, thought Deus. Rich was nearing his final destination, and Deus did not want to miss the Air Elemental's grand exit. Deus grasped the figure tightly in his right fist, visualising its counterpart picking his way cautiously through the trees as he did so.

"Little one, I give you life,
I name you Rich Benson.
His body is your body,
His breath is your breath.
His passion is your passion,
His blood is your blood.
Though separate you were,
Now you are one.
So mote it be."

With a gasp of air, the Action Man gave a shudder. Smiling to himself, Deus set the figure on the floor and released it. "Time to go to war, little man…" he muttered slyly. Deus watched carefully as the Action Man began to mimic Rich's movements perfectly, weaving its tiny way across the ground, walking around the invisible trees. After a short while, it knelt down with one hand outstretched over what must have been the site of the fire, Deus guessed. A moment later, little Rich stood up and stepped forwards, pensively still for what seemed like an eternity. *What the hell was he doing?* wondered Deus impatiently. After about five minutes, Deus was still watching the figure standing in the same place, occasionally turning its head as if something was buzzing around it. "Come on!" Deus breathed, giving the figure a sharp jab in its camouflage jacketed back.

The Action Man whirled round, tiny eyes wide with fear. Deus smiled at how perfectly the figure had absorbed Rich's personality. He could just see the real man in the forest, all alone and trembling hopelessly. The little man cast about the floor for a second, before stopping dead in its tracks, miniature chest heaving with apprehension. The fear radiated from it, snaking outwards like oil in water. Now was the time.

As the toy stood in the centre of the room, Deus knelt in front of it, breathing deeply and flexing his fingers. He knew what he was aiming to do, but was only aware that it had worked when the cowering figure looked right at him in frightened awe. Deus knew now that a huge pair of smoky hands were hovering above Rich, talons trembling menacingly. Man and avatar stared at each other, both tensing for the oncoming confrontation.

Like two bullets fired into a duel, both men sprang into action at the same moment, the miniature man sprinting across to the right as Deus slammed down with his left hand, knowing that in the forest on the other side of town, the exact same thing was happening, only magnified in size and force. As the tiny figurine scrambled towards the edge of the room, Deus viciously palmed it in the back, sending it sprawling to the floor. To Deus' surprise, the Action Man cried out in pain as it rubbed its eyes frantically but it was not Rich's voice. The scream was high pitched and grating like a tortured animal. The piercing sound was enough to halt Deus in his onslaught for a second as he wondered if his god-like manipulation had enabled the avatar to feel pain. Was it just mimicking Rich's cries of anguish, or had Deus somehow created a living creature with a soul and essence of its own? As the figure flailed helplessly on the floor, Deus decided that he didn't care. He was out to kill a real human, so why should he care about a piece of plastic?

With renewed hatred, Deus pinched the figurine's leg and dragged it back towards the centre of the room, ignoring its puny attempts to fight back, little fists bouncing harmlessly off his skin. Once Deus had hauled his victim across the floor, he held the struggling figure down with one hand, and pounded his other fist into the Action Man's head. Although the plastic avatar yielded no blood, Deus was sure that Rich would be in a bad way after the crushing blow. Lifting his fist once more, Deus felt a futile kick underneath his palm. If that was all the strength Rich had, his demise would be quicker than Deus had anticipated.

Grinning to himself, Deus slammed his fist down once more, only to be caught off guard. The miniature figurine forced its way from underneath his palm and rolled away to the side, Deus smashing the floor so hard that the wooden floorboard cracked and splintered as he struck it. Angered that the figurine had avoided what was to be the final blow simply because of his own carelessness, Deus shot out both his hands and grabbed the avatar from where it was standing, regarding him fearfully from across the room. Once more, the figure let out its high pitched wailing as Deus waved it uncontrollably, shaking little Rich with a vengeful energy that could rip the plastic arms from the moulded body.

Raising the toy above his head, Deus began a twisted dance of rotation, manoeuvring his hands and inverting the figure with malicious precision, each turn designed to cause as much pain and discomfort as possible. It would have looked to an outsider like an elegant art form if it weren't for the continued cries of the Action Man, the shrill notes of pain cancelling any delusions of sophistication. *This was going to be quite interesting,* thought Deus. He could use this torture to test the limits of humanity. How long could the figure endure such torment before the real Rich Benson's spine gave in and snapped like a matchstick? As soon as Deus had allowed this thought, the Action Man seemed to stop struggling. Was it over? Had the body of his murderer taken all that it possibly could? Deus couldn't help but smile as he ended one of the lives that had ended his.

There was the slightest whisper, perhaps little Rich's last breath escaping from the fragile body, and the air in the room seemed to draw itself in, closing down to honour the passing of its supposedly all-powerful representative. Shaking his head solemnly, Deus waited for the satisfaction that he assumed would come once Rich was dead. It had to, he would be one step closer to being the only Wiccan on the planet, the sole wielder of elemental power. To feel nothing would be absurd.

The air in the room exploded outwards as the Action Man screamed once more. What was left of the furniture shook, and the scraps of poster fluttered against the walls. Deus' hands seared as a network of lacerations forked across his palms like red lightning, causing him to discard the figure in shock. He felt pain! Rich had damaged him, not only making him bleed, but making him feel it too. Rather than falling to the floor, the avatar floated gracefully, arms outstretched in triumph, as if purposefully mocking the Spirit Elemental, but Deus did not care that his captor had escaped, nor did he care how it had happened, he was blinded by rage, pure and simple. After watching the avatar hop gently to the floor, Deus cruelly grabbed its arm, and twisted until it snapped.

Chapter 29 – Haematite Secrets

For the whole of the next day, Deus sat in the pitch darkness of his room, deep in contemplation. He could have easily smashed the Action Man to pieces and ended Rich's miserable life, but he was so infuriated that he had left the little man to die a slow and agonising death in the cold forest night.

Now that he had paused to think, he began to wonder about his creation. Since clawing his way out of the ground, all he had felt was the need for self-preservation, but where did this drive come from? It was as if all of the knowledge was locked away in the back of his mind, like the powers he had, but unlike his powers the mystery of his origins had remained inaccessible. Chase Rivers had been killed when Matt, Josh, Scott and Rich had initiated themselves as Wiccans. Judging from the scrap of paper he had found in the clearing, he had been the necessary sacrifice to make the ritual work, but that still didn't explain how he had come back to life as Deus, or what Deus actually was. It was this that he now sat trying to understand.

Every so often, a flicker of memory would flash into Deus' mind, but like fireworks they were gone in an instant. There was waking up in some sort of hall, blinking the light out of long-unused eyes. Four figures were standing over him, he guessed they must be Rich and the others, except they weren't dressed in the usual hoodies and jeans. They weren't even wearing their Wiccan cloaks - instead the four were adorned in old-fashioned armour like gladiators, great plumed helmets resting on blurred faces. The vision was accompanied by a complex mix of emotions, swirling and twisting around each other in an inseparable compound. There was an immense feeling of pride, entwined with a heavy sense of guilt, shame and defiance. It was hard for Deus to sort the feelings into any sort of chronological order but at some point he had felt them all until they had become his core, black and dangerous.

In another flash of his history, there was a book and a young man surrounded by a circle of stone pillars. He did not recognise the man, but his clothes and hairstyle were both very dated. Maybe the 1600s? Maybe even earlier. But Deus was sure that was impossible. It couldn't be one of Chase's memories unless it was some sort of fancy dress party, but when would the pathetic loser ever have been invited to one of those? He saw himself tuck a velvet-wrapped package into the cover of the book before handing it over to the mysterious man, then flickering onwards through the vision.

"They kill the host, I kill them and choose my warriors," he whispered without even understanding the words.

Next was an image of a vast room, like some sort of meeting room covered in bodies. Men in suits stained dark crimson, and blood on his own hands. It was as if Deus had lived many different lives, all of them leading towards something, but how would he know if he had reached what he was supposed to be looking for? All of the thoughts had given him a headache, and he wasn't sure if he was supposed to be able to have headaches, which made him angrier.

A loud knocking disturbed the Spirit Elemental from his tempered musings. It took a second bout of thumping before Deus realised it was his own front door. *Who would be knocking for him?* Unless it was someone for the charred remains that used to be Heather. Deus cursed to himself before clambering to his feet and shaking his legs about to regain some feeling in them. Stalking to the window, he

could just make out the top of somebody's head. The hair
was black and cut short, and from the way the person
stood, he could tell that it was male, but there were no
other distinguishable features that Deus could place. He
turned and made for the stairs, half expecting the knocking
to sound again as the man grew more impatient. The Spirit
Elemental was already forming a game in his mind that
would ease the torment in his mind. He would hear this
man's excuse for calling at the house, and judging the
quality of the reason, the caller would be punished
accordingly. A smile spread across his face as he
approached the door, but he could already see that the man
had vanished. *Damn it!* If only he had been quicker, he
could have had some fun.

As he was turning to return to his solitude, Deus saw
that a note had been posted through the letterbox. It was
written in untidy and hurried scrawl, probably done just
now as the man leaned against the door. *"I need you. I will
find you."* Deus screwed up the scrap of paper angrily. Just
what he didn't need now was more cryptic information that
didn't make sense. And the fact that it didn't make sense
was even more infuriating. This in turn led back to the
question of his origins, and the cause of his incessant
pounding headache. With a yell of anguish, he swept his
arm across the hall table, spilling and smashing the contents
onto the ash stained carpet. Fragments of vase and wilted
flowers settled as he stormed back to his room.

What he really needed was something to jog his
memory, something that could possibly hint at how he
came to be this way. All of a sudden, Deus rolled his eyes.
How could he have been so ignorant? The Book of
Shadows would help him out, after all that was where the
initiation ritual had come from. If only he had thought to
look at it last time he was in Rich's bedroom. Opening the

door with a nod, Deus hurried out into the darkening evening. There were two suited men walking down the street as the Spirit Elemental raced along, forcing his way past them regally. As he swept away, he didn't notice one of them take a notebook from his pocket and begin scribbling.

After ten minutes of stalking across the town, Deus once more stood in the cluttered room, absorbing the resonances that remained there. Of course, Rich's was the strongest, but the others were also very prominent. It echoed the atmosphere of the typical schoolboy hangout and Deus could imagine them all in there late at night, talking or watching television and smoking.

It did not take long for Deus to find the Book of Shadows, and to his relief it did not have the same simple incantation that had protected the Air Elemental's transcript notebook. After flicking past Linking and Binding rituals Deus settled on The Initiation Ritual. With a jolt, another image flashed across his mind's eye. A hand was writing out the very same ritual onto a blank page. He must be picking up on when Rich copied his book from the original, Deus thought to himself as he scanned the words that had led to his creation. As Deus reached the bottom of the ritual, he noticed that the last line was missing, torn from the page with careful precision. After delving into his pocket, he pulled out the scrap of paper that he had found in the clearing, already knowing that it would fit perfectly onto the bottom of the page. "The willing fifth, you must sacrifice to gain true power." So who had torn the line off, and why? Had the line been removed before or after the accident on Halloween? Perhaps Deus should have questioned Rich and Josh in detail instead of lashing out at them. Deus slammed the book shut - it would be of no further help until he had found out the truth behind the missing line of the ritual.

Sighing deeply, Deus surveyed the room once more, everything glowing with an aura of yellow, a sign of Rich's presence. It was interesting to see which items the young man had favoured the most, judging by the strength of the aura. The clothes that littered the floor and the bed all emanated a strong golden colour, whereas some of the weighty textbooks looked like they had never been touched. There were also wisps of blue and red indicating places where Josh and Matt had stood or sat. If only there was music, this could have been a smoke-filled disco, he mused.

Suddenly, he noticed something interesting. Amongst the faint swirls of yellow, blue and red, there was a strong pulse of green radiating from a spot somewhere on the shelf. Green meant Scott, and the deep vivid shade meant that whatever was on the shelf had been touched by him recently. It wasn't just a graze either, he had held onto this object tightly. His curiosity baited, Deus walked over to where the aura originated. It was a fist-sized lump of stone, slightly heart shaped with veins of deep red running through it. Deus recognised it as Bloodstone, a tool commonly used for storing information. Scott had hidden something inside the Bloodstone! Maybe it was a message for Rich, in which case Scott obviously did not know what had happened to his friend. With a smirk, Deus reached out and touched the Bloodstone, hoping to see an amusing show of sickening emotions as Scott wondered where his companion was.

As soon as warm flesh touched cold stone, a moving tableau projected itself out of the Bloodstone and into the room, the figures occasionally flickering like holograms and old film. Scott was sitting on the floor, leaning back against the bed and Matt was there too, staring sceptically at him.

Deus narrowed his eyes malevolently as he saw that the other two were also there. Rich was heavily bandaged and sitting on the bed, but Josh looked unharmed. So both of them had survived. Deus clenched his teeth so hard that one of them cracked. With disgust, he spat the bloody lump onto the carpet as the scene unfolded before him.

"Chase is too powerful!" cried Scott, panicking. "There's no way we can stop him on our own." Deus cringed as he heard Chase's name. He had told Josh specifically that his name was now Deus. He hadn't even had the decency to tell the others: as if not dying wasn't bad enough, he had simply gone on calling him Chase. Nobody said anything for a few seconds, until Scott piped up again, calmer this time. "If only there was something we could do. Some place we could go."

"We don't really know how Chase managed to survive," said Rich, looking down at him knowingly. "Perhaps we should go to the clearing as soon as possible, see if we can find some clues." Deus snorted as he saw Matt shake his head. It was obvious what they were doing, they were putting on a show just for him.

"Um….what time should we go?" asked Josh after what seemed like an age. The Water pest looked like he was internally duelling with himself. *Yes*, thought Deus. What time do you want to be humiliated when I don't show?

"Oh I dunno, how about tonight at, let's say midnight?" Matt said casually.

"Ok, it's a deal!" exclaimed Scott happily, and the picture show flickered into non-existence. So they were going to be at the clearing at midnight were they? All four of them? Alive and well? Ha! They could freeze to death under the cold November moon before he would give them what they wanted. Deus would disappoint them to give them false hope, then the torture would start again to an even more ferocious degree. No more leaving people for dead. Deus would not move until he saw each and every one of them die. With a yell of rage, Deus threw the Bloodstone as hard as he could at the opposite wall, where it smashed apart, littering the carpet with fragments of stone and chippings of plaster. To his surprise, another image shimmered to life from the ruins of the Bloodstone.

Scott was standing on his own, staring straight at Deus. He had a mournful yet defiant look on his face as he began to speak.

"I knew you wouldn't fall for it. Matt was too obvious, but we had to try," he began, with a sigh. "We aren't going to the clearing, we'll be at the compass points. I'm assuming you know where those are, as you know pretty much everything else about us." Deus frowned as Scott went on. He was intrigued as to why his enemy was giving the game away so readily. "It's odd to think that after all the damage you've done, here I am talking to you like an old friend. But let me assure you of one thing, you will never be one of us. I don't know why or how you came back, but we *made* you. You'll never be anything more than some *thing* we created by accident, simple as that. And if that's not enough," the young man glared. "I *knew* something was going to go wrong that night. I saw a sign, and I still went ahead with it, that's how worthless you are. If you were waiting for a "come get me", that was it." Scott vanished, leaving Deus fuming. People did not speak to Gods like that! This fragile mortal had challenged his spiritual prowess and would pay with his life. Slow and painful was out of the question, Scott had now sealed the fate of the four: they were all going to die tonight in a blaze of retribution. The clock on the wall showed 11:28, that left just over half an hour to get to the forest and the North Compass point where Scott Fielding would meet his death.

Ed's Downfall
November 16

Chapter 30 – Medicine Men

The hospital room was bare save for a single card. Ed Russell was lying in the bed, the fleece blankets worn with use tucked tightly around his waist, not quite covering the bandages that crossed his chest.

The two lowest ribs on his left side were cracked, the strips of linen acting as a binding harness to keep them in place whilst they healed. The university had been very organised in getting him to hospital, and thinking of a rational explanation for how he had ended up through a window. They had blamed alcohol, although it was clear that Ed was anything but drunk. His parents had driven over as soon as they had been contacted and regrettably, their son had fallen back on the university's excuse, preferring the simple booze fuelled route through the glass rather than the bizarre truth. At least it was more believable, Ed thought, remembering back to his A Levels when he would gloss over the anguish of coming out with a heavy coat of vodka. It was a wonder his parents still spoke to him really, considering the amount of times they had dragged him home in the early hours of the morning, crying and nonsensical.

He wasn't sure he really understood the truth himself. He had told Chase how he felt, then remembered his back slamming into the grass outside the print room, a thousand diamonds sandwiched between his flesh and the soil. It also seemed to be raining fire, but that part must have been shock.

The confusing thing was he couldn't actually remember Chase hitting him that hard – certainly not

enough force to knock him back so far. Ed had tried to
convince himself that he had been leaning over, or caught
in the middle of a turn, but deep down he knew that wasn't
it. He had been standing completely still, watching Chase
deal with the unfamiliar feeling of affection.

At this moment, the door opened. Ed looked up,
expecting to see his parents or maybe even his sister, but
instead it was a nurse flanked by two official looking men
in expensive suits. Both men had a small lapel pin – a
purple circle with a silver S.

"Mr Russell," the Nurse began. "These men are
from Spyrus." She paused for effect, as if she had just
introduced royalty. When Ed continued to look thoroughly
unimpressed, she continued. "The company is piloting
some of the painkillers we put you on. These gentlemen
would just like to ask you a few questions, if that's alright?"

Before the young man could even answer, the nurse
nodded at the suited visitors and left, closing the door
behind her without a second glance. Ed would have said
yes anyway, anything to stop him dwelling on the confusing
events that had befallen him. One of the men perched on
the end of the bed, whilst the other hovered at the foot and
it struck Ed that they resembled the 'good cop, bad cop'
pairing that he was familiar with from his Media Studies
course. One man to chat casually, the other to break even
more ribs if necessary.

"So what can I help you with?"

"Like the nurse said, we are just here to ask you a
few questions about the painkillers." This was Good Cop,
not as warm as his stereotyped counterparts. Ed nodded,
suddenly wishing he had asserted himself and told them to
leave. "What dosage are you on?"

Ed gave as many answers as he could, whilst Good
Cop rattled off the questions in businesslike monotone.

Bad Cop barely moved throughout the process, and it became easy to simply forget he was in the room. The enquiries drew to a halt, and finally Bad Cop spoke.

"So what happened to you?" he asked in a voice that suggested he was straining to sound as casual as he could. Ed decided he might as well tell the truth this time, as the strangers were in no position to judge him. If anything they might think he had gone mental as a side effect of their drugs – at least that would be a refreshing dose of humour after the mind numbing interrogation.

"A boy blasted me through a window," he said with a wry smile. It felt relieving to voice his absurd theory.

"Chase Rivers?"

Ed jerked upright suddenly, sending waves of throbbing pain pulsing across his chest. "How did you...?" The two men glanced at each other, a smirk of satisfaction creeping across Bad Cop's face. He leaned forwards, placing his stocky arms either side of Ed's legs, a viper wrapped in finest silk.

"Did you see anything? Flashes or sparks?" Bad Cop now had a hungry gleam in his eyes, and the young man found himself shrinking back against his pillow. Maybe the flaming raindrops weren't shock after all? Ed hesitated, unsure of what to say, how much to reveal. Bad Cop didn't wait. "And where is Chase now?"

"How should I know?" Ed snapped, thinking about how their encounter *could* have turned out. In the ideal world, he would know exactly where Chase was now – at his side. "Look, what is this about?" Bad Cop tilted his head, caught off guard. Good Cop seized the opportunity to jump in with a hastily prepared explanation.

"Chase is also on one of our products," he blurted. "We just wondered if you witnessed any adverse... effects?"

"No I haven't. I'd like you to leave now." After a cowing glance from Good Cop, both men nodded, their demeanour returning to the previous air of casual interest.

"Well if you remember anything, please let us know," Good Cop said, offering a business card. When Ed made no effort to take it, the man placed the small rectangle on the corner of the bed. Both Spyrus men left the room, but Ed could still feel the heat of their excitement long after the footsteps had faded from the corridor. He had the feeling that as soon as they got outside, both of them would launch excitedly into conversation, or perhaps pull out their mobiles and phone their bosses.

It was funny, Ed mused, how even a simple conversation with two strangers became all about Chase. *It all came back to Chase.* Ed couldn't get him out of his mind – if anything, his obsession had only heightened since their encounter but there was no reason for it to. Any normal person would never have spoken to Chase again after that, but the young man knew this was far from a normal attack.

Ed took a quick glance at the door, listening intently to be sure there were no approaching footsteps in the corridor. When satisfied, he gently peeled back the bandages, clenching his teeth to stop himself from crying out. With each layer, the mauve bruising darkened, a discoloured rose against a pale canvas, blooming out from the point where Chase had hit him.

He unwrapped yet another layer of linen until the bandages became loose enough and slipped down into his lap, and Ed gasped in shock. This was the first time he had seen the full extent of his injury, and to his horror, in the centre of the damage was a perfect hand print, shining raw where the skin had been grazed.

As he looked at the mark, the purple shadows seemed to writhe beneath his skin, twisting and spreading as if they were taking over his body, consuming him. He tapped the palm of the hand scar with his index finger, and was pleasantly surprised as his entire arm began to tingle softly. It was as if the wound was charged somehow, or a bit of Chase remained there to remind Ed of him.

The young man lay back and closed his eyes, his own palm resting over the imprint of Chase's.

Chapter 31 – The Other Side

The next day, after another check from his doctor, Ed was
discharged from the hospital. Of course he lad a lengthy list
of prohibitions – no sports, no alcohol, no operating heavy
machinery. *Pity,* the young man mused wryly. *Pissed Tractor
Ball would have to wait a few weeks.* Remarkably, the doctor –
another employee of Spyrus judging by his lapel pin –
hadn't even commented on the spread of the bruising, even
though it now resembled a drop of violet ink swirling in
pale rose water.

As it was, he now stood in the hospital car park, the
grey morning chill biting his skin. Ed was wandering what
to do first, a conflict of desires battling inside his head. On
one hand, all he wanted to do was go home, stick on his
Crystal Homicide EP and lie in bed with a huge slab of
chocolate, but he could feel something tugging him in the
opposite direction. It was like there was a compass needle
threaded into his heart, pointing resolutely towards the
street where Chase lived. If he didn't follow it, the needle
might spin out of control and rip his heart to pieces.

Ed began to walk through the identical streets until
at last, the city centre apartments and shops gave way to the
more suburban rows of houses with manicured gardens
and territorial fences and walls. It was funny how man
staked out his land with ornaments – it seemed that
security had fallen to decoration. With each step, the aching
in the young man's soul grew until he could feel his
heartbeat fluttering as if it had gained an extra beat from
somewhere. He rounded the corner of the next street and
his insides churned, even though this warning was
unnecessary. Long ago, when he had first taken a liking to
his shy colleague, he had found out where he had lived,
even making excuses to walk past the house, hoping to

catch a glimpse. He remembered the evening when he had seen the object of his affection briefly as he was closing his curtains, but it had been enough to fuel Ed's dreams for the next week.

He now stood outside Chase's house, shuffling nervously from foot to foot, his chest pounding with excitement and need. The house was still and all the curtains were drawn. Ed knew that Chase only lived with his mother, but he had never seen her. There was no car in the driveway, but the young man did not know if this was auspicious or not. Perhaps Mrs Rivers didn't drive?

He stepped onto the front path, taking it further than he ever had – previously he hadn't dared to be on the same side of the road, let alone actually step onto the property.

Ed knocked once and waited. Nothing stirred, not even a sound of footsteps hurrying down stairs or inner doors opening. Almost too quickly, the young man pounded the door again, craning his neck to see through the frosted glass into the entrance hallway. When still there was no answer, a wave of panic swept over Ed. What if the two of them had just missed each other, and Chase would never know that he was here? Perhaps Chase was at this very moment on his way to find Ed and apologise, then when he returned he thought Ed didn't care? The enamoured young man couldn't risk that, so he hastily pulled an old receipt from his pocket and scrawled a message as best he could whilst leaning against the wall with broken ribs. *"I need you. I will find you."* Ed didn't bother signing the note as he pushed it through the letterbox. Surely Chase would be feeling the same gut wrenching tugging wouldn't he? They were connected now: they had to be. It was the only explanation for what he was feeling.

As Ed was wandering aimlessly back along the street, passing through the shadows of the beech trees that lined the road and feeling like he had left part of himself behind on Chase's doorstep, he was struck by a fleeting idea. What if all of this was a test? What if Chase was making sure that Ed meant what he had said in the print room, treating him mean to keep him keen as it were? Well there was no way that Ed was going to be subdued or led astray from his goal. If Chase wanted a show of dedication then Ed would give it to him.

Around twenty minutes later, the young man crossed the threshold of the UCE campus, heading towards the halls of residence where he lived. All the halls at this end of the campus were named after famous women – archaeologists and the like – and Ed lived in Van Ristell Hall.

Up ahead, there was some sort of commotion outside Garnsworthy Hall. He couldn't make much out but it looked as if there was a lot of junk spread out on the grass, with huddles of people hovering at the side. A couple of the figures were wearing the tell tale uniform of Campus Security, so it must have been relatively serious.

He drew nearer and noticed his feet starting to squelch into the grass, as if the area had just suffered a localised torrential downpour. Gradually, all of the spectators filtered away and the security officers strolled back in the direction of their small portakabin that served as their base of operations, busy scribbling into their notebooks.

Only one person remained, hanging around the debris that Ed could now distinguish as somebody's belongings. There was part of a chair; heaps of sodden mush that had once been paper, and various items of clothing sprawled on the waterlogged ground like emaciated and twisted bodies. A ground floor window nearby was broken – a burglary? The remaining figure scooped something off the ground and tugged it into an ill-fitting hoodie, and that was when Ed recognised him. *One of the four.*

There was a group that he had often seen around campus although two of them weren't actually students. One of them was the bassist from *Crystal Homicide*, who he had reviewed once for The Rag, but the other three, he didn't know. They had always kept to themselves, but Ed knew for a fact that Chase had been desperately trying to break in with them. Ed had often seen him ignored and abandoned, usually resulting in Chase standing alone, watching them as they walked away, talking conspiratorially. Countless times, Ed had wished he had the courage to walk up to the lonely teen and put a comforting arm round his shoulder. Despite their constant coldness towards Chase, perhaps this one might know something? Ed hurried forwards.

"You! You know Chase." The guy jumped slightly before whirling round. He looked cold, and out of place in his too long hoodie and jeans that were tight around the shins. Ed saw him look up and down, taking in the bandages that were visible at the bottom of Ed's top.

"Yes," he stated.

Ed stepped forward eagerly. "I know you do," he began. "I've seen you lot together. Do you know where he is?" He was conscious that he was speaking too quickly, but even the slightest bit of information about Chase would do. He just wanted to find him. To Ed's dismay, the other man shook his head.

"What happened to you?" he asked, changing the subject with a nod towards Ed's injuries.

"Chase broke my ribs," Ed stated as he gingerly touched his bandages. He was getting impatient, and idle chat was wasting precious time. Time he could be spending with Chase. "He wasn't himself," he added as an afterthought, not wanting this outsider to think that Chase was some sort of monster. There had to be a good reason for his violent outbreak after all.

"Yeah, I've noticed that too. So why do you want to find him?"

"I need to apologise," Ed said, noticing the other man's incredulous expression. "I think it was my fault," he continued.

"What do you mean?"

"He was normal one minute, then he just lashed out, like he was a completely different person. I think I somehow turned him into something bad."

Josh shook his head. "What did you say to him?" he asked.

"It doesn't matter." Ed was now certain that this young man didn't know where Chase was, and couldn't tell him anything useful. He tapped his feet impatiently, hoping for a pause where he could cut the conversation off.

"Well you've just got to put it behind you. I'm sure he will be back to normal soon, then you two can sort it out and make up or whatever." At this, Ed's temper began to rise. This wasn't some stupid high school crush! The plebeian in front of him obviously had never experienced anything as real as the connection that he and Chase now shared. This was love!

"You don't understand," Ed said awkwardly. "I looked into his eyes and… I've got to find him. I can't stop thinking about him. Do you know where he is?" Again the other man shook his head. "I'll find him. I have to know what he did to me. It's like he took something, stole my heart. I'm not complete without him…" Ed's voice petered out as he turned, downcast. The other man stepped forwards and grabbed his arm.

"Look, Ed?" he began. Ed didn't question how this guy knew his name, after all his picture was in every issue of The Rag. "Promise me something?" Ed watched him curiously as he continued. "Promise you won't go looking for Chase. When he's ready, he'll come and find you, I'm sure of it. But for now, he's done some things that… well, you're not the only person he's hurt, and people might be after him."

"To hurt him?" Ed said wide-eyed. His mind flashed back to the men at the hospital, although they were professionals – why would they want to hurt an innocent teenager? But they had been asking questions about him, and Ed couldn't think of anybody else. "To hurt Chase? No, they can't, I need him." He continued to babble as the other man increased his grip.

"Ok, you are freaking me out now," he said, a concerned look in his eyes. Ed tried to squirm out of his grip, unwilling to hear what he knew was coming. This guy was going to denounce Chase, to say he wasn't worth it. Maybe he was jealous and wanted Chase for himself. *I'd rather die than see anyone else with him,* Ed thought scathingly. "Whatever Chase said to you," the other young man continued. "Whatever he did to you, *he wasn't himself.* You have to remember that. Now go home and cool off. Do anything but don't get mixed up in this." Ed broke his grip, noticing the sincerity burning in his features, like a dormant power waiting to be awoken.

"That look, you have it too," Ed commented, half in admiration and half in disgust. He was impressed, but at the same time, didn't want anybody else to share what made Chase unique. "Not as much as Chase, but it's there.

Like something boiling away behind your eyes." Ed paused
for a second then writhed in pain, his face contorting
against his will. It was like his body had momentarily been
taken over by something else desperate to be heard. "The
Gods are coming, and they are vexed!" he spat, before
gasping. Ed looked down at his own hands, expecting them
to rise up and act without his consent as his mouth had
done, but they remained still. With a final horrified glance
at the other guy, he turned and ran, head full of confusion,
determination and fear.

Chapter 32 – Depraved And Fatal

Ed had not stopped until he was safely shut in his room, curled on his bed with his arms wrapped around his knees. He had cried until his eyes were dry and red, his face stinging as his body forced out tears that weren't there. He felt like he was stuck in an ocean of despair, torn between the two tides – high desire and low fear.

At times, all he could think about was Chase and being with him, but then those feelings subsided and he was overwhelmed by the hopelessness of the truth. *This wasn't natural.* His wound was abnormal. The Chase that had cast him so roughly aside was not the well-mannered boy he had fallen for, and he knew it. *Something was very wrong.* Was there any way to break free from this hold? Ed didn't want to say the word magic, but it felt like he was no longer in control. Like he was poisoned somehow.

To make it worse, the bruising across his chest had spread again, now creeping around the curve of his ribs to the right and onto his back. On the left side, the tendrils of deep purple had crept up and were now perched on his shoulder, eagerly waiting for their chance to flow sinuously downwards and consume his left arm. The patterns looked like veins shining through his skin, and perhaps that was what it was – perhaps his blood was contaminated with lust and desire and his body was falling to temptation.

He rolled awkwardly onto his feet, feeling his cracked ribs grating inside him as his torso twisted. He grimaced as he looked over to his bedside table, which held a single framed picture. At the beginning of the year, all The Rag staff members had had their pictures taken for the back page of paper. Ed had sneaked the original photo of Chase to keep for himself, and many a night had he stared into those clear grey eyes, waiting for sleep to take him.

Well no longer. He swept the picture forcefully off the table where it landed heavily onto the floor. Chase was still smiling his hesitant grin even as the cracked frame laced spider webs over his youthful features. In a moment of clarity, Ed decided he was done with his fantasy boy – now he just wanted to be free of this heart-wrenching obsession. He was going to confront Chase not for love, but for answers.

Half an hour later, and Ed was standing once more at the front door to the Rivers house. The afternoon sun was fading and the sky was taking the indigo tint of early evening. He had knocked again, and like before, he was left standing there. *I'm not going to give up this time,* he thought resolutely as he thumbed through his wallet and pulled out a bankcard. The lock on the front door was simple, and Ed was determined to get in whether Chase was there or not.

He slipped the card into the sliver of space between the door and the fame, sliding it downwards towards the locking bolt whilst keeping a watchful eye over his shoulder for anybody alerted to his criminal actions. After manoeuvring the card side to side for a few seconds, he was greeted with the reassuring clicking sound as the lock slid open. Ed pushed the door and slid inside, easing it shut behind him.

The first thing he noticed was the smell. It was coming from a door to the left and it was the acrid aroma of something burnt beyond recognition. He had been there many times himself when he had put toast under the grill and forgotten about it. Chase was obviously no better at cooking than he was at responding normally to confessions of attraction.

He skirted past the kitchen door without looking inside and headed straight for the stairs. If there was anything of use here, it would be in Chase's room, which as a result of his numerous reasons to pass by the house, he knew was at the front of the upper floor. He flitted stealthily across the landing and braced himself before stepping into the place where Chase spent most of his time.

Ed's eyes widened as he stepped into the darkness. Everything was pitch black, the walls, the floors, even the velvet curtains that hung over the window blocked out all light, seemingly sucking it out of the sky and swallowing it. He had never figured Chase for living like this, but you never could tell from looks alone, after all, Chase didn't *look* like a violent dick but here Ed was, broken ribs and all. He immediately felt guilty for referring to his paramour as a dick, and could sense the unquenchable and unreasoning desire rising within him once more. It seemed that his depressive mood was ebbing, the waves of lust threatening to drown him again.

He shook his head and busied himself with looking around the room for any clues as to what might have happened to the boy who lived here, and what in turn had been passed on to Ed, the unwitting victim of... he still wasn't sure. There were a lot of torn scraps of paper littering the floor like fallen leaves, and as Ed knelt to rifle through them, he saw that they bizarrely had poster prints on one side, and photographs printed on the other. He collected a handful of images and sat cross-legged in the centre of the room as he flicked though them.

They were mainly pictures that he himself had asked Chase to take for The Rag, a picture of the new block they were building for the Science Department, the captain of the chess team who had just become national champion and other such trivial items. There was even a picture in which Ed recognised himself caught ostensibly peeking out from behind a tree in the background. It was picture of those four again, although why Chase had bothered taking a photograph of them, he couldn't imagine. It was like Chase was blind to their true feelings about him, couldn't see their faces when his back was turned, and didn't know that they paid him no heed when he wasn't there. *Out of sight, out of mind,* he mused. *Just like me to him,* he added bitterly. The mood was still low enough to allow him a passing practical thought. The picture had rusty looking stains on it, but apart from that, there was nothing out of the ordinary.

Disappointed, he dropped the pictures and returned to looking around. There was an Action Man kicked under the bed, and when Ed retrieved it, he found its arm hanging limply, snapped beyond repair. He sat it gently against the wall and continued his search, moving methodically around the room, hoping for some sort of clue, but always left empty handed. There was a bizarre candle holder on the windowsill that looked like a specimen jar full of crimson water, but if it meant anything, it remained a mystery. As he searched, he was aware of the wrenching of his soul becoming fiercer, probably because of his proximity to so many of Chase's belongings. They seemed to amplify his own emptiness tenfold.

Eventually only the chest of drawers beneath the window remained untouched. Ed walked over to it, feeling the heat within him rise even more. There was a line of what looked like ash across the top surface, and he held his hand over them, absorbing the energy that seemed to radiate from them. He opened the first drawer – empty. He had only two chances left to succeed in his quest for knowledge.

The second drawer yielded an uneven pile of old bank statements and university letters. There was also Chase's passport, which had no stamps in it, but boasted a cute picture of him with longer hair that covered one of his eyes. Ed pocketed the passport and slid the drawer shut, his palm gripping the handle of the bottom drawer eagerly. He took a deep breath before gently pulling it open.

Pants. Of all the things, Ed had discovered a draw full of neatly folded boxer briefs. His heart first skipped a beat, and then beat so hard that the young man could feel his ribs scraping together again. He knew his search was over because even if he wanted to, he would be physically unable to root out anything that might incriminate his unrelenting passion.

He reached in and grabbed a random pair, squeezing them tightly in his fist and revelling in the smooth texture of the cotton that seemed to flow across his fingers like he was squeezing a ripe piece of fruit that oozed sweetness. He breathed them in deeply, laundry fresh but the unmistakable essence of the person who inhabited them still present.

Lost to the world, Ed clutched the shorts to his chest and fell back onto the bed, sinking into the duvet, completely surrounded by Chase. He tucked his hand into his waistband and closed his eyes…

In The End
November 17

Chapter 33 – Searching For Humanity

It was midnight in the forest. At the most Eastern point of the trees, the moonlight was forcefully illuminating Altair as he fumbled with his elemental necklace. It was made a lot harder by the fact that his arm was still in a sling, but eventually he managed to slip the cord over his head and place the amulet on the soft earth before his knees. Next, he set up a small tripod and poured some pale yellow liquid into a glass dish. The Air Oil quickly began to send plumes of rosemary-scented smoke twirling and dancing around the tree trunks, oblivious to the sincerity of their purpose.

Altair took comfort in the knowledge that at the other compass points, Dylan, Dex and Phoenix were doing the exact same thing.

"Ina kioymarinatoh firel paroywonelrai oyfia Ainarai tohoy firel kiunasarel oyfia firel fioynarai," he whispered, hoping that he had got the words right and that his broken nose hadn't distorted any of the syllables. Altair leant back on his heels, casting around for some sort of sign. When explaining the plan, nobody had told him what would happen to show if it had worked or not. Unless something had gone wrong? What if even now, he was the only one of them left alive, and Chase was stalking his way maliciously through the forest, intent on finishing the job he started previously? Altair had only just managed to stave off the ethereal hands - he was certainly in no shape for a face to face confrontation with the Spirit Elemental. Altair sat back and waited for a moment, before tutting quietly to himself and picking his way carefully into the trees. Once more, he would stumble blindly into the darkness.

On the opposite side of the forest, at the West compass point, Dylan was kneeling in front of his own elemental necklace, the strong aroma of lavender and willow bark stinging his nostrils slightly.

"Ina kioymarinatoh firel paroywonelrai... shit!" he started, as two of his candles sputtered out. His left side was instantly plunged into darkness, and Dylan was constantly aware that the clock was ticking as he untangled himself from his cloak, fishing for matches. He couldn't help feeling a little cheated, after all this was *his* plan and he was probably the only one who was having trouble with it. This should have been his chance for glory, to displace Dex as the plan man. Instead the other three were probably standing in the clearing right now, arms folded wondering why Chase had got away because he hadn't done his part of the ritual in time.

Once the candles were relit, he reeled off the correct phrase in hesitant Theban Locte. As soon as the last word had left his lips, a column of blue energy shot from the centre of his circle and snaked away through the blackness, crackling and hissing with pure power.

Altair stumbled in surprise as a blazing yellow stream of energy shot past his head. That had to be the ritual working! His confidence renewed, he was sure now that at least the others had managed to perform their parts of the ritual unharmed. Maybe things were going to turn out alright after all. With increased vigour, Altair made his way through the trees, no longer worrying about getting lost. He simply had to follow the glowing aftermath of the Air Energy he had released. It would lead him to wherever Chase was held captive. He picked up his pace, breaking into a run as he crashed through the tangles of bracken that lay across his path and then he collided with a dark figure, also hurrying through the darkness. All jubilation and hope

that Altair was feeling was knocked out of him as he fell
badly onto his broken hand in a tangle of cloaks. Tears
were forced from his eyes as he gritted his teeth, trying not
to shout out as the icy needles of pain shot up to his
bandaged shoulder. A grim thought floated into Altair's
consciousness. What if he had collided with Chase himself?
He could have been on his way to finish him off and now
Altair had just presented himself on a silver platter. A
bandaged, mud-stained silver platter.

Altair was torn from his thoughts as a hand started
groping across his chest, grasping a handful of material and
pulling upwards. Panicking, he did the first thing he could
think of and screamed at the top of his lungs. The air
blasted out of him like a shockwave, and the other guy was
thrown backwards, his cloak swirling outwards amidst a
shower of falling leaves, the dry curls cracking and
disintegrating in the sonic onslaught. The mysterious figure
cried out as he fell to the ground, arms outstretched in
defence.

"Ouch! Christ, dude, it's me!"

Altair sighed with guilty relief as he recognised the
voice. "Sorry Josh... I mean Dylan." Altair chuckled
slightly as he eased himself off the ground. Dylan tutted
with mock disapproval.

"What would Dex say if he could hear you now?
Using the wrong names and everything! And what was up
with the air force? I was trying to help you up, you idiot!"
Altair blushed as Dylan gave him a reprimanding slap on
the back.

"I thought you were Chase. Plus one of my eyes is
bruised shut, and it's dark so really I'm not to blame."

"I'm starting to wish I was Chase - that hurt, man."
The two of them hugged unashamedly, both aware that
either one of them could have discovered the other's body.

Joking around was the only way they could get over the immense feeling of gratitude that the other one was alive.

Suddenly, both men recoiled at the same moment. A deep burning sensation was in the pit of Dylan's stomach, and he knew that Altair was feeling the same. It was Phoenix's calling candles. Had the ritual worked? Dylan closed his eyes and rotated his head, searching for the ethereal essence that Phoenix would be emanating. Within seconds, he had found it, and closer than he had expected, the soft red glow was only about fifty metres through the trees ahead of them. Dylan opened his eyes and looked worriedly at Altair, who was staring gravely back.

"Phoenix…" he said emptily. It was as if time had suddenly rushed upon them. Phoenix was calling and what they found in the clearing would be the end one way or another. Either Chase would be contained and Phoenix and Dex would be waiting, or the monster was victorious and Phoenix had managed to light the candles with his dying breath. Altair nodded shakily through his bruises and the two of them headed cautiously towards the clearing.

Phoenix was lying on his back, eyes closed, trying to block out the excruciating pain lancing through his spine. The only sound in the clearing was the soft crackling of the calling candles he had lit, permeated occasionally by the metallic pounding as Chase tried once more to force his way out of his imprisonment in the air. Each time he touched the shimmering violet energy, a cascade of sparks shot out and fluttered around briefly, before fizzling into the darkness.

"You think I'm powerless in here?" Chase taunted as Phoenix instantly felt a presence trying to force its way into his mind. He strained to keep the invading thoughts at bay, knowing that if he gave in, the Spirit Elemental could gain control of his entire body. Phoenix would be powerless to stop himself from committing suicide or even murdering his friends.

As if on cue, Altair and Dylan emerged through the undergrowth and spotted him lying on his back. The pressure on Phoenix's mind relinquished and faded, allowing him to relax and concentrate on hiding his injuries from the others.

"Saved by the bell-ends..." muttered Chase viciously under his breath as the newcomers hurried towards their comrade. Altair looked worriedly through his bandages, casting a dark glance at the prisoner as he passed, but Dylan walked up to the ethereal cell, defiantly staring into its occupant's eyes. Although no words passed between them, Phoenix knew that Dylan was relishing in his enemy's capture. After all, Phoenix mused, despite it being Altair that had suffered the most injury literally at the hands of Chase, it was Dylan who had taken the guilt - not to mention he had lost nearly all of his possessions when his room was turned into an aquarium.

Phoenix heaved himself awkwardly onto his elbows, watching Altair looking hopefully around the clearing, already knowing what he was searching for. He was looking for Dex. Phoenix was glad that he had always managed to maintain an unreadable expression, even in the most dire of situations. It was a talent he had unwillingly gained after his parents had divorced when he was eleven. The constant flow of family and friends telling him they were sorry, and that it wasn't his fault had forced him to show as little emotion as possible. If nobody saw that you were upset, they wouldn't fuss over you. It was a benefit back then, but was it really helping now? If Altair had come into the clearing and seen him crying his eyes out, he would have known instantly that something terrible had happened. Phoenix couldn't help feeling that his stony faced indifference was leading Altair along, dangling false hope in front of him like a carrot. Altair's eyes settled on him.

"Where's Scott?" he asked, the name petering out as if he had already guessed the answer. Phoenix looked down, afraid of giving the truth away whilst Dylan approached silently. Nobody spoke for a few moments, all three of them knowing what had happened but none of them daring to say it. It was as if they could go on denying it for as long as they wanted, but as soon as the words left someone's mouth then it was a cold, hard fact. The silence was harshly shattered by Chase's piercing laughter. The sound was so unexpected and unwelcome that Altair jumped a little when he heard it, turning in unison with Dylan to angrily face the monster. Phoenix however, remained staring stolidly at the ground. Chase stopped laughing and grinned widely, rivalling any clown for being the character of nightmares.

"Scotty isn't coming…" he began, cruelly pausing for the harsh reality to sink in. "But don't worry, he's gutted that he couldn't make it." He burst into hideous laughter again as he mocked the dead Elemental. The cruel cackling intensified as Dylan furiously sent a cascade of boiling water droplets bouncing harmlessly off the violet energy shield.

Dylan turned back toward Phoenix, who had finally brought himself to look at them, the shining of his eyes the only betrayal of emotion. With grim realisation, he gave one single nod to confirm Chase's words. Dylan felt as if the bottom had dropped out of his stomach, his soul pouring out into the air, even his ability to speak flowing into ineffect. Altair, however, would not believe it even still, shaking his head blankly.

"No…." he murmured. "He's just caught up somewhere. Scott can't die, that's just… that's…" Altair faltered, his words failing as he searched his heart for an explanation. Phoenix gritted his teeth impatiently before holding up Dex's athame. Altair's eyes widened as he recognised the unmistakable hilt etched in the shape of a maple leaf.

"Dex is gone," stated Phoenix bluntly.

"For God's sake, call him Scott! Scott's gone...." The pain was too much for Altair as the tears broke, streaming down his cheeks and soaking his bandages. He sank to his knees, holding his head in his good hand, the other arm slung tightly against his chest.

"He knew..." Dylan said pensively as he stared at the ground. Phoenix looked up at him questioningly but Altair continued to sob quietly in to the uncaring soil. "Earlier, he... I mean Scott said goodbye to me like he knew he wouldn't see me again. He knew he was going to die." Altair's sobs grew louder.

"The only thing Scott knew," cut in Chase, "was that *I* was going to die. He did this on purpose. It's his fault."

"Bastard!" Altair spat. "That's not true."

Phoenix shook his head. "We'll never know for sure," he said. He paused for a second as if to think of the right words before continuing. "I know this is the last thing anyone wants to hear, but we still have to think about Chase. Without all four of us, the Expulsion of Malevolence won't work." Dylan frowned, Phoenix's bluntness continuing to grate against his own feelings of regret and sadness, but what his friend had said was true. He had written the expulsion ritual for the four of them, and Scott's essence was an integral part. Before he knew what he was doing, Dylan turned and walked back toward the violet cell. "What are you doing?" Phoenix whispered hurriedly, as if not to upset Altair further. Ignoring his question, Dylan trudged across the springy grass but then halted, narrowing his eyes before turning back.

"Chase's tattoo," he said, trying to contain his concern. "Did he have it before all this?" Altair looked up as Phoenix thought of his reply.

"It's not like I asked him to get his kit off, why do you ask?"

"Because," Dylan said dramatically as he pulled his Element pendant from beneath his top. "It's the same as one of these, but with a different line through the middle. He knows more about our little endeavours than he's letting on."

This time, Dylan marched forwards until his nose threatened to graze the faintly crackling energy field that surrounded the Spirit Elemental. Chase looked down at him, mouth curled into a sneer as he waited for Dylan to speak. After drawing a deep breath, Dylan looked into those eyes, cold and unblinking.

"Where did you get your tattoo?"

"I honestly can't remember." Dylan looked for the signs of sarcasm that he was expecting to see, but Chase's smirk was gone. *Was he telling the truth? Maybe the tattoo was something he woke up with?*

"Why are you doing this?" Dylan said, straining to hold back his anger and his tears.

Chase rolled his eyes, the acid wit returning. "Oh please! If this is your plan, I'll kill myself now..." he called across to Phoenix.

"We are Elementals, all of us," continued Dylan hopefully. "Together we could achieve so much more! Combining our expertise could lead to something great. We could govern the world, why do any more of us have to die?"

Deus snapped his head up awkwardly, somehow

shocked by Dylan's words. Governing the world sounded oddly familiar but he knew it was not a phrase he had heard since his awakening in the cruel dirt tomb that lay torn open a few metres from where he floated. Once again, he saw the haunting images of the gladiators standing tall, the leather-bound book and the young man looking on in awe. So this was another piece of the puzzle that was Deus. Did this pathetic human know something about his origins? He did not think so, it was probably mere coincidence that he had chosen those words. If Scott had said them, then it would have been different, he was the one with the brains, but Josh was simply a follower of something he did not understand, gifted power at the sacrifice of another. It was then that Deus noticed Josh staring up at him, eyes wide like the mischievous puppy dog that thinks that digging up the garden has somehow pleased its master.

"You idiot!" he scathed, trying to disguise the fact that Josh's speech had rattled him. "I'm not some simple-minded creature capable only of destruction. Even Frankenstein's monster had feelings. I'm a being of Spirit and emotion. I could light up this whole world with love if I wanted, but I'm intelligent enough to realise that it's a pointless endeavour. Did you ever stop to think what the world would be like if there was no war?" Josh took a step backwards, his brow furrowing in curiosity. "Without conflict, everyone would live in perfect harmony... except harmony isn't balance is it? Where would hatred and jealousy fit into the perfect world? If there was no envy and anger then your pathetic lives wouldn't have come this far, you'd all be stuck in caves, satisfied with hunting and gathering. Did you ever ask why you four chose to initiate yourselves?"

Dylan was stunned at Chase's philosophy. He had never expected the Spirit Elemental to be so profound, he thought that the creature's power lay only in the ruin of everything else. Why had they decided to try the initiation ritual? Why had all of this happened, really? It was because the four friends had wanted to be better than everyone else. Boiled down to the twisted bones, Chase Rivers had been killed as a result of greed and anyone else would probably think that Dylan and the others deserved everything they got.

Suddenly aware that he had drifted off, Dylan hastily changed tack. He had tried pleading, but it was clear that Chase was going to show no mercy so perhaps he could be won over by different means. After all, power was the language of the Gods, he reasoned. Perhaps Chase could be intimidated?

"You think we're so different, don't you?" he began, whispering so the others wouldn't hear. The Spirit Elemental folded his arms and glared. "You're not the only one who's tried dark rituals."

Chase arched his eyebrows sceptically. "And what exactly have you tried, mortal?"

"Caput Mortum would have killed you wouldn't it?" As the Water Elemental spoke, Chase smiled cruelly.

"Ha! Maybe, maybe not. What stopped you? Somebody tell you it would ruin your soul?"

Josh opened his mouth with unashamed wonder. "Wouldn't it?"

"What does your heart tell you?" The Water Elemental considered for a moment. This wasn't the direction he was aiming for. He knew he was being drawn into a conversation he didn't want to be in, but what if there was a possibility? To behold that limitless power even for a second more…

"It felt like…"

"Like ecstasy, an endless pleasure trip," Chase cut in, knowingly. "That's what I feel like every day. Don't hold back next time, if you think you can handle that much raw power." Josh thought deeply. What if these rituals only had the terrible reputation because their creators had second thoughts about sharing their power, and rather than scrapping the rituals they surrounded them with threats? Or on the other hand, Chase might be luring him into trying something else and tainting his soul completely? What if it was already too late and his core was black and shrivelling like a tarred lung? "Although," the Spirit Elemental added. "When I get out of here, I'm going to kill you in a heartbeat, regardless of how much power you think you have."

"You're full of shit," Josh accused, suddenly enraged that the monster could still think they were a pushover after they had trapped him. Chase looked taken aback for a split second before regaining his sneer, obviously thinking that he had triumphed the conversation into submission. Dylan used this opportunity to continue driving his verbal wedge in. "I think if you really wanted to kill us you wouldn't be in this situation." For all his confidence, Dylan was now extremely glad that he was protected by the violet energy as Chase's eyes flashed, sending another shower of sparks to the ground.

Teeth bared intimidatingly, the captive leaned closer. "You dare to undermine my power?" he hissed malevolently, his voice coated with venom.

Dylan did not flinch. "How did you try and kill Altair? You used hands made of air. And me? You tried to drown me in my own room. And by the looks of Phoenix, you fought him with fire. Were you trying to be all clever and destroy us with our own elements or did you secretly hope we would survive?"

Chase's face contorted with rage. "I am in control!" he screamed. "Nothing dictates my actions. Your survival is through no fault of mine."

"Then why didn't you flood Phoenix's room with water?" Dylan asked. "He would have been powerless to stop you, after all what could Fire do against Water?" He paused, watching Chase's deep grey eyes narrow. "I think subconsciously you wanted to give us a chance out of respect. That's all it takes Chase, one tiny glimmer of a feeling can bloom into salvation. Humanity is complex." Dylan finished, hoping that his words had some impact on the raging spirit. To his surprise however, the other man was grinning slyly, the arrogance of understanding clearly playing across his face.

"Don't think I don't know what you're doing..." he began. "You're trying to convince me that there's some part of him left inside. You think he wouldn't want you to die as much as I do? You treated the Rivers boy like shit, never spoke more than two words to him and here you are appealing to him for help? Let me assure you, my better nature is long dead, but you'd know all about that wouldn't you, seeing as you killed him."

"You're wrong!" Dylan challenged. "Chase may be dead, but why do you still look like him? You even speak like him sometimes, as if you *are* him. I heard you in my room. If you were so powerful, you would have changed the way you are instead of keeping the face of someone you seem to loathe so much."

Chase gritted his teeth. "Humans are weak. You see and hear what you think you should." He folded his arms, offering no more to the discussion. Conversation closed. Defeated, Dylan lowered his head, avoiding Chase's gaze, which was once more smug with victory. He had honestly thought that he could have made the Spirit Elemental think that something inside of him was staying his hand. If that were the case, he might have seen his vengeance as a lost cause, but of course he had seen through the ploy.

The energy field started to crackle once more but Dylan did not look up. Chase was obviously trying to break it again.

"Perhaps there is some truth to your words..." Chase said uncharacteristically softly. Dylan stepped forwards, eager to hear what could be some sort of confession from the spirit. "With power as great as mine, I could have crushed you all in the blink of an eye, but I wanted to see what you could do. Giving you the chance to defend yourselves showed me the extent of your powers."

Dylan nodded. "Thank you for giving us a chance," he began. "Now when we destroy you, I won't feel like we were unfair to you, Chase." Suddenly a pale hand shot down and grabbed the front of Dylan's cloak, the icy flesh brushing against the skin of his neck, draining all of the warmth from his body. Too shocked to make a noise, Dylan looked up into the glowering face, still behind the purple barrier, but somehow he had managed to force his hand through. Dylan was lifted off the ground effortlessly, his feet dangling, hopelessly scratching against the carpet of burnished leaves that coated the floor. Their faces millimetres apart, Chase glared at him.

"It's Deus..." he whispered. "Now say hello to Scott..." Dylan found his voice just as his energy began flowing out of him, through Chase's arm and into the Spirit Elemental. It was as if for that one moment the two of them were joined in unholy union. Chase was deep within Dylan's core, rooting out his life force and Dylan was forced to stare subconsciously through the screaming vortex into the centre of evil. Chase's core was a pitch void, a single violet orb with hints of red, blue, green and yellow swirling around it like an atmosphere, the elements keeping the evil within alive, incubating it. The intimacy of the matrimony disgusted him, the spirit's every movement probing and scratching against the inside of his body, hollowing him out. The intense draining link was enough to make Dylan's gorge rise: the thought of his body being invaded was too much for him as he wondered if Chase was feeling the same at the other end. Before he blacked out, Dylan managed to loose a strangled cry, and Phoenix and Altair were soon by his side, pulling him away from the harsh grip and the sickening violation. The three of them fell to the floor with grunts of pain as the grasping arm retreated back inside the violet shell. "Aww, maybe next time..." Chase simpered with mock pity. Panting and rubbing his neck weakly, Dylan strained to look up at the others, who were now hurriedly dragging him as far away from Deus as possible.

"I know what we have to do..." he coughed.

Chapter 34 - Contact

"Anything that touches something else will maintain that contact through the ether. This is the Wiccan Law Of Contagion."

The Book Of Shadows

From the bushes at the side of the clearing, Ed watched, silently crouching in the dirt with baited breath. Ever since he had looked into Chase's eyes, he had been unable to tear himself away from the feeling that he was somehow incomplete. He had seen something in Chase that he lacked, some sort of force that he had been unaware of previously. Now it was eating at his consciousness, invading his every thought. He needed the other man to be whole again.

He had awoken in Chase's bedroom, sweating and chest heaving as his heart threatened to leap out and fly away. He had no choice but to follow it and had been inexorably drawn to the forest, as if a magnet was embedded in his chest. He could not fight it and he didn't understand why. Once there, he had immediately seen the firefight between Chase and one of the others, the one in the band. Both of them had used some sort of extraordinary weaponry that he couldn't make out from his hiding place. Now the rest of the group were here, including the guy that he had spoken to on campus, and Chase was stuck in the air somehow. There was a scuffle, and the three men on the ground had retreated. Now was his chance.

Catlike, Ed crawled out from the undergrowth, coming up behind the floating man, and thankfully out of view of the others. Ignoring the pain in his bandaged ribs, he crept closer. Chase had not noticed him. At this distance, he could see that the cell that the other man floated in was made of sparking purple energy, but that was impossible wasn't it? It must be an electrified cage of some sort, probably hung from one of the looming trees.

"Chase?" he whispered. The young man wheeled round instantly, his naked torso glowing with the violet energy. Ed couldn't help noticing the definition of the other man's chest before moving his lingering gaze upwards. Chase's disdainful glare softened once he noticed who was standing before him. Perhaps he was back to normal? "I found you. I did, I found where you are."

The frustration that Deus had felt when Josh was ripped from his grasp immediately faded as he saw Ed looking up at him, eyes filled with wonder. Of course, this human's essence was nowhere near as strong as one of the Elementals', but it would be enough, he reasoned. This crackling prison had contained his current form as Deus, but he also had traces of energy from Chase and his mother. He had used this to grab Josh, but it obviously hadn't been enough. If he could absorb someone else's energy, then perhaps he could pass through entirely. Finally the ritual he had done with the dog's heart was about to pay off.

Deus paused for moment, concentrating and focusing his mind. At the sight of Ed, he could feel Chase's consciousness struggling for control again, the hope that this man represented was obviously still strong but this time Deus managed to quench it before it broke out. Once the incessant scratching at the back of his brain had ceased, he plastered the most Chase-like expression he could think of across his face.

"Ed! Thank God you're here," he said desperately. "These guys think I'm some sort of monster, they're gonna kill me." Ed looked outraged as he remembered what Josh had told him. He said people were after Chase, he never mentioned anything about killing.

"I won't let that happen," he whispered. "You can't leave me again. I need you, I found you." Deus frowned as the human scanned his violet prison, searching for a way to break him out. Those words... it must have been Ed that left the note at his door. His sadistic charm had obviously had more of an effect on the mortal than he realised. "I can't seem to find a way to open this thing," Ed continued. "I'm sorry I made you this way Chase, if I made you angry by what I said, but..." his hand automatically reached for his bandage. The man paused, as if waiting for some sort of verification. It looked like Deus would have to lower himself to actually apologising if he wanted to free himself. What would Chase say in this situation?

"Look, I'm sorry I hurt you," he began, forcing the words out awkwardly as if they had a bitter taste. "They were after me even then. I panicked, thought you were in on it and wanted to get at me."

Ed let out a sigh of relief. "I knew it had to be something like that. You wouldn't hurt me would you, not now we have this connection."

"What connection is it you think we have?" Deus snapped, causing a shower of sparks to drift silently the ground like purple snowflakes. Ed stepped backwards, a confused expression on his face.

"What I told you before," he began, suddenly unsure of himself. "You have to complete me, Chase. I saw it. You are the one... I worship you Deus." Ed gasped once more as unfamiliar and unprecedented words spilled out of his mouth. Deus narrowed his eyes, waiting to see what would happen next. Would Ed recover from the temporary slip he had made? The Spirit Elemental had never really considered how his immense powers would effect those he came into contact with. For a mere mortal with no craft endowment, the energy must be overwhelming. He was in Ed's mind, had been since he had seen him in the print room. The capturing of the heart in the jar had only exacerbated feelings that were already fostering in the young man's soul. Ed had backed away to the treeline, clutching his ribs once more.

"I don't know," he muttered wildly. "How can that happen?"

Deus clenched his teeth, stretching his arms behind his head as he contemplated his course of action. It wouldn't be long before Josh and the others returned with their next attempt at vanquish and now he was losing this pathetic creature to doubt. He had to find a way to get the other man close enough.

He looked down to where Ed was standing, gawping at him silently with his mouth open. *Was this guy actually serious?* Even now, after everything, Ed was staring at him, drinking in the sight of his biceps flexing behind his head, revelling in the sparse patches of smooth hair that shaded his armpits - and Deus had found his way in. He had cast aside the trivial conversation that Chase had had with Ed before, but now it would provide him with his freedom. He knew that as long as he had Chase's body, Ed would never be lost to him. Closing his eyes, his vision was replaced with a black and white image, like an x-ray of the man in front of him. There was a bright patch of rosy light over Ed's heart, flickering with his increased heartbeat. Perfect. The guy still had feelings for him even after he had been smashed through a pane of glass. It seemed Ed would overlook domestic violence for anyone with a six-pack. Or an infinite wealth of elemental power and a heart in a jar. Concentrating, Deus angled the pink energy from Ed's chest, down over his stomach and towards his crotch. It was exactly like the flashes of emotion Chase had seen in the Print room, but intensified tenfold.

Ed watched silently as Chase closed his eyes. Was he giving in? Perhaps the other three had beaten him badly and he could take no more? The young man seemed to look frail and defeated, a slight frown on his features, which made him look even cuter. Ed's heart began to race uncontrollably, then suddenly his muscles jolted causing him to gasp. Intense heat flowed through his body as he shuddered involuntarily with the force of the energy. It couldn't be... had he?

Deus opened his eyes and smirked as he saw Ed buckling slightly, helplessly overcome. After a second, the human looked up at him, breathing deeply.

"What have you done to me?" he panted. "Why do I feel like this?"

"I didn't do anything," the Spirit Elemental lied. "You said you loved me before. I guess you still do. That's why you found me here. You came to rescue me." Resisting the urge to laugh at his choice of words, Deus studied the other's face. Part of what he had said was true. It was Ed's love that had brought him here. As Deus had told Josh less than an hour ago, he was a creature of Spirit and emotion, not vengeance. Ed's love for Chase had transferred onto him, and whereas the same situation with two humans would last a couple of days perhaps, such strong feelings between a human and a God were amplified. Ed was infatuated. "Come on, I can give you what you want."

Still reeling, Ed considered his options. Yes he had been hurt, but wasn't this what he wanted? It felt like the man in front of him was the missing piece of a puzzle he had only just realised was incomplete. For so long he had pictured himself and Chase together, as more than just colleagues. More than just friends even, and now here it was on a plate in front of him. As if to emphasise the appeal, Chase lowered his head through the shimmering wall of light and raised his eyebrows, moving his lips slowly. Ed was completely lost as he leaned forwards and pressed his mouth against Chase's, his tongue forcing its way inside with reckless lust.

Deus was only vaguely aware of a muffled yelp as he bit down and began to suck.

Chapter 35 – Deus Ex

Breathing deeply, Altair stared down at Dylan who was still massaging the spot where Chase had grabbed him. A patch on his neck had gone grey, as if that area had died when the Spirit Elemental had touched it.

"We have to do the Expulsion of Malevolence…" Dylan continued. Altair glanced at Phoenix, who met his gaze. The shards of moonlight were the only thing altering the Fire Elemental's features as, typically, no emotion passed across his face. Despite the lack of outward signs, Altair could tell that Phoenix was feeling exactly the same as he was. The Expulsion of Malevolence would not work, *could* not work without the power of Earth that Dex would have supplied. Surely Phoenix was right when he had stated it earlier? Dylan spat ashamedly into the mud and wiped his mouth, desperate to rid himself of the desolate poison of Chase's touch. "I know it looks hopeless, but trust me. I think I see a way round Scott's absence, but I won't be sure unless we give it a go."

Altair nodded, his trust in his old friend unwavering after all they had been through. Dylan had fought off death for both of them, his armour dented and worn but his stance resolute. Altair would not give up on him. Phoenix, however, was frowning stubbornly.

"I'm not going to do anything unless you explain why," he stated with blatant obstinacy.

Altair gritted his teeth, fighting his sudden desire to swear. "Scott wouldn't have to explain himself," he said, voice hovering just below the red zone of calm. "Anything is worth a shot, we can't just leave him here. You saw what he did just now. It won't be long until he can pass more than just an arm."

"Energy is limited!" protested Phoenix, his rationality fading. "I don't see why we should waste it on something tha-"

"Will you shut up and trust me?" growled Dylan, finally rising shakily to his feet. "I'm not gonna explain it to you now because if that... thing knows then he might be able to block it." Dylan cast a dark glance to where Chase hung, now with his back to them. "All I'm going to say is that I saw something just now that makes me think it's worth a try, ok?" Phoenix raised his eyes and began to concentrate on looking anywhere but directly at Dylan. It looked as if he had just seen the most interesting thing in the world, and was trying to figure it out, brows furrowed and tongue in cheek as if he was concentrating.

"Fine," he muttered casually, sounding as if he no longer cared what happened. At this reluctant hint of acceptance, Altair offered his strong arm down for Dylan to grab hold of. Raising him to his feet, the three of them turned towards the prison, faces set with determination.

"What the hell is that?" Altair exclaimed, taking in the scene that was unfolding in front of him. There was someone else in the clearing, a man, and Chase was *kissing him?* Altair cast a worried glance at the other two, who wore similar expressions. Chase was leaning ever further through the energy barrier as he sucked harder and harder at the other man's face, the poor guy's arms flailing helplessly. The three Elementals ran forwards.

As he drew closer, Dylan recognised the newcomer as the man he had spoken to before, Ed from the uni paper. He could also make out the dark shade of blood running down Ed's cheeks as he clawed frantically at Chase's torso, which was now fully out of the ethereal prison. The Spirit Elemental wrapped his arms around the other man's waist and hoisted his bucking form off the leaf-strewn ground as if he weighed nothing. Dylan threw out his hands and his companions slowed to a halt, staring with sickened awe. *How could he have possibly been compared to that?* the Water Elemental thought, whilst simultaneously wondering if Chase was feeling the sensation that he had got from the Caput Mortum. As they watched, Chase stepped completely out of his cell, which fizzed into emptiness as soon as he left it. He dropped Ed's now limp body into the mud and turned to face the onlookers, twin trails of blood curving from the corners of his mouth. He licked his lips loudly.

"Who's next?" he rasped, the last of Ed's life gurgling in his throat. Altair looked at his friends, who gave him an encouraging nod. They were still going to go ahead with Dylan's idea. Altair in particular wanted the spirit to know that he would not be beaten into submission. As the three of them stood resolutely facing their nemesis, he couldn't help coaxing the breeze to ruffle their cloaks dramatically. Phoenix's hair blew out behind him, the wiry patch where he had been burned evident amongst the clawing strands. Chase, however, rolled his eyes with his characteristic *are you serious* expression.

"I see. The fate of the world is in the hands of a bunch of movie stars," he scathed. "Well go on then. Give it your best shot before I crush you." Chase clenched his fists as the three Elementals raised their hands, palms open.

Dylan glanced nervously to his companions from his position in the centre of their defiant line-up. Altair was watching him nervously, but Phoenix was staring straight ahead. Dylan wasn't sure, but he thought he saw the Fire Elemental's hand quivering slightly. Was Phoenix scared? Eventually, Phoenix turned in his direction and gave him a solemn nod. Altair saw it too and the three of them took the deep breath before plunging over the cascading

waterfall of serious power. This would be the first thing
they had attempted together since the initiation ritual, and
they all still bore the pain of how that had ended.

"Elohelmarelnartosar, elexapareloh firel elvirinaloh
oyfia Dielunasar!" they shouted, Altair's voice ringing
louder than the other two, his useless arm testimony to his
commitment. The air crackled and the trees began to writhe
violently as the energy awoke. Chase cast a worried glance
around the clearing, his ash-coloured eyes widening as he
took in the sight. It was as if the whole forest was
screaming the words with Dylan, Phoenix and Altair. As
the final echoing syllable ricocheted around the trees and
faded into the darkness, Dylan screwed up his face with
one last contortion of effort and his palm began to glow. It
was happening to the others too, but before he had time to
even think about letting concern creep into his mind, a jet
of blue energy erupted from the centre of his hand, fluid
and sinuous. The stream twisted over and over, splashing
back into itself almost playfully as it wound over to Chase,
snaking around and around him. Seconds later, it was
joined by a tendril of hazy golden smoke and a raging blast
of scarlet flame, the three vipers of raw power orbiting
Chase, dancing and teasing him by occasionally brushing
against his skin, explosions of sparks spluttering with each
contact.

The breeze died down and the trees stopped waving,
leaving the clearing once more in a state of serenity. Like an
engine powering down, the ritual energy left Dylan and he
looked at the others, blinking and shaking his head. Altair
was staring at him questioningly, but Phoenix had his arms
folded, a smug grin on his face like he was desperately
holding back an "I told you so." The only sound that broke
the imposing silence was Chase's harsh laughter.

"Well, fuck me!" he exclaimed gleefully ignoring the fact that he had looked more than a little threatened just moments ago. He now ignored the three swirling strands of elemental power that still wafted eerily around him. "That was exciting, wasn't it? I don't know what you were expecting, but that certainly did it for me." His eyes narrowed as he focused solely on Dylan. "Was it good for you too?" he teased with a sickening rendition of sultriness. Dylan locked eyes with the Spirit Elemental, squaring him up, deadly serious.

"I've seen into your core…" he whispered, instantly silencing Chase behind the swirling tendrils of power. "Do you know what I saw? There was your energy, but there were four other forces in there too. That reminded me of what you said before you tried to kill me. Do you remember what that was?" Chase glared at him but remained silent. "I'll tell you then. You are Spirit. You are Fire, you are Water and you are Air. But most importantly, you are Earth…"

Chase frowned, suddenly looking uncomfortable. He tentatively touched a hand to his mouth and then examined his fingers to see if he was bleeding. There was a deafening cracking sound and his head snapped backwards, a high pitched screaming rising from the depths of his throat as a column of bright green energy burst from his mouth. The trail blossomed and grew as it curled around his head and joined the other three as they merged together into a single enveloping sphere. Chase was once more lifted into the air. The Elementals had to shield their eyes as the force field began to glow more and more fiercely until it was a pure dazzling white, Chase's silhouette suspended in the centre, arms outstretched and head tilted backwards. He was still screaming.

And then there was blackness. It happened so rapidly that Phoenix had to squint to be sure of what he was seeing. Chase had dropped to the waiting soil and the energy had vanished, like a light bulb that had just blown, yet there was still something, someone hanging in the air where the young man used to be. The figure was tall and muscular, perfectly formed but dressed in unusual garb. As his eyes grew accustomed to the gloom, Phoenix realised that the man was wearing armour and a helmet, like a character from Greek mythology. The helmet came complete with a large plume, and the whole outfit was embossed with purple gilt, shining in the occasional patches of moonlight that lanced through the clouds. Veins were visible as the warrior gripped a large shield in one hand, a needle-point spear in the other. The features of the warrior's face were unclear, but Phoenix was sure that they were strong and regal, streamlined with chiselled perfection.

"Foolish humans." All three of them heard the voice, but Phoenix was certain that the warrior's mouth hadn't moved. "That shell was weak. I am better to be free of its rank emotion." There it was again, echoing inside his head as if each stinging syllable the warrior growled was meant specifically for him. "I am the scourge of all the worlds, yet on this Earth my black heart is set." The warrior turned its head and looked directly at Phoenix, causing him to recoil in fear. It was like he was being read from the inside out. He was certain he saw the gladiator smirk before the roving gaze passed on. When the mysterious being turned to Dylan however, it paused. The gladiator raised his arm, the spear trained towards where the Water Elemental stood transfixed. "This one has been tainted by darkness…" the voice reverberated. His roving gaze moved on to Altair, who was visibly quaking, trying to avoid the warrior's piercing scrutiny. "Await my return, for my exile shall not last. There are those that look for my coming. I am the herald of your despair."

With his last word, the forest seemed to implode and the gladiator was gone, nothing but a ring of flames and the smell of ozone rapidly being replaced by that of smouldering leaves. The three of them stood stunned, staring at the circle of fire that completely enclosed but did not touch Chase's body as it lay where it had been dropped like an old rag. Dylan immediate ran over to where Ed lay, bending to check his pulse. To Phoenix's surprise, Altair spoke first.

"That…" he faltered. "That was Deus, wasn't it? Not the Deus that Chase called himself, but the actual thing. The evil inside of him." Phoenix had to admit that it made sense. Altair turned as Dylan came jogging back. The bandaged man gave him a jerky one-armed hug.

"He's dead," Dylan said, shaking his head. "Chase bit his tongue out. Must have sucked the life out of him." A shudder ran through the three of them, each imagining what that must have felt like.

"Who was he?" Phoenix asked.

"I think he knew Chase before… don't think he knew what was going on though. He probably was just looking out for his friend and got caught up in this mess." Dylan deliberately held back on explaining about his conversation with Ed earlier. After all, what did it matter now? The poor guy was dead. Nobody could change that. There was a moment of silence. However, Altair couldn't help feeling that they had won, despite all the setbacks.

"You did it, Josh!" he said tentatively.

Josh nodded modestly. "We did it. All three of us together."

"But it was your plan." Rich went on. "You were the one that convinced us to do the Expulsion. Scott would be proud of you. You more than filled his shoes, right Matt?"

The Fire Elemental looked quizzically at the others. "So we are back to normal names now are we?" he said with a hint of sarcasm.

Rich looked taken aback. "Well it's over, isn't it?"

"What did he mean 'tainted by darkness?'" Matt asked, turning his attention to his Water brother. Josh was lost for words. He couldn't bring himself to explain the torment he was feeling, not just about the death and the suffering he had witnessed, but the constant battle in the back of his mind, a single feeling screaming for him to seek out and use as much power as possible. To his relief however, his best friend once more came to his rescue.

"You felt it when Deus looked at you," Rich reprimanded. "It felt like he was trying to search out our weaknesses. He was obviously trying to frighten Josh. But it doesn't matter now, he's gone." Deep down, Matt felt sorry for him. Poor, sensitive Rich, who could barely make a decision for himself. He almost felt bad for crushing him with his practicality, but still, it had to be done. He had to be sure that some things stayed buried.

"If that was Deus, then yes, he's gone for now at least. But we don't know about Chase." Josh looked at Matt for a second before raising his hand to his chin and pacing off, deep in thought.

Rich's eyes widened. "What do you mean?"

Matt shook his head. "I mean," he began, "that Chase might not wake up at all. He isn't empowered anymore, that's clear. But did he die before or after he became empowered? If everything has kind of reset itself, then he could still be dead if he was dead before the spirit took him." He watched Rich's face as his words sank in.

He could almost see the proverbial cogs turning inside the Air Elemental's head, a decision on the tip of his tongue. He decided to help him along, and nodded gently. "Yes, I think you should go and ask Josh what he thinks." Rich nodded eagerly and turned away, making for his trusted friend who was now on the other side of the clearing.

Now was his chance, Matt thought, rolling his eyes at how long it took to get rid of Rich. After checking that the Air Elemental wasn't going to turn back, he hurried to where Chase lay. He was still wearing the black outfit with the torn trousers, but the colour had returned to his flesh, rosy pink once more conquering lifeless grey. It did not look like he was breathing. Matt knelt down for a closer look, thankful that Chase's eyes were closed. The younger man could have been sleeping peacefully, but how could he be, after going through what he had? Matt felt guilty for his part in Chase's torture, and guilt for what he knew he might have to do to save his own life.

He glanced across the clearing, where he could just make out the two ghostlike outlines of his companions, deep in conversation. The crumpled body of Ed lay not far off, and thankfully his face was tilted the other way. Turning back to Chase, Matt cast his eyes over the length of suffering that lay before him. Something glinted in the moonlight.

Matt shifted around the body to get a better look and froze, heart thumping inexplicably loud, caged beneath his ribs. Tied around Chase's wrist was Scott's Element pendant, the crooked line in the circle unmistakable. Matt shifted awkwardly as he remembered how Chase must have gotten hold of it – ripped from the body of Scott. Matt deftly untied the simple knot and pocketed the necklace, as if keeping it would somehow keep their fallen comrade with him somehow.

With a morbid desire for certainty and security, Matt gingerly stroked Chase's cheek with his finger. He jumped backwards, almost crying out as the young man twitched, his smooth chest rising and falling with a single breath, the muscles rippling themselves into life. Matt moved around behind Chase's head just as his eyes snapped open.

Screaming filled the air. Screaming and purple fire, then blackness. For an indeterminate amount of time, Chase Rivers was nothing. Nothing floating in nothing. It was as if he was suspended in space, black and empty, yet unable to twist and spiral in the freedom. As strange as it was, he had felt like this before, although he was unable to recall when or why. Something brushed against his cheek, warm and living. He opened his eyes, but for a moment thought he was blind, the night sky just as black as his eyelids. He was sprawled on his back, lying on what felt like leaves, and for some reason he was topless. The chill of the early morning played across his skin tantalisingly. It seemed like he had felt nothing for so long, and now every touch was exciting and new. Slowly, he sat up and squinted across the clearing, vaguely picking out two figures standing next to the tree line, enveloped in the darkness underneath the sprawling canopy. He should call out to them. Perhaps they would know what happened to him. And then he remembered. Everything flicked through his mind like a sped-up film, his death, his rebirth, the face of his mother as she burst into flames and every other act of malice that Deus had committed whilst using his body as his twisted sanctuary. The ghastly montage ended with the image of Ed sinking to the ground, his jaw gaping and hot blood pumping through ruined lips. It was worse than simply seeing these actions however, as Chase could feel the intent behind every one of them: the hatred, the greed and the corruption. *Oh God, his mother.* The sour taste in his mouth made him retch, but nothing came out. He hadn't eaten for some time but the stinging still hit his throat as if he had just thrown up.

And yet beyond the compound of regret and disgust, there was a feeling of hope effervescing up inside, waiting to burst into the fireworks of euphoria. He was alive! The sting of death was becoming soothed by the prospect of new life. He had been in a terrible accident, but now he was fine. It happened all the time in hospital didn't it? People were always waking up from comas or being resuscitated after flatlining weren't they? Chase knew that his accident was different somehow, and that his revival hadn't exactly been conventional, but it didn't matter. He had been given a second chance. For the first time in so long, he felt warmth spread across his cheeks as the flicker of a grin threatened to invade his face. It was a new start, a clean slate. He would make more of an effort to talk to people, to get out there and make friends. It finally seemed to Chase like they were a possibility after his reprieve.

Chase was suddenly horribly aware that somebody was standing behind him, looming silently. In a second, the breakout of colour left him and he felt warm breath against his ear, and two hands gripping his shoulders, dangerously close to his neck. Fear took him. Instantly, he regretted his jubilation at life. He was sorry that he had thought about the silver lining of this stormcloud, and he was left with the bare truth. He was cold, alone and had been through a soul-destroying ordeal. All he wanted was to be at home, tucked up in his bed. He didn't mind spending most of his time alone if it meant he wouldn't have to be here now, feeling like he did.

"I'm sorry Chase," the familiar voice said. Chase knew it was one of them but couldn't quite place which one. "I can't let you tell anyone what happened. Just understand that this is necessary. Think of it as helping me out one last time." The voice belonged to Matt Blake, and Chase remembered something else. He opened his mouth as the hands slid upwards and tightened.

Rich and Josh froze as the crack shot across the clearing like gunfire. They snapped their heads in the direction of the sound, and saw Matt crouching next to Chase's still body. After glancing at each other for a split second, the two of them began to jog towards their friend. All sorts of ideas were flashing through Rich's mind, but all of them ended with one image, the armoured form of Deus, cold and uncompromising.

Matt started to walk solemnly towards them, rubbing his hands awkwardly against his thighs.

"He's dead. We couldn't save him," he stated with minimal emotion. "At least he's at peace now," he added as an afterthought. Rich looked from Matt to the body and back again, straining to understand what had happened. It seemed like only yesterday he had been in exactly the same position, staring bewildered at the corpse of Chase Rivers. He had desperately hoped that they could have saved their young victim. In Rich's head, that would have somehow absolved them of some of the guilt that now hung over them.

"What was that noise then?" he asked.

"I dunno. A branch or something? A bird maybe." Matt replied, unwavering in his monotone. Rich certainly hadn't felt anything in the air that could snap a branch or scare birds. By his side, Josh broke out of his pensive stance.

"What's that you've got?" he nodded towards Matt's left hand, which was clearly grasping something. After a brief pause, Matt opened his palm, revealing a thin strip of paper.

"It's the missing piece of the Initiation Ritual. Chase must have had it." Josh froze as their supposed companion held out his hand. It was one line of a book, just like the one torn from the bottom of Scott's Book of Shadows. Josh had completely forgotten about it until now, but he could clearly see that the paper had writing on it. Writing that none of the other books had… Rich snatched the paper from Matt's hand, glanced at it and then passed it to Josh who read about the willing fifth and the sacrifice for true power. Sacrifice. What had Chase said earlier? "I get some message telling me to go to the forest, so I do and I get fucking scorched." It was all coming together in his mind. Chase hadn't turned up by accident, someone had drawn him there. Maybe somebody *did* know that he was going to die, but it wasn't Scott… Suddenly, Josh remembered Chase's phone, which was safely tucked into his belt. Obviously, he hadn't worn his ritual cloak and tool belt since Halloween, and had completely forgotten that the phone was in there. He fished for it, holding the device triumphantly. Rich's eyes widened.

"Chase's phone," the Water Elemental said sheepishly. "I took it just in case."

"In case of what?" exclaimed Rich. Josh ignored the question, everything falling horribly into place inside the pools of his memory. At last, he understood what he had seen after the Absinthe, the flaming bird made sense now. He switched the phone on and went into the memory. The last message was from an unknown number and told Chase to go to the forest, with the enticing prospect of being 'part of the group'. As he read it, he felt sickened that the poor kid's loneliness had been used as bait. Josh's thumb hovered over the redial button, afraid of what would happen if he pressed it. He was aware that both of his friends were staring at him in a state of confusion. Or at least one of them was.

"You know what the last thing I said to Scott was?" he said calmly. "I said that you can never blame just one person for something like this. I just realised I was wrong." He pressed the button.

Chapter 36 – Revelation, Resolution And Warning

*"Intention is another key aspect of Wiccan lore. If someone draws a
Pentagram on the ground, which is then discovered by someone else,
which way up is the symbol? Is it the right way up, with Spirit
overseeing the elements and therefore good, or is it inverted with the
elements ruling over the freedom of Spirit? Only the one who drew it
can say, as only he knows his intentions when he did so. However,
make no mistake. Intention cannot excuse evil, no matter how craftily
it is disguised."*

The Book Of Shadows

Matt Blake was rooted to the spot, the Crystal Homicide
ringtone blaring from his pocket, two pairs of eyes boring
into him like the murderer they now knew he was. He was
in no denial of that fact, but surely his intentions counted
for something?

"I never said anything about a missing piece of the
Initiation. That means you took it." Josh snarled the
accusation and it was true. Matt had ripped the line out of
Scott's book. He had been the first to copy the original,
and had seen the line probably before Scott had even
realised the true implications of its words.

"I did it for us…" he began his defence. "I knew
that if any of you saw that we needed a sacrifice to make
the ritual work, you would pull out. You're all so unwilling
to do exactly what it takes. You should be thanking me. I
took the line for the greater good. You thought Chase
finding us was an accident, a coincidence, but without
Chase Rivers, we would be just like he was. Average and
unremarkable." Upon hearing this, Rich exploded, rushing
towards Matt and pounding against his chest, fist clenched,
a forceful echo of Halloween.

"Without Chase Rivers, Scott would still be alive," he cried. "How dare you weigh our power and their lives against each other?"

Matt gulped, but he did not step back from the attack. "I didn't know he would come back. I thought once he was gone, that would be the end of it. A tragic accident, but we would get over it. People always get over it…" Matt's voice petered out as he realised he was failing to win them over.

"Murder is still murder," Josh said softly. "No matter what you dress it up as."

"The line said willing!" Matt yelled in a last ditch effort. "Chase didn't have to come to us, he *chose* to of his own free will."

"That's not the same," sobbed Rich. "He didn't know what was going to happen to him. He might have chosen to follow your directions, but he didn't want to die!"

Matt saw that he had lost, and ditched all hopes of reconciliation. "Fine!" he sneered. "Have your moral high ground, but you can't do anything about it. Even if you do manage to convince anyone to believe you, both of you are still just as culpable as me. Accessories go down with the culprit." Rich took a step back, hot tears streaking down his cheeks.

"You killed Chase, that's all the Police would find." Josh piped up hopefully, only to be shot down instantly.

"What about Scott? What about that Ed chap? Not to mention that we are all wearing cloaks and carrying knives, candles and vials. At the very least, they'll bang you up for insanity," Matt said with a slight smile.

"You complete bastard," Rich spat viciously, before jamming his palm into Matt's ribcage, the force of air lending strength to his strike. The Fire Elemental was sent sprawling to the ground, bitter resentment poisoning his face. Josh grabbed Rich by the wrist and pulled him backwards before he struck again. He stared down at their pitiful acquaintance with a numb sense of defeat.

"You're right," he sighed. "Go wherever you want, Matt, but if I ever see you again, I swear I'll kill you." Josh turned his back on his old friend, and led Rich towards the edge of the clearing.

"But we are like Gods!" Matt shouted dejectedly. Josh faced him pityingly.

"That's what Deus said, and look where it got him." Rich shrugged, aware that Josh had turned away from the other man's greed, flushing awkwardly. The two of them left the clearing and Matt lay backwards, collapsing between the remnants of Chase and Ed as if his whole life had disappeared. His world had shrunk beneath his feet. He had thought he was doing the right thing to help his friends, but now he had lost everything, exiled and unable to go to anyone for help. What he had told Josh was also true for him, for who could he turn to now? He tilted his head and stared into Chase's open yet lifeless eyes, his neck twisted horribly, and he cried, wishing it was him that lay there, unable to feel the pain he felt now.

Rich and Josh walked for twenty minutes in silence, neither of them knowing what to say. They had reached The Haven before they stopped.

"Thanks for covering for me back then," Josh began solemnly. "If Matt knew about the Caput Mortum, it would only make things worse." His best friend looked at him thoughtfully for a moment before replying.

"Is it true?" he asked. "What Deus said. Are you tainted by darkness? I mean do you feel-"

"I don't know what I feel," Josh snapped abruptly. Upon seeing the other man's eyes widen, his temperament softened. "I mean, it's complicated. One minute I'm fine, then the next minute I keep thinking about what it would be like to have gone through with it, to have a taste of what Chase had."

"Nobody could possibly want to end up like that."

"I mean the power. Obviously Chase, or Deus or whoever abused it, but to have that much… I would use it properly. At least at times I think I would. Other times I can't imagine having those abilities and – well you see my problem. It's like I'm strapped into this rollercoaster and it's started climbing up the slope, and only now am I thinking 'What the hell am I doing?'"

"I'm never using my power again," Rich sniffed. "The cost of it was too much. It disgusts me." Josh nodded, but before he could answer, the wind picked up, instantly violent. There was a flash of light, a booming thunderclap and then silence. The two of them stared open-mouthed, for there was someone standing in the centre of The Haven. Someone who had not been there before.

The strange man looked older than them, perhaps mid twenties, but he was wearing bizarre clothes. He was wearing what looked like a woollen jumper, but his top had no right sleeve, and his right shoulder had some sort of tattoo. It was still too dark to make out properly, but it looked to Josh like a small circle with two lines cutting viciously through the centre. In his hand, he was clutching what looked like a wooden sword. The man's eyes were a vibrant green, two emeralds glinting in the ever-brightening sky. He was staring wildly around The Haven, as if he did not know where he was, or what was going on. As he spotted Rich and Josh, he jumped slightly, taking in their cloaks with apprehension, but as his gaze moved up to their faces, his eyes glinted with a flash of recognition. The stranger stepped forwards and bowed low before talking to them.

"Altair of Air and Dylan of Water," he said hurriedly, with an accent that was hard to place. "You are in great danger! Where are Dexamenas of Earth and Phoenix of Fire?" His eyes darted between them, almost too fast to notice. The two friends stared. Who was this newcomer and how did he know who they were?

"Why do you want to know?" Josh asked, sounding calmer than he felt. The mysterious stranger looked at him, face set with sincerity.

"Because, my Lord Dylan. A war is coming…"

COMING SOON

SPYRUS

ACKNOWLEDGEMENTS

Mark, Sam and Ian – All this is us

Roberts, Pinkus, Buttler, Jagger, Bugler, Wells, Speed and Foxton – You guys made me love writing

Brammers – You did it first then told me how

Lesley – For the sage financial advice

Looby, Jess, Miguel, Mr Heff and Tubbs – UCE belongs to you

Rummy, Taps and Imhotep – Your trailer made it more real

Mark, Tessa, Looby and Rummy – You read it first and helped shape it into this

Pigeon – Just because!

Tina – Because who wouldn't want to kiss you when they're drunk?

Emma, Liam, Liam, Nik, Mark, Dave, Ali, Gemma and Moko – Everything I know about Uni life started with the guys in B5

Turner – I gave you a doctorate, you can thank me later

Marilyn – You're not real. Doesn't stop you though

LJ – For the last minute blurb correction

George, Matt, Lewis and Jude – Thanks for the advice on the colours, I hope your controlled assessment went well

Bunty – For being a page Nazi

Firainarkorsar faroyrai elvirelraiyohfirinanargia

About The Author

Philip T McNeill currently teaches English in a
Gloucestershire Secondary school. He can often be found
writing or drawing whilst he should be paying attention in
meetings.

Check out his web comic 'Clamp Oswell's College Years' at
www.clamposwell.com

@g3mcneill
@clamposwell

5458260R00180

Printed in Great Britain
by Amazon.co.uk, Ltd.,
Marston Gate.